Hannah's Wishes

Agnes Alexander

Thank you for your help with Sewing my living Room Curtin —

Love
Lynette
AKA
Agnes

Dedicated to Jarrett Pierce Nifong who graciously allowed me to use his first name for the hero in Hannah's Wishes.   --Love, Aunt Lynette aka Agnes Alexander

Chapter 1

Hannah Hamilton sat in her upstairs bedroom with the door closed, but she could still hear the voices floating up from the formal parlor below. If she hadn't done so already, she was sure Aunt Verbena Wedington would serve her friends the delicious tea she saved for special occasions and special visitors. Hannah loved that tea, but had only been privileged to have it when a visitor caught her downstairs and her aunt had no choice but to let her be served with them. Verbena said they could never have the tea when they were alone or at meal times because it was expensive and must be saved for special guests. Hannah was never allowed to come down when these special guests were entertained unless she was being displayed as one of the crosses widowed Verbena Wedington had to bear in the middle years of her life.

Though it was Wednesday, the one day of the week Hannah was usually permitted to have a full day in the lower part of the house, she'd been hurried back to her room after breakfast where she'd been tucked away upstairs long before Aunt Verbena's company arrived. At least she wasn't gagged or threatened as she had been when she was younger and had tended to be rebellious. After being tied and punished with a few licks of Aunt Verbena's big wooden paddle, when she was small it didn't take her too long to learn to be quiet when there were visitors in the house. Sometimes, she wondered why her aunt hadn't just put her in some kind of orphanage or institution, but she'd finally come to the conclusion that Verbena only let her live there so she could pull her out and show the society neighbors and special church friends what a long-suffering and generous person the widowed aunt was because she hadn't turned her back on her poor crippled niece. Hannah learned to accept this humiliation as her aunt bragged how she'd given the young lady a good home and good Christian training for more than a dozen years and would probably have to for the rest of her life.

Of course, Hannah knew differently. Verbena Wedington didn't really want her niece around, but for some unexplained reason, the widow didn't seem to have a choice in the matter. The neighborhood women, as well as Verbena's Bible study group and church friends, knew Hannah had a withered foot and lived at the Wedington estate through the generosity of her aunt. For this reason, Hannah realized her aunt would be disgraced if it became known the woman sent her poor crippled niece away. Hannah also knew that probably wasn't Verbena's only reason for giving her a home, but she'd never been able to figure out what the other motive could be.

As soon as she was married and had a job, Hannah's oldest sister, Lydia, occasionally sent money to their aunt for Hannah's keep, and now that her sister, Drina, had married a rancher in Arizona, she would probably send money, too. Of course, Hannah had never seen a penny of Lydia's money and would not see any Drina sent, either. This probably played a factor in the decision her aunt made to give her a home. If there was anything Hannah was sure of about her aunt's character, Verbena Wedington was greedy. Though she may not know all the reasons, ever since she was four years old, Hannah had lived with her mother's sister in her elegant, though slightly decaying, Savannah home. Hannah was now seventeen, and would have her eighteenth birthday in a couple of months. Not that it mattered. Even though she would then be considered grown, there was no way she could leave this house. As a single woman confined to a wheelchair, she had nowhere else to go. She was stuck, and she knew it.

Shaking the voices downstairs out of her head, Hannah rolled her chair to the small table in the corner of her room. Opening the drawer, she pushed aside some of her sewing threads and pulled out paper, pen, and her ink well. She would write Drina another letter, though she hadn't heard from her sister since she went to Arizona to marry the rancher, Aaron Wilcox. This would be the fourth letter she'd written her sister, but Drina hadn't written back. She'd promised to write as soon as she was married to let her sister know about her new life as a ranch wife. Hannah now wondered if something had happened to prevent the wedding from taking place. It was hard not knowing what was going on with the sister she most idolized. It wasn't that she didn't love Lydia, her oldest sister, but Drina had been the one to look after Hannah when she was little and Hannah came to depend on Drina for this care. Too, they were closer in age.

Oh, how Hannah wished she could walk! If she could, she'd have gone to Arizona with Drina. She knew she could never live with Lydia because her older sister was married to a gambler and they owned part of a small saloon in Savannah. Hannah had never seen the place because her Aunt Verbena would never allow her to go to such an unsavory establishment. As her aunt often said, it wouldn't be proper, and her friends would be horrified if they heard the young innocent girl had gone to a saloon. But this wouldn't have deterred Hannah if she could walk. She knew if she could get out of her wheelchair she would not only visit Lydia's saloon, but she'd also go to Arizona to visit Drina. She didn't think there would be any disgrace in Aunt Verbena's friends' eyes if she went to a ranch in the west. She knew without a doubt both she and her aunt would both be happier not living together.

Hannah sighed. There was no need to keep the thoughts of visiting a saloon or moving west in her mind. These were just more of her wishes that would never come true. Shaking her head she picked up the pen, dipped it in the inkwell and wrote, *Dear Drina...*

♥♥♥

Verbena stood at the front door and watched as the last woman in her Bible study group walked across the yard to join their two friends who waited in the carriage. She breathed a sigh of relief. At least they'd be gone if Reginald decided to come by today. She certainly didn't want them to see him here. She knew how the women talked, and if they had any inkling that she and Reginald Phillips had any sort of relationship, their tongues would get sore from wagging.

Reginald was a member of her church and the manager at the bank where she did business. Though several widows and spinsters had tried to catch his eye, for some reason, he'd been showing her a lot of affectionate attention for the last couple of months. Especially since Barnaby Phillips, his older brother and the banker who had been in charge of Verbena's account, had died. She sometimes wondered if Barnaby had confided to Reginald the content of the papers concerning Hannah's placement with her, but she realized that was impossible. When Barnaby fell sick and knew he was going to die, he'd given her his copy of the document. She'd come directly home and burned it. There were now only two copies in existence. She had one in her safe and Burl Hamilton had the other one somewhere on his farm. She often wished she could get her hands on it, but knew Burl would kill her if she tried to find it.

Verbena was wise enough to realize Reginald was probably as much interested in the money he thought she had as he was in her. Still, marrying him might make a good match. He was rather wealthy himself. The only thing holding her back from returning his interest was Hannah's presence in the house and the last remark he'd made about her niece being there. He blatantly asked Verbena if she'd ever thought about seeking a husband for Hannah. He even suggested a couple of young men who he thought might be someone to consider as husband for the girl. Verbena hadn't cared for this comment, and the fact he'd suggested Calvin Sawyer as one of the men disturbed her, though she never let on she had the same idea herself.

Calvin Sawyer hadn't always been the feeble-minded man who lived with his sister, Hilda and attended church with her occasionally. A few years ago, he had been accosted on the street outside a saloon and was beaten nearly to death. In fact, everyone thought he would die, but somehow the doctor managed to save his life. In spite of all the surgeon did, there was no way he could fix the brain damage the young man had suffered at the hands of the ruffians. He now thought and acted like a six- or seven-year-old instead of a young man turning twenty. Not only that, but he had developed a love of strong drink. Especially beer. He often slipped away from his sister and either bought or managed to get others to buy drinks for him in some of the more unsavory saloons. The barkeeps were aware of his problem and often sent someone to get his sister to come and take him home. Calvin did have one good thing going for him. He was more handsome than the average man. Until he spoke and gave away his disability, many young women tried to get him to notice them in a romantic way. Of course, he never returned their flirting, though his body was that of a man, his mind hadn't reached the age where he was at all interested in girls other than as playmates.

Though she was a little ashamed of herself, she had no intention of telling Reginald or anyone about the plan she'd been working on to marry Hannah off to Calvin. A plan she had to move a little faster on, since she realized Hannah's birthday was coming up soon. The first step had been accomplished. For several months she'd been planting in people's mind the fact that Hannah was slow and no normal man would ever be interested in her. She knew many people already believed the young girl was feeble-minded simply because she couldn't walk, and she was sure her friends wouldn't think she was awful for suggesting her young crippled niece could be a wife. A couple of them had already said it would be good for Hannah to have a man to look after her.

Verbena wasn't sure if Reginald's remark about marrying Hannah off was because he didn't want the girl to stay in her aunt's home, but she had a feeling it was. She just hoped he never got it in his head to help her get Hannah married before she turned eighteen. She was afraid he might say something about the matter in front of Hannah and mess up the plan. Therefore, she decided not to let her niece come downstairs whenever he visited. If he asked about the young woman, Verbena would always have an excuse to explain her absence, which was easy for her to do.

But none of this kept Verbena from wondering what it would be like to have a husband in her life again. Hector Wedington had not turned out as she had thought he would when she married him. He spent most of his time taking care of his business and refused to let her have a child, no matter how hard she begged. Then when she became pregnant in spite of what he said, he'd pushed her down the steps late one night when she'd got up to get a glass of milk. She broke her leg and had inside injuries from the loss of the baby. The doctor said she would never be a mother again because of these injuries. After Hector's death a few years later, she played the grieving widow well and none of her friends ever guessed she was glad he was out of her life. She thought things would be better with him gone, and in a way it was, but all her family and friends would've been shocked to know he left all his money in trust at the bank and only allowed her enough monthly allowance to scrape by on instead of the amount they figured she had at her disposal. Other than the financial situation, only four people knew the real story of what had happened to Hector Wedington. Her sister, Ella; her brother-in-law, Burl Hamilton; her banker, Barnaby Phillips; and herself. Now, her sister and the banker were dead. Burl's silence had been bought a long time ago. She knew as long as she kept up the tax payments on the farm, he would never say a word.

Sighing to push away these thoughts, she closed the door and turned back into the house.

Jarrett MacMichael sat behind his desk in the Flagstaff, Arizona office of MacMichael and MacMichael Investigations and stared at the wire in his hand. It was long for a telegraph, but it certainly spelled out everything Aaron Wilcox wanted him to do. Go to Savannah, Georgia, and check out a man named Burl Hamilton; Hamilton's daughter, Lydia; and Hamilton's sister-in-law, Verbena Wedington. Make sure Hannah Hamilton, who lived with Mrs. Wedington, was being taken care of. Wire him back as soon as these questions were answered, and Wilcox would make a decision about whether to bring Hannah to Arizona or find her a new place to live in Savannah.

Rubbing the stubble on his chin, Jarrett wondered what this Wilcox fellow was up to. *I'd think he was trying to check up on this family for some sinister reason if he hadn't said make sure Hannah Hamilton was being taken care of.* He wondered how old Hannah was. Probably a little child, if somebody had to look after her. That was fine. He liked kids, most of the time.

He wasn't sure what it was, but something about this request intrigued Jarrett. He sat back in his chair and thought about it a minute. The door opened and his partner walked in.

"Well, little brother, I go to the gun shop to get a new sight for my rifle and come back to find you haven't moved from your seat the whole time. Must be planning on a special evening with the lovely Felicia."

Jarrett shook his head. "Nope. It's not that. You know I've been corresponding with Aaron Wilcox."

"Yep."

"I got another wire from him today."

Everett lifted an eyebrow. "Oh, what did he say this time?"

"He wants to hire our firm, and as I've told you before, I'm thinking about taking this on."

"Still think it's a one-man job?"

"I do. I know I can always send for my *big brother* if it gets to be too much."

Everett chuckled. "Sorry if I offended you."

"I guess I shouldn't be so touchy. After all, I'm thirty years old and two inches taller than you. You may have ten minutes on me, but I could take you any day of the week."

"You really think so?"

"Absolutely." He tossed the wire to Everett. "Read this and see what you think."

Handing the wire back to Jarrett, Everett said, "Since there's nothing pressing around here, except Miss Newell's idea of maybe marrying up with you, I don't see any reason why you can't go to Georgia and check this out. It looks like good money."

"Felicia Newell has nothing to do with this. You know I see her when I see her. It's nothing, and I have no intention of ever marrying her. You know why."

Everett chuckled. "I guess I do. There have been a few other men going down to Chester Street now and then."

"Yeah, you included."

"Can't keep something that sweet all to yourself, brother."

"Will you quit yammering about Felicia Newell and say what you think about this job?"

"Since you insist. You know we haven't had a big job since we brought the Norton gang down. I figure I can handle anything that comes up here, including Felicia Newell."

"Go ahead and try to get Miss Newell interested, but I think she has her heart set on me."

"Confident, aren't you?"

"Damn right I am." Jarrett shook his head. "But as far as this job for Wilcox is concerned, I think you're right about me taking it. Of course, you and I both know you're not right about Miss Newell wanting you instead of me."

"We'll see about that after you leave."

Jarrett ignored his statement. "Going to a southern state I've never visited might be interesting. I'm sure my absence will make the lady's heart grow fonder."

"Then, I say take the job and let Felicia make up her own mind which of us is the better twin."

Making a quick decision, Jarrett glanced at the wire again, folded it and put it in his pocket. He then pushed himself from the chair, ran his fingers through his hair and put on his tan Stetson.

"I'll go to the telegraph office and let Wilcox know I'll take the job as soon as he sends the money as a retainer. Then, I'll make arrangements to get a train ticket to Savannah and gather up the other things I'll need for this trip to Georgia. In the meantime, I'll make sure Felicia has a night to remember me by."

Everett laughed out loud. "You do that, brother."

Hannah had heard the group of women leave from downstairs more than an hour earlier. Though it was Wednesday, her day to be downstairs, her aunt hadn't sent her butler up to carry her down. She rolled her chair to the window and looked out, wondering if Aunt Verbena would make her stay here till morning. It wasn't that the sparse room was uncomfortable. She had a fairly soft bed, though there could be more feathers in the mattress, and the mirror over the small dressing table was cracked in three places. Hannah had a hard time bending her head so she could see if all her pale blonde hair was in place. A ladder-backed chair sat near the window, but was only used when Lydia came to visit or Hannah was banished to her room without her wheelchair for some minor incident. Thankfully, that hadn't happened for a couple of weeks. It meant she was getting better at answering her aunt's questions the way the older woman thought they should be answered.

On the opposite wall from the bed was a wardrobe. It wasn't large, but there was plenty of room for her two decent dresses she owned—one of which she had made over from the one she'd sewed for her aunt two years earlier and the older woman had grown tired of. Though she sewed often for other people, Hannah hadn't had a new dress from new material in over a year.

Sewing was the one talent Hannah had that her aunt was proud of. The girl was a superb seamstress. Verbena and many of her friends sported dresses sewn by Hannah's hand. Though her work was shown off and bragged about continually, she received no pay for her labors. If one of the women would slip her a few dollars, when her aunt found out, she'd take it, saying it was still not enough to pay for the supplies such as thread, pins, needles and such that had been purchased to finish the product. Even with her aunt confiscating most of her money, Hannah somehow managed to save enough money her aunt didn't know about to help pay for the material to make Drina a wedding dress to take with her to Arizona. Of course, she couldn't shop for the cloth. Her sister Lydia paid for the balance, bought it and smuggled it in without her aunt knowing. Hannah had kept the dress hidden in her wardrobe and had worked on it after she was sure Aunt Verbena went to bed. Since she hadn't heard from her sister, Hannah now wondered if Drina wore the gown to get married.

It had been so long since Hannah had been allowed to construct herself a new dress she'd grown two inches, and her shape had become that of a woman. The dress was now too tight in places, and it was above her ankles. This spring she did get to make over an old one her aunt had discarded, but it was a little faded before she even got it, and it didn't fit her well since her body had changed its shape. She wondered if it would be prudent to ask her aunt for new material. Would Verbena think up some punishment and dare her to tell her sisters?

A knock on the door interrupted her thoughts. She turned as her sister Lydia came in.

"Lydia!" A big grin crossed Hannah's face. "I didn't know you were coming today, but it's wonderful to see you."

"Good to see you, too. It's been a while since Aunt Verbena allowed me to come see you without an appointment." Lydia reached down and hugged Hannah.

"I know. I think it's been over a month."

Lydia laughed and dropped to the ladder-backed chair. Her purple satin skirt spread out around her. "So, what's new in your life, little sister?"

"Oh, Lydia, what could be new in my life? I sit in this room unless Aunt Verbena sends Tobias up to carry me downstairs. Most of the time I sew, but occasionally I read or just sit here and look out the window."

"I'm sorry, honey. I wish I could do something about it, but you know when I tried get you to come live with me, Aunt Verbena went to court and told them that you were too young and impressionable to live above a saloon. The judge agreed."

"I know, Lydia. I wasn't complaining."

"If anyone has a right to complain, it's you. I'd try to get you out of here again, but I know they still won't let you come live with me. I'm sure everyone would agree that a saloon is still no place for a … young lady like you."

"You mean a *crippled* woman like me, don't you?"

Lydia looked hurt. "I didn't mean that at all, Hannah."

Hannah dropped her eyes. "I'm sorry, Lydia. I know you didn't. I'm just a little grouchy today."

"It's all right, dear. Now, let me tell you why I came to see you today."

"Please do."

"I got a letter from Drina. She was concerned about you. She said you hadn't answered either of her letters."

Hannah looked confused. "I haven't gotten any letters from Drina. I've wondered why she hadn't answered any of the ones I've sent her."

Lydia frowned. "She said she'd written you twice."

"And I've sent her three letters. I wrote a fourth one today while Aunt Verbena's friends were visiting."

"Something doesn't sound right. What did you do with the letters you wrote?"

"I gave them to Aunt Verbena to mail for me."

"I might have known. I'd bet everything I own she didn't mail them, and she didn't give you the ones Drina sent to you."

Tears came to Hannah's eyes. "Do you think she'd really be that mean?"

"Of course, she would. Aunt Verbena would have no qualms about doing such a thing!"

There was a knock on the door.

"Yes," Hannah said.

"It's me, Miss Hannah. Miz Wedington told me to bring you down."

"My sister is visiting."

"I know, Miss, but she said to bring you down anyway."

Hannah looked at Lydia and shrugged. "I don't have a choice. She'll get mad if I don't obey. Maybe we can visit downstairs."

"I understand. She's probably trying to get rid of me, but I'll come with you." Lydia paused. "Wait a second. Didn't you say you wrote Drina?"

"I did."

"Give the letter to me and I'll make sure it gets in the mail right away."

"Oh, thank you, Lydia. It's on that small table over there."

Lydia picked up the letter, put it in her draw-string purse and they headed downstairs.

When they reached the informal parlor, Tobias put Hannah on the settee. She thanked him as she always did, and he nodded, then went back up the stairs to get her wheelchair.

Verbena came into the room. She was tall and thin, and as was her style, she walked with her back stiff and her shoulders thrown back. Her gray hair was piled on top of her head in a tight bun and her thin face was accented with piercing brown eyes. She brushed imaginary lint from her tailored blue dress with the handmade lace collar. Hannah had completed the outfit only a week ago. With a sour look on her face, she said, "I thought you left, Lydia."

"I'll be leaving shortly, but Hannah and I hadn't finished our visit."

"We'll be a having our evening meal soon."

Lydia looked at the timepiece pinned to the bodice of her dress. "It's only four-thirty. Do you eat this early?"

Verbena pursed her lips, but didn't reply.

Lydia went on. "I got a letter from Drina. She asked about you, Aunt Verbena."

The older woman looked a bit interested as she turned toward Lydia. "Oh? What did she say?"

"She said she hoped you were well and still enjoyed all the ladies you entertain in your fine house."

"That was nice of her."

"She also asked about Hannah and she wondered why her baby sister hadn't answered the letters she'd sent her."

Verbena's eyes widened, but she muttered, "There have been no letters from Drina."

Hannah glanced at Lydia. She was uncomfortable with the way the conversation was going, because she knew her aunt would take it out on her if Lydia made her mad.

Lydia must have sensed her sister's discomfort, because she said, "Well, it's a long way to Arizona. I'm sure it would take a long time for a letter to reach Savannah."

Verbena visibly relaxed. "That's probably true."

Lydia stood. "Well, I don't want to keep you from your meal." She leaned over and kissed Hannah's forehead. "I'll see you soon, dear."

"Thank you for coming, Lydia."

Tobias came in with the wheelchair and Verbena said, "Tobias, see Lydia to the door."

He put the chair down in front of Hannah. "Yes, ma'am."

"Good-by, Aunt Verbena."

Verbena only nodded then turned to Hannah. "I hope you haven't gotten any ideas from her. You seem to change every time she visits you, and that's why I'm not fond of her coming. Your sister is not a good influence on you."

"No, ma'am," Hannah muttered and held her breath. Was her aunt going to come up with some punishment for her because Lydia had visited? Then Hannah realized she didn't care. It would be worth it, even for the short time she spent with her sister.

But her aunt actually almost smiled when she said, "Mrs. Bessie Calhoun, the new preacher's wife was so taken with the dress I'm wearing that she said she'd love to have the seamstress make her one. Of course I bragged that my niece was the seamstress with so much talent that she could design clothes for anyone. I told Mrs. Calhoun I felt sure you'd be happy to sew a dress for her."

Hannah realized she wasn't going to be punished and took a relieved breath. "Of course. I'd be happy to sew her a dress."

"I knew you would. Therefore, I made arrangements for her to bring the material she wanted it constructed from by here later this afternoon. I thought it'd be a good time for you to get her measurements. That's why your sister couldn't stay any longer today. It wouldn't be fitting for someone like Lydia to be visiting when the preacher's wife arrived. I'm sure she can come back by to see you in a month or so."

Hannah didn't answer and Verbena went on, "Now straighten your dress and smooth down your hair. Reverend Cedric and Mrs. Bessie Calhoun are two people I want you to always look presentable in front of when they see you. Mrs. Calhoun should arrive at any moment. I'm not sure whether he'll be with her or not, but either way, I want you to look nice."

Of course, her aunt hadn't taken into consideration that Lydia was busy at her work and it wasn't easy for her to get away, or that the sisters were enjoying the visit with each other, but there was no way she'd bring either fact up at this time. Hannah knew she had no other choice, so she gave the older woman one of the practiced false smiles she'd been able to master through the years of living with her relative. "That's fine, Aunt Verbena. I look forward to meeting Mrs. Calhoun and the Reverend also, if he accompanies her today."

"That's a good girl, Hannah. Just remember, you must always be polite to my friends."

"Yes, ma'am."

Chapter 2

Four weeks later, a rented buggy pulled up in front of a two-story Victorian home with its gingerbread trim and decorative porches both downstairs and up. There were several huge oak trees in the yard with streams of moss hanging from their limbs and a flower garden with an explosion of deep pink and white azaleas off to the side.

Though the beautiful spring day should have made him glad to be in Savannah, Jarrett MacMichael frowned. There was no obvious reason for his concern, but he couldn't get over the feeling that something was amiss. His detective mind told him to keep his eyes open, because something wasn't right here. He just wasn't sure what, but he intended to find out.

First of all, he wondered why anyone would worry about a person living in this luxury? Was there a tyrant in the house? If so, would the young Miss Hamilton be afraid to tell him if something bad was happening to her? Would he have to dig for clues to this whole situation, now that he was here? And the most immediate problem, would the aunt who they said owned the place admit him into her house? To top it all, would this trip to Georgia be a waste of time? He hoped not. It had taken more wires and a couple of letters to cement the deal with the Wilcoxes. That had happened four weeks ago, and now that he was in Savannah, Jarrett wanted to accomplish the quest he was hired to do. Though, after looking this place over, he couldn't help having some reservations. In the last wire from Wilcox, he had said the main goal was to escort Hannah Hamilton to Hatchet Springs, Arizona if the girl was able to travel. Jarrett decided the first thing he had to do was to find out what 'able to travel' meant.

That presented him another problem. Though Jarrett kind of liked them, he had no experience with children, to speak of. His sister Charlotte's twins were toddlers, and lived on a small ranch near their grandparents. Jarrett had seen them only one time, this past Christmas. Though he figured he might could handle a little boy, he wasn't sure about taking care of a girl. If he had to take the child back to Arizona, he decided the smart thing to do was to hire a nurse to accompany them. He was taking Aaron Wilcox at his word that money was no object in the completion of this task, and his expense account was the largest Jarrett had ever had.

Looking again at the stately home, he wondered what he should do first. His plan had been to simply walk in and explain that he was checking up on Hannah Hamilton for her brother-in-law and his wife; but for some reason, he didn't think this would be a smart move, and he hesitated. His instinct had served him well in the past, and he decided to heed it this time. This meant he would have to change his strategy.

He could turn around, go back to the livery and exchange the buggy for a saddle horse. He could then go visit the farm where Mrs. Wilcox's father lived and see what he could find out about Burl Hamilton's relationship to the child, Hannah. But that would waste time he hadn't prepared for. Besides, after the trip to the farm, he'd still have to come back here to speak with the girl. That is, if she wasn't too young to answer his questions.

He decided he'd stay where he was and play it by ear when he got into the house. He'd invented stories on the spot to tell people before and it had worked out well – most of the time.

Securing the horse and buggy to the hitching post at the end of the yard, he walked up the pristine walkway. Bracing himself for whoever or whatever was inside, he used the big brass knocker.

In a matter of minutes, a nice looking, middle-aged Negro man, almost as tall as Jarrett, opened the door. "Yes, sir."

"Hello, sir. I'm Jarrett MacMichael, here to see Miss Verbena Wedington."

The man stepped aside and let Jarrett into the entry hall. "I'll inform her you're here, sir. Please wait."

Jarrett nodded. When the butler left, Jarrett again wondered why someone living in this type comfort would need help. He shook his head and looked around the elaborately furnished entry. To the left of the front door was a parlor. He could see the furnishings were of carved woods and the chairs were upholstered in velvets and heavy damask materials. The painting over the settee was framed in a heavy gold leaf and he was sure it was of good quality. The tables in the room had marble tops and the oil lamps were of cut glass, including the one hanging from the ceiling. On one of the tables sat a marble statue approximately fourteen inches high. It looked to be of exceptional quality. The woman who lived here had to be wealthy.

The butler returned. "Miz Wedington said to seat you in the parlor, sir."

Jarrett was surprised when, instead of going to the left, the butler opened the doors on the right, exposing another parlor. This one wasn't as elegant as the first, but it was still well furnished. He followed the butler inside and took a seat on the black horsehair sofa.

In a few minutes a tall, neatly dressed older woman came into the room. She didn't smile as she entered, but she did hold out her hand.

"Miss Verbena Wedington, I presume." Jarrett stood and took her hand. "Jarrett MacMichael, ma'am."

"It's Mrs. Wedington, Mr. MacMichael." She stared at him

"I'm sorry. Thank you for seeing me without an appointment, Mrs. Wedington. It was gracious of you."

Verbena's stern look softened a little. "Since you're a stranger to me, may I ask why you're here, sir?"

His instinct told him this woman couldn't be fully trusted. Now was the time to fall back on his inventive mind. He just hoped he'd be able to convince her he was a gentleman. A rich one, at that. "I'm so sorry, ma'am. I should have stated my business earlier. I'm here from Flagstaff, Arizona to meet with two men who want me, along with a friend of mine, to invest in a new hotel in Savannah. The town is growing fast and they're sure it will be a prudent investment. I'm sorry I'm not able to give you the names of these men, but I'm sure you'll understand."

"Yes, I do appreciate why you can't name the people you're going into business with."

"Thank you for understanding. Many people wouldn't." Jarrett gave her a big grin. "Now, to explain why I so rudely dropped in on you without informing you first: This afternoon was the only free time I'm afraid I'll have for several days and I wanted to keep a promise to a good friend of mine."

She frowned, but said nothing.

Jarrett went on. "Of course my friend doesn't mind if I give you his name. It's Aaron Wilcox."

"I don't believe I know Mr. Wilcox."

"He told me you hadn't met personally, but you do have a connection. Mr. Wilcox's wife is your niece, Drina Hamilton Wilcox."

She looked puzzled. "But Drina went to Arizona to marry a ranch man."

Grinning at her expression, he said, "Oh, he's a rancher, all right. Aaron Wilcox owns one of the largest ranches in Arizona, but his real wealth comes from his interest in an Arizona silver mine...and I think he also has some connection to an uncle who runs a shipping business in Galveston." At least part of this was true. Wilcox did own a huge ranch.

Surprise spread across her face. "Oh, my. I never dreamed..."

"When Aaron told his wife I was coming to Savannah on business, she insisted I visit you and find out how things were going with you and her sister, Hannah. She wanted me to see if there was any way she could help you with her sister's care." Now he'd thrown out the name and the idea that there might be money involved, he was anxious to hear her reply.

Verbena's eyes seemed to glow. "As you must know, looking after Hannah has been a trial for me, but as a good Christian woman, there was no way I could turn my back on the child. As it turns out, she hasn't given me that much trouble. Of course, I can always use financial assistance. Hannah's father is in no position to help at all. Her sister, Lydia gives me a little money occasionally, but she can't be relied on." She paused and Jarrett waited. She then went on, "I'm delighted to learn Drina has married so well. The poor girl had a rough life living here in Georgia with her papa. She deserves to be comfortable now."

Jarrett wanted to ask her why she hadn't helped her niece when she needed it, but he only smiled. "Yes, she's very happy."

He decided it was time to push his luck. "I don't want to impose, but would it be possible for me to meet Hannah? I've heard so much about her…"

Was it fright that crossed Verbena's eyes? If not, what could it be? He knew instantly that she didn't want him to meet the girl.

Finally, she mumbled, "This is the time of day that Hannah takes a nap. I really don't want to disturb her because she needs her rest."

He was sure the woman was lying. He pushed her further. "Oh, I didn't know she napped."

"Oh, yes. With her condition, she tires easily."

Jarrett wondered what the condition was, but he didn't ask. "I see. Then I must not keep you any longer today. I'll try to find time to return, but now I need to go make some arrangements about finding a place to eat my supper. I was looking forward to some good southern food and the place I chose at dinner was a disappointment." He stood. "I'll tell Mrs. Wilcox that you and Hannah are doing fine."

"Wait." Verbena touched his arm. He could tell she was afraid something profitable was about to get away from her. "Why don't you come back and join me for supper? I'm sure Hannah will be able to join us, and you can meet her then."

He was surprised at the invitation, but tried not to show it. "That sounds wonderful. I'd enjoy sharing a good home-cooked meal in your home. I'm not that fond of restaurant food."

"Very good. Shall I expect you to return about six this evening?"

"Would it put you out if I came at seven? I need to meet with the business men to let them know I'm tied up tonight." He asked this to see if his changing the time would upset her.

It didn't. "Seven would be perfect."

He smiled at her. "I'll see you at seven, Mrs. Wedington. Thank you very much for the invitation. You've especially kind to invite me."

She walked him to the door and he knew she was still watching when he drove the buggy away.

♥♥♥

Hannah sat at the small window in her room and watched the tall, handsome man walk in long, determined steps to the street and climb into the buggy. Though she couldn't tell if he was handsome just by viewing him from the back, she was sure he was by the way he carried himself. She wished she could see his face. As she watched the man drive away, she wondered who he was and why he was visiting Aunt Verbena and even if he'd come again. If so, maybe she could meet him next time. Hannah wasn't used to her aunt having male guests. Unless it was the doctor, or the preacher, or occasionally Mr. Phillips, it was a rarity for a man to come to the house. That was one reason this man intrigued her so, but she guessed she would never know anything about this stranger except that he was probably a good looking man.

Nobody she knew had indicated they suspected she'd ever noticed a man's looks, but she had. It was her foot that was useless, not her eyes. Of course she kept this fact about herself as her secret. She wasn't about to tell people how she wished she could meet a handsome man someday, because she knew they would laugh at her and say a crippled had no right to think such thoughts. Some people even thought that because her foot was crippled her mind was also, so how could they ever accept that she wished for a normal life like any woman?

Her door opened without a knock and she turned her wheelchair around. Verbena walked in. "I see you lollygagging at the window instead of finishing up Mrs. Calhoun's second dress. You've had a week to work on it and you know she's coming tomorrow to get it."

"Yes, ma'am. It's all ready with the exception of finishing the hem. I ran out of thread and was going to ask Tobias or Minerva to request some from you when they brought my supper."

Her aunt grunted then said. "I'll be having company for supper and you're to join me. I'll send Minerva up with some warm water. I want you to wash up and get out of that old faded dress. Put your best one on. The blue one you made from the one I recently gave you. You'll also need to brush your hair and braid it or tie it back, or something. When you're ready, I'll send Tobias up for you. I want you to look respectable when my guest gets here tonight."

Hannah couldn't believe that she was being invited to have supper in the dining room with her aunt and a guest. It hadn't happened in a long time that she'd been invited to eat in the dining room. And it had never happened with a guest. Before she could stop herself, she blurted, "May I ask who will be joining us?"

Verbena pursed her lips. "I guess I might as well tell you. You'll find out soon enough. It's a Mr. Jarrett MacMichael. Seems he's friends with the man Drina married, and he came by to speak to us. I felt you should meet him so he could tell Drina's husband you were well taken care of here."

Hannah didn't notice the fact that her aunt said she was well taken care of because she couldn't help the excitement that she going to get to meet someone who had news of Drina. "Oh, how wonderful. I can't wait to hear how Drina's doing. I haven't heard from her since she left."

"According to Mr. MacMichael, she's doing fine—so don't start making a pest of yourself by asking him questions." She paused and looked back as she was half-way out the door. "Now calm yourself down and start making yourself presentable. You look like a ragamuffin, and I don't want him to see you like that." The door closed.

It was all Hannah could do not to shout out loud when she found herself alone. She was going to get word about Drina from someone who actually knew her husband. Reminding herself to contain her enthusiasm so she wouldn't get into trouble with her aunt, she rolled over to her dresser and picked up the hairbrush. If Aunt Verbena wanted her to look her best, then she'd do all she could to accomplish it. It was the least she could do since she was to be allowed to join her aunt and her guest at supper. She began to form questions in her mind. She wanted to ask just the right things so she could learn all she could about her sister and her husband. She smiled as she leaned over so she could see how her hair was shaping up in the unbroken corner of the mirror.

♥♥♥

When he left Verbena's house, Jarrett decided he had time before supper to check on Burl Hamilton. Maybe a meeting with this man would go as well as the one with Verbena Wedington. As he came into the yard, he couldn't believe how rundown the farm appeared to be. He reined his horse up and threw the bridle around the leaning hitching post near the front porch. At one time, the farm house had been lovely, but today it had shutters hanging at angles beside the filthy windows and there was a missing step leading to the sagging front porch. Several windows facing the wrap-around-porch were patched with some sort of heavy paper. He thought he saw someone peek out one of the windows, but when they didn't come out, he wasn't sure.

A scrawny hound dog came running around the edge of the porch. He growled and barked at the intruder. Behind him, a dirty farmer with a ragged pair of overalls and a floppy brown hat pulled over his eyes yelled, "What're you doing here and what do you want?" In his right hand he had a shotgun.

Jarrett knew he had to be careful. This man didn't look like he'd mind raising that gun and putting a bullet in anyone who he took a notion to shoot, including Jarrett. "I've come to talk to a man named Burl Hamilton. Is that you?"

"Who wants to know?" The dog continued to bark. "Shut up, dog." The old man raised his leg and kicked the animal in the side. The pitiful looking hound ran off toward the woods whining. Another dog crawled out from under the porch and followed the hurt one.

"I'm Jarrett MacMichael."

"That don't tell me nothing. I never heard of you. Are you from the county?"

"No. I'm from Flagstaff, Arizona."

"You the man Drina run off and said she was gonna get married to in Arizona?"

"No, but I know the man."

"He ain't sending her back here to me is he?"

"Not that I know of."

"That's too bad. I could use somebody asides Lulu to do some cooking round here." He spit a stream of tobacco juice on the ground and let his gun relax. "Told the fool she should've stayed here where she had a decent home. At least until Lydia decides to leave that outlaw she married and come back where she belongs."

"Do just you and Lulu live here, Mr. Hamilton?"

Burl shook his head. "Nah. I got a couple of maids and a butler just like that shriveled up old sister-in-law of mine. Not to mention the beautiful young wife that loves me more than anything." His voice was sarcastic. "What does it look like? Seen anybody else around?"

Jarrett ignored the sarcasm. "What about your other child, Hannah? Doesn't she live here with you?"

"Hell no! And she never will. I didn't want her when I had her. I give her to her aunt when she was little. Ain't seen her since, and don't want to." The man seemed to get a better grip on the gun. "What business is if of yourn, anyway?"

Jarrett knew he had to be careful. This man was unpredictable. "You're right, Mr. Hamilton. It's none of my business." He laughed.

"Well, I'm tired of your foolish questions and there ain't nothing else for you to talk to me about." He raised the gun and pointed it at Jarrett. "Now, why don't you jest get back on that horse and ride outta here afore I take a notion to shoot you?"

"I'm sorry I disturbed you, Mr. Hamilton, but I thought you might like to hear from your daughter, Drina."

"Don't care nary a thing about hearing from her. She weren't worth much 'cept she'd put a decent meal together now and again. Let that cowboy she married put up with her stupid ways till she decides she wants to come back and cook for me." He cocked the gun. "Now, git."

"Yes, sir. I'm taking my leave." Jarrett climbed on the horse.

"And don't come back."

Jarrett didn't say anything, but he had no intention of ever returning to this farm. He figured he'd seen what he needed to and had gotten all the information he'd get from Burl Hamilton.

Chapter 3

Jarrett couldn't believe his eyes when Tobias showed him into the formal parlor that evening. One of the most beautiful young women he'd ever seen sat on the settee with her slightly faded royal blue skirts billowing around her legs. The neck of her dress was scooped, and he noticed the smooth, white skin on her neck. Her long, luscious blonde hair was pulled back and tied with a ribbon matching the dress. Her blue eyes looked at him with interest. Though Jarrett was used to beautiful women, for some strange reason, this woman made his heart flutter.

He glanced away thinking this couldn't possibly be the girl, Hannah, everyone was talking about. Or could it? If so, there was no way this lovely young woman needed anyone to look after her. Of course, he noted silently, there were probably a gaggle of young men who would like the job. If it wasn't for his affair with Felicia at this time, he'd be there in the mob to assist this lady, too…and maybe he would be there regardless of Felicia.

Verbena stood and held out her hand. "Mr. MacMichael, I'm delighted you came. It's a pleasure to have you join my niece and me for supper."

Knowing he had to stay on Verbena Wedington's good side, he took her hand and lifted it to his lips. "It's my pleasure, dear lady. I've been looking forward to seeing you and meeting your niece."

She grinned and nodded toward the settee. "May I present my niece, Hannah Hamilton?"

He was surprised at the revelation that this was the girl he'd been seeking, but he was able to hide his amazement. He took Hannah's hand and kissed it lightly as his heart did another little unexpected flip. "I'm delighted to meet you, Miss Hamilton."

"And I'm pleased to meet you, Mr. MacMichael."

When she smiled at him, he could hardly believe the strange feeling that ran down his spine. This shouldn't be happening. He was here to do a job. Not be stirred by a beautiful young lady. Though stirred, he was.

His thoughts were interrupted when a pretty, slightly rotund Negro lady came in with a tray. "Here's the tea you requested, Miz Wedington."

Verbena gave her a hard look. Jarrett knew the mistress wasn't pleased that her maid spoke in front of a guest. It didn't surprise him. From first meeting her, he'd already gathered Mrs. Wedington was stuck on correct protocol and demanded those around her use it at all times. She was also probably still stuck in the past when those of color were only slaves. It probably bothered her to have to hire them to work in her house now.

Verbena turned to him. "Please have a seat, Mr. MacMichael and Minerva will serve the tea."

He chose a chair where he could observe Hannah Hamilton without it being obvious he was doing so. He needed to figure out why Wilcox thought this lady needed his help. Though, he didn't mind giving that help, if it was necessary. In fact, he'd look forward to rendering it.

"Thank you," he smiled and said when the maid handed him the filled tea cup. Jarrett didn't particularly like tea and would have much rather had a cup of strong coffee or a stiff drink of whiskey to get him through this supper, but he would make do since he had no choice in the matter. He was on a fact-finding mission, and he wouldn't do anything to jeopardize that.

"I hope your meeting with your business partners went well this afternoon."

"Yes, Mrs. Wedington, it was satisfactory." He threw Hannah a smile and she returned it, then ducked her head as if she was embarrassed or afraid. He wasn't sure which.

"My husband, Hector Wedington, was an astute businessman. I miss him so very much. He was always doing special things for me." She waved her hand toward the marble statue. "For instance, he brought me that lovely piece of art when he returned from a business trip to New Orleans. He knew King David was my favorite Bible character and he wanted me to have the special remembrance. I cherish it, not only for its beauty, but because Hector was so thoughtful."

Jarrett drew his attention back to the older woman. "That is a lovely piece and I agree it was very thoughtful of your husband to purchase it for you. More husbands should think of their wives in such a way."

"Are you married, Mr. MacMichael?"

"No, ma'am. Not yet."

"I'm sure you'll make a wonderful husband when you meet the right woman." She sighed. "God forbid if something were to happen to you, she'd always cherish your memory."

Jarrett had no intention of marrying any time soon, but he didn't tell Mrs. Wedington this. Instead, he asked, "Have you been alone long?"

"Almost seventeen years." She sighed and gave him a crooked smile. "You would've liked Hector very much, Mr. MacMichael. You remind me of him."

"You flatter me, but I appreciate you saying such a nice thing." Was this woman actually flirting with him? To change the conversation, Jarrett turned to Hannah. "I'm sure you miss Mr. Wedington, too."

Hannah looked a little scared, but then she shook her head. "I never met him."

Before he could ask why, Verbena said, "My dear husband passed away before Hannah came to live with me."

"I'm sorry." He changed the subject because Hannah looked uncomfortable. "It does look like your late husband was a good businessman. You have such a lovely home. May I ask what type of trade Mr. Wedington was in?"

"I don't mind at all. My husband was extremely judicious when it came to business. When he saw the war brewing, he was smart enough to invest in the right things. At first, he and his partner bought a small fleet of ships, then he bought stock in one of the companies that made buttons for uniforms, and I think he had something to do with the productions of gunpowder. I'm not sure what else he was involved in, but I'm sure there were other businesses over the years. Of course, the war was hard on many of us and we lost a lot of our material wealth. Yet, with Hector being so diverse with his investments, we fared better than most people."

"I'm sure that was a blessing for you and your family." Again, he glanced at Hannah. Why was she acting so nervous? He hoped it wasn't because of him. He didn't want to make the lovely woman upset in anyway.

"Of course it was. My parents were dead, but I had my sister, Ella. She stayed with Hector and me until she married Burl Hamilton. They had three children, all girls, and Hannah is the youngest. After her death, Hannah came to live with me as a small child. She's like my own daughter." Verbena set her tea cup in the saucer and placed it on the table. "Now, Mr. MacMichael, I've told you about my life and I'd like for you to return the favor."

Now what was he going to do? Tell her the truth about himself? He didn't think that would serve his purpose since he knew he wasn't a very interesting person. He'd followed his father's footsteps and became a rancher for a short time. For some reason, the profession hadn't taken with him, and he decided to become a lawman. For a while he worked as a marshal, but he didn't like the rules, though he did like the part of tracking down a criminal. It was then he decided to go in business with his twin brother, Everett. Five years ago, the MacMichael & MacMichael Detective agency was born.

Instinct told him Verbena Wedington wouldn't be impressed with this story, so he decided to do what he called *improvising*.

Taking a breath he said, "I'm afraid I'm not very interesting, but I'll tell you some of the highlights. There were two boys in my family. I was the youngest, and as lots of families, we were considered part of the poor working class. One day my brother, Everett came home from school with a bloody nose and a broken arm. He had taken a biscuit with nothing but butter on it for lunch and some of the boys made fun of him. They told him his mother didn't care enough to give him a good meal and they made him cry. Of course, he fought with them, and lost. Dad was furious. He decided then and there that his family wasn't going to stay poor. He went to the mountains and staked out a gold mine. Needless to say, it was the smartest thing he ever did. It made us wealthy."

At least part of this was true. He did have a brother named Everett. He decided not to mention his younger sister, Charlotte.

"Is your father still living?"

"Unfortunately, no. He and mother were both swept away in a flash flood on their way home from a trip to Denver. They shouldn't have set out for the estate with the rain coming down like it was, but my father felt he could beat the storm and they were anxious to get home." He wondered what the folks would think if they knew he'd killed them off in this story. Instead of being dead, they were happily working on their ranch near Phoenix.

"I'm so sorry. How about your brother?"

"Everett is happily married to a woman he met when he went to England on business. Her daddy is a lord, or a count…or some type of royalty. They live in England and have a little princess of their own." He wondered how Everett would feel if he knew he'd graduated him from the detective business, married him off, and elevated him to royalty in England

Verbena's eyes lit up. "Really? Royalty?" He nodded, and she went on. "Have you visited them?"

Hannah looked interested, but there was something in her eyes that made him wonder if she knew he was telling a tall tale. He gathered that this young lady was no fool. He answered Verbena's question with, "I'm so busy with my own enterprises that I've only had time to visit them once. They have promised to come visit me in the next couple of years. Everett wants to show his wife and daughter his country."

"I think that's wonderful."

There was a knock on the parlor door, and Minerva poked her head in. "Supper is ready, Miz Wedington."

"Send Tobias to get Hannah."

"Yes, ma'am." She scurried away.

Jarrett couldn't help wondering why the man was to come get Hannah. The fact was, he'd been looking forward to offering her his arm so he could escort her to supper. Jarrett's question was answered in a matter of a moment. Tobias returned pushing a wheelchair. Jarrett was stunned as the butler pushed it up to the settee and reached down to lift Hannah into it.

So that was her problem. She couldn't walk. He never would have guessed.

Verbena stood. "Shall we go into supper, Mr. MacMichael?"

"Of course." He stood, and since he had no alternative, he offered her his arm. They went out of the parlor leaving Tobias to push Hannah's chair behind them.

♥♥♥

Hannah wondered about Mr. Jarrett MacMichael. Yes, he was as handsome as she thought he'd be now that she'd seen his face. In fact, he was the kind of man she often dreamed about and wished she could meet. Yes, he told a good story about his life, but something didn't ring true to her. Was he trying to impress Aunt Verbena? If so, why? What could her aunt do for him? And why hadn't he mentioned her sister? She'd kept quiet just like her Aunt Verbena had told her to, but she didn't intend to let him get through the meal and leave this house without answering a question or two about Drina.

Verbena moved to the head of the table and Jarrett held the chair for her. She motioned for him to take a place on her right. Tobias rolled Hannah's chair to the side of the table on her aunt's left.

For a moment, no one spoke, and Hannah decided to take advantage of the situation. If her aunt didn't like her speaking up, she might have to pay for her boldness later, but she was going to take a gamble since this might be the last chance she had to talk to Mr. MacMichael. After all, she'd done what her aunt told her to do in the parlor, which was to sit quietly and speak only when spoken to. She took a breath and in a quiet voice she said, "Mr. MacMichael, I understand you know my sister, Drina."

"Actually, I haven't met her, but I know her husband, Aaron Wilcox. When he told her I was coming to Savannah, he said she insisted I visit you, because she misses you a lot."

She thought he started to say something else, but checked himself before it was out.

Her aunt shot her a look that seemed to say, *stop talking now*. Hannah ignored it. "Did he say how she was doing?"

"He told me they hadn't been married long, but she was settling into ranch life well and was making friends in town and on the nearby ranches. He did say she was happy—with the exception of missing you."

"I miss her, too." If he only knew how much…but she couldn't explain. Not with Aunt Verbena glaring at her.

He nodded. "He said you were her younger sister, and she wanted me to visit you when I arrived here. I think she was a little concerned about you."

Again, the frightened look crossed her face, but she said, "Oh? Why is that?" She noticed Verbena pursing her mouth, but the aunt didn't say anything.

"Aaron told me your sister said you hadn't answered the letters she'd sent you, and she was afraid you'd fallen sick, or something."

She couldn't help but throw a glance at her aunt. The older woman still didn't look happy about the conversation, but Hannah said anyway, "I've written her, but I guess with the distance, it takes a long time for a letter to get there. As for me being sick, you can see I'm fine."

"Yes, I can see that, and when I wire Aaron the details of our business here, I'll tell him to let his wife know I've met you and your aunt and that both of you are well and seem to be doing fine. I'll also tell her to be on the lookout for a letter."

Minerva entered the dining room carrying a tray with a large beef roast. She acted as if she didn't know what to do with it.

Verbena looked at Minerva then glanced at Jarrett. She asked, "Mr. MacMichael, would you mind carving the meat?"

"I'd be honored, ma'am."

"Put the roast in front of Mr. MacMichael, Minerva."

"Yes, ma'am." She sat the platter at his place.

Soon, the plates were served, and Hannah didn't get a chance to ask their visitor any more questions. Her aunt monopolized the conversation and her eyes seemed to shoot daggers every time Hannah started to say something. She figured she might as well give up. She was probably going to have to stay in her room for at least a week—maybe a month—without her wheelchair for what she'd already said to the man. But it was worth it. She found out that Drina was happily married. That was what was important.

After the dessert was served and eaten, Hannah wiped her mouth with the linen napkin. Knowing she'd not get another chance to talk to Mr. MacMichael, Hannah said, "Aunt Verbena, I'm a little tired. Would you mind if I go to my room after supper?"

"I think that's a good idea, Hannah. I know being here is tiring on you." Her voice was sweet, which was something unusual. Verbena then turned to MacMichael. "Hannah tires easily and needs lots of rest."

Hannah knew her aunt was saying this because she wanted to impress their guest. She didn't care. She was tired of seeing Verbena make a fool of herself flirting with this handsome younger man. The sad thing was, he seemed to be enjoying it.

"I understand about needing rest." Jarrett turned and smiled at Hannah. "I appreciate you coming in to have supper with me, Miss Hamilton. I hope to see you again before I return to Arizona."

"I hope so, too, Mr. MacMichael." Hannah returned his smile, but said nothing else.

"Before you retire, could I ask you another question?"

She glanced at her aunt expecting her to butt in and tell him she'd answer his questions, but when Verbena said nothing, Hannah nodded. "Yes."

"Does your other sister live here in Savannah?"

"She does. She and her husband have interest in a saloon here in town, but I'm afraid I don't know the name of it."

Looking at Verbena he asked, "Would you happen to know, ma'am?"

"Of course not." She sounded indignant, but turned toward Hannah. "I'll call Tobias to see you to your room."

Jarrett quickly moved behind Hannah's chair. "I feel I'm the reason you're tired, Miss Hamilton. May I have the pleasure of seeing you to your room?"

"That's not necessary." Verbena stood. "Tobias is used to helping Hannah."

"It's no trouble, Mrs. Wedington. I'm sure Miss Hamilton's room is here on the first floor, so it's no trouble at all."

Hannah didn't say anything. She waited to see what he would do when he found out her room was on the second floor.

After an awkward moment of silence, Verbena said, "Well, there wasn't a room downstairs that would suit my niece, so she has a more suitable room on the second floor."

Jarrett frowned. "So you put her on the second floor? Isn't a lot of trouble getting her chair up and down the stairs?"

When Verbena said nothing, Hannah muttered, "It doesn't seem to be a lot of trouble. Tobias carries me up or down, then goes back for my chair."

"So, as you must understand, there's no way I can permit you to see Hannah to her room. It wouldn't be proper for you to go upstairs with her." The older woman stiffened her back.

He looked at her and surprised Hannah by saying, "From what I have observed, I'm younger and stronger than Tobias. Don't you think I'm capable of carrying Miss Hamilton?"

"But, it's not seemly." It was obvious Verbena was becoming upset.

Jarrett ignored her, walked to Hannah's chair and picked her up.

She was startled. Though she was concerned about what her aunt would do, she couldn't help but be a little excited since, for the first time in her life, she was in a handsome man's arms. This was going to give her something to dream about—but what were the strange feelings that almost overwhelmed her when she felt him pull her against his hard chest? There was also the smell of spice, and a manly, musky odor, and maybe the remnants of cigarette or cigar smoke.

He headed toward the stairs saying to Aunt Verbena, "Tell Tobias to bring the chair." Glancing down at Hannah he added, "Now, direct me to your room."

Hannah had no choice. "It's the last door on the right."

When they were halfway up the steps, he whispered in her ear, "Are you going to be in trouble because I insisted on bringing you to your room?"

Surprised that he was that intuitive, she whispered back, "I might."

"I'll see if I can smooth it over with your aunt." He turned down the hall toward her room. "I'll be coming back, because Mrs. Wilcox is convinced you're not happy living with your aunt. Don't say anything to her, but that's why I'm here. I need to find out what's going on."

Hannah's heart began to pound. "Tell Drina to please not worry about me. I'm doing all right."

"She and her husband don't want you to just be 'doing all right', they want you to be happy."

There was the sound of footsteps behind them. "I think Aunt Verbena is coming."

"Then, don't say anything to her, and we'll talk later."

She was sure he gave her a little squeeze.

Jarrett could hardly believe his eyes when he carried Hannah into her room. Compared to the opulence of the rest of the house, this room looked barer than any servant's quarters he'd ever seen. "Are you sure we're in the right room?"

"Of course, this is the right place." She laughed a little. "You can put me down over there on the chair by the window. Tobias will get me in my wheelchair when he brings it up."

He put her in the chair she indicated and turned to look around the room. He was beginning to understand why Wilcox had told him to be sure Hannah was being taken care of. He didn't have a chance to ask her why the discrepancy in the furnishings between these and those downstairs, because Verbena came trotting in.

"Mr. MacMichael, I can't permit you to be in my niece's bedroom. You must leave immediately."

He tried to look shocked. "I'm so sorry if I offended you, Mrs. Wedington. I knew Tobias was busy and I truly thought I was helping you by bringing Miss Hamilton to her room. I guess I'm just the type of man who sees something that needs doing and I take it upon myself to do it. That's one thing that has made me successful over the years."

She seemed to relax a little. "I guess I can understand that. But would you kindly come downstairs now?"

"Of course, I will." He turned to Hannah. "I bid you good night, Miss Hamilton. It was a pleasure meeting you."

"I enjoyed meeting you, too, and please tell my sister's husband that I'm doing fine and am looking forward to hearing from her."

"I certainly will." He knew he had to get Verbena Wedington back on his side and keep her from taking her irritation out on Hannah. Offering his arm to her, he said, "Now that your niece will soon be settled, may I escort you downstairs? Maybe we could have an after dinner drink and discuss something I think would be prudent to both of us."

She looked a little surprised, but smiled and accepted his arm.

He didn't want to act as if he was ignoring Hannah, but he couldn't help it. He couldn't let the aunt think he was appalled at the furnishings in the small bedroom or think he had an interest in Hannah's wellbeing. Though the room was clean and probably had everything one needed to survive, it was not the kind of room the niece of a wealthy woman should be living in. Wilcox was right. This needed investigating.

Verbena spoke and broke into his thoughts as they stepped into the hall. "May I ask you something?"

"Absolutely."

"Would you like a special after dinner drink?"

"Of course, I would. That sounds great."

"I'm sure you don't do a lot of drinking, but my dear Hector would often have a spot of brandy after a good meal. Maybe you would like that?" She smiled at him with the question in her eyes.

He thought he'd managed to get back on her good side. Just to cement the idea, he reached over and patted her hand. "My dear, you've just said the magic words. You're right, I don't drink a lot, but a nip or so at a time like this seems to be called for, and I'm delighted you suggested it."

He would have sworn she giggled.

Hannah reached down to remove her shoe and stockings. Though she wore stockings on both legs, only her left leg had a shoe. Her deformed right foot was encased in a small satin slipper that she'd sewn to keep it warm since no shoe fit the withered foot.

There was a knock at the door. She took a deep breath. "Come in," she said, expecting her aunt to walk in.

Instead, Tobias rolled in her chair. "Here you go, miss."

Surprise crossed Hannah's face. "I figured my aunt would keep the chair downstairs since I'd been so bold as to speak to her guest."

Tobias smiled. "She might have if that Mr. MacMichael hadn't noticed it in the dining room and offered to bring it up."

She giggled. "He did that?"

"He sure did, but you know Mrs. Wedington wouldn't permit him to bring it up here. She called me and told me to bring your chair up, then she called Minerva to bring drinks to the parlor. Can you believe that? She told her to bring him brandy and her sherry. Minerva was as shocked as I was."

"Do you know who this man is, Tobias?"

He shook his head. "I don't know any more than you do about him, but your aunt shore seems to like him."

"I know she does."

Tobias chuckled. "Of course, I don't mind. It makes her easier to get along with, and that's a good thing."

She laughed. "I agree."

"I better get back. You know how she is. She don't want me being up here any longer than I has to be."

"I do know that, and I thank you for all you do, Tobias. I wish things were different, but you know you and Minerva make my living here bearable."

"We's will do anything we can for you, Miss Hannah. You knows that."

"I *do* know that, Tobias and I appreciate it more than I can say."

He grinned at her and went out the door.

Chapter 4

Lydia looked at the tall, handsome man who tossed his tan Stetson in a nearby chair and took a seat in the red-and-black upholstered chair beside her desk. He'd requested a private meeting with her, but she'd at first refused. He then sent word that it was about her sisters. She'd changed her mind and had him shown to her office. After doing this, she did ask that Ramon, the big man who worked in the saloon to protect the women, to stand by in case she needed him to come to her aid.

She didn't normally have to take these precautions because Bradly was usually here to be at her side when something unusual like this unexpected visit came up. But with Bradly out of town, she decided to obey her husband and be overly careful this time. She just hoped he was doing the same thing in New Orleans, where she felt there would be much more danger.

After a quick introduction she said, "Would you please explain why you said your business with me concerned my sisters, Mr. MacMichael?"

His voice was strong and direct when he said, "I've been hired by Aaron Wilcox to investigate what's going on with your sister, Hannah. I appreciate you seeing me very much, Mrs. Patterson. I think talking with you will help me gain a perspective into this investigation."

She eyed him with interest. "I've heard that name, but I don't know Aaron Wilcox personally or why he'd be interested in Hannah."

"I'm sorry. I should have explained my connection to Wilcox. As you probably know he's married to your sister, Drina. She's concerned about Hannah, and her husband hired me to check things out for her. I must say, after what I saw at Verbena Wedington's house, I think your sister has a reason for this concern."

This surprised her. "You've met Aunt Verbena?"

"Yes. I had supper with her and Hannah last night."

Lydia couldn't help smiling. "That's a rarity. Aunt Verbena doesn't often let Hannah come down to supper when she entertains."

"I told her I was a friend of Wilcox and I specifically asked to meet Hannah."

"And she took your word for it?"

"Your aunt is easily impressed. She thinks I'm a rich businessman visiting in Georgia from Arizona to invest in a big hotel that is to be built here in Savannah."

"That *would* impress her." She gave him a hard look. "If that was just a lie you told her, who are you really?"

"I'm going to be honest with you, Mrs. Patterson and hope I can trust you to keep it quiet. I'm a detective. I have an agency in Flagstaff with my twin brother. Wilcox contacted me and asked that I come here to investigate how his wife's sister was getting along." He picked up the drink she'd served him. "I hope *you'll* be honest with me about how things are, Mrs. Patterson. Though I've only seen her once, I'm not so sure your sister has it very good at your aunt's fine house."

"You're right about that, but every time I ask her, Hannah says things are all right. I think she might be afraid of what Aunt Verbena will do if she tells me the whole truth."

"Do you think your sister is being mistreated?"

"The only thing she's ever confessed to me is that when Aunt Verbena gets mad at her, she sends her to her room, but keeps her wheelchair downstairs so she can't even get to the window to look out. She also told me once that when she was little she was often spanked, but that ended when our dear Auntie figured out Hannah could sew. She's turned into a wonderful seamstress. I think this made Aunt Verbena ease up on her a lot. Because our aunt wants to always impress her friends, she keeps Hannah busy sewing expensive-looking dresses for her and many of the women she socializes with. Of course, Hannah isn't allowed to sew a dress for herself except every year or so, and she isn't allowed to sew anywhere in the house except her room. Verbena doesn't want the mess downstairs. When the women come to try on their outfits, our aunt does have Hannah down in the parlor to fit them. I'm sure it's because she doesn't want her friends to see Hannah's room."

"Is sewing the only thing Hannah likes to do?"

"She loves to read, but because of all the sewing, she hardly has time to indulge something for her own pleasure."

"How about her education?"

"Aunt Verbena was like our mother. She insisted on the three of us getting as much education as we could. But our aunt wouldn't permit Hannah to attend school. She said the other children would make fun of her, and nobody had time to push her wheelchair there and back daily. She did have tutors come in and teach her. Of course, her reading has broadened her education a lot. She's read all the classics from our aunt's extensive library because that's what she's allowed to read. I do slip her in a romance novel now and then. She hides them because our aunt would never permit her to read what she thinks is nothing but trash. She doesn't complain when she reads Shakespeare as long as it doesn't interfere with her sewing."

Jarrett hadn't seen any books in the room, but that didn't mean they weren't hidden there somewhere. He changed the subject. "What do you think of the way Hannah's room is furnished?"

She grinned. "When did you see her room?"

Jarrett explained how he'd carried Hannah to her room over Verbena's protests.

Lydia laughed out loud. "You are a sly one, Mr. MacMichael. I bet the straight-laced Verbena had a fit."

"Please, call me Jarrett, and I think the lady calmed down when I escorted her downstairs and had an after supper brandy with her." He smiled. "Though there's a sizable difference in our ages, I got the strange feeling she likes me."

Lydia laughed again. "I can't think of Aunt Verbena liking any man, but because you're able to charm her, I think I like you, Jarrett. And that means you should call me Lydia."

"Thank you, I will. Now, can I count on you to help me find out what's going on in the Wedington house?"

"Yes, you absolutely can. What do you want me to do?"

"First of all, tell me when and why Hannah went to live with your aunt."

"I'm not positive, but I think our mama had something to do with it."

"Oh?"

"Mama was sick for a long time, and I think she somehow knew she wasn't going to live to see any of us grow up, but because of Hannah's withered foot, she was mostly concerned about her. When Hannah was about six months, Aunt Verbena came for a visit. Mama sent Drina and me outside, and the two of them had a long discussion. I was about seven and Drina was four. Mama lived almost two years, but she couldn't do much around the house. I began to help her with the work and Drina helped look after Hannah. When Mama died, Aunt Verbena told us at the funeral that she would be taking Hannah to live with her one day. Pa told her to get out of our lives because he'd take care of his little girls himself. At the time, I think he really meant to do so, but things changed. Though he'd always been hard on us, he'd never been mean until Mama died. After that, he grew resentful of the fact that his little daughters couldn't keep the house and everything up like our mama did, though we tried. We were just too young. A year or so later, Aunt Verbena made another trip to the farm and they had a long talk. Again, I don't know what transpired, but she left without Hannah."

She took a deep breath and when he didn't comment, she went on, "Things got worse after that. I was trying to do the cooking and some of the cleaning, and Drina did what she could, but she was so young…and it was mostly her responsibility to look after Hannah, who was still a baby and wasn't able to do anything. Pa kept saying she'd be walking soon and she could help with the chores, too. As you know, that never happened. When she was four, Aunt Verbena made her third trip to the farm. That time, she left with Hannah—and we saw very little of our sister after that. When we'd go into town with Pa, which wasn't often, he'd sometimes drop us at Aunt Verbena's and we'd visit until he came to get us. We loved those times, and so did Hannah. Of course, Aunt Verbena probably didn't enjoy them very much."

"I'm surprised your aunt let you visit like that."

"I know. She never seemed to like us coming, but she hasn't once refused to let us visit Hannah in all the years our sister has lived there. On her birthday, she even lets us take Hannah out on the veranda if the weather is nice."

"When is the next birthday?"

"In a few weeks. Since it's a special birthday, I plan to take her out to a restaurant if I can convince Aunt Verbena to let me do so."

"One should be allowed special consideration on their birthday." Jarrett turned his head and thought a minute. "Do you think the reason she's never prevented you and your sister from visiting Hannah has something to do with the talks your aunt had with your mother and father?"

She shrugged. "I've never thought about it that way, but it could be."

"One more question, Lydia. Does Hannah ever visit you?"

Shaking her head she said, "Aunt Verbena would never allow her to come to a saloon, and she never visited Drina at the farm before she left for Arizona, either." She thought a minute, then added, "When Hannah was small, our aunt would dress her up and take her to church and on outings, but when she grew bigger and Aunt Verbena couldn't pick her up any longer, our sister was confined to the house. She hasn't left that house except maybe to sit on the veranda a few times since she was about eight or nine years old."

He looked stunned. "You're kidding."

"No, I'm not. It's the gospel truth. I've tried several times to get Aunt Verbena to let me take her for a carriage ride at least, but the answer is always that it wouldn't be suitable for Hannah to be seen with a woman who works in a saloon."

"Is there anything else you can tell me that you think I should be aware of?"

"I don't know if it'll help you or not, but one time I tried to get Hannah away from Aunt Verbena so she could come live with me. Of course, the judge agreed with my aunt that I wasn't a fitting influence on my sister. I haven't tried since, because I knew it would be useless."

He nodded. "I'll check those court records and see what all was said." He then picked up his hat from the extra chair and stood. "In the meantime, I'm going to do some searching around. It looks to me like the answers to all our questions goes back to the conversations your aunt had with your mother and father. I'm going to see what I can dig up."

As he started to the door, Lydia said, "I just thought of something else, Jarrett." He looked at her and she went on. "This will help you understand a little about how devious Aunt Verbena can be. I got a letter from Drina. She asked me to find out why Hannah hadn't answered any of the letters she'd sent her. When I asked, Hannah said she hadn't heard from Drina, but she'd written our sister three times and had given the letters to our aunt to post. I took the last letter she wrote and posted it myself so I know it will get to Drina."

"Hannah said something about that, but I could tell your aunt wasn't pleased, so I changed the subject. I'm glad you said something about it again. It does give me an insight to Verbena's thinking. I'll make sure I don't let anything slip that she could use against Hannah." He put on his hat. "If you like, I'll report back to you about anything I can dig up."

"I'd appreciate that very much, Jarrett."

Lydia sat at her desk after he closed the door. She thought about all the things she and Jarrett had talked about. *At last*, she thought, *somebody who will see that Hannah is really taken care of, since my hands are tied.*

She stood and went to the door. "Ramon!"

The huge man appeared from the end of the hall. "Yes, Miz Lydia."

"The man who was here is Jarrett MacMichael. It turns out that he's a friend of the family. When he returns, make sure he gets any information he wants and then send him to me immediately. He's doing an important job for my family."

"I sure will, Miz Lydia."

"Thank you, Ramon. You can go back downstairs now. If I need you again I'll let you know."

He nodded and headed for the stairs.

Lydia closed the door and again sat at her desk. Though she was deeply concerned about Hannah, she had a responsibility here. She had to clear her mind of family and get back to those account books. Something wasn't adding up right and so far she hadn't been able to find where the missing money had been spent.

♥♥♥

Hannah sat on the side of her bed. It looked like a beautiful day outside from what she could see. She'd have liked to spend the afternoon looking from her window. She thought about trying to hop over to the chair, but she was afraid to do it. The last time she'd been brave enough to attempt it, she'd fallen. Hearing the fall downstairs, her aunt had come up to the room and told her she didn't appreciate the jumping over her head and she was not to do it again. She'd then stared at Hannah as she lay in the floor and said, "So you'll remember not to try that silly jumping on one foot again, you're going to lay there until I decided to send Tobias up to help you get up."

After her aunt left, Hannah tried several times to get herself up. She finally made it by pulling herself by her elbows to the bed, but she was exhausted. At supper time, Tobias arrived with a tray containing her food. He said he'd also been told to help her get up if she was still in the floor.

"I'm so sorry, Miss Hannah. If I'd knowed you'd fell, I'd have come up here and got you out of the floor afore you got so tired, no matter what Miz Wedington said. She didn't tell me till a little while ago that you had fell. I can't believe that woman would do this to you. It's cold in here, and I bet you're about to freeze."

That day, her aunt had been mad because Hannah had the audacity to tell one of the older woman's friends that she had two dresses to sew and couldn't get around to another one for at least a week. Because her aunt said she had to get the dress done, Hannah ended up working night and day to finish it.

Today, her aunt had banished her to her room because she'd asked if she could make a new dress for herself. "I've outgrown the last one I made and the one I made over is faded and ill-fitting. At this moment, I don't have one to sew for you or someone else," Hannah explained in a soft voice she hoped wouldn't sound demanding.

Undoubtedly, her aunt thought differently, because she said, "The dress of mine that I gave you to make over last winter is still good and fits you well enough."

"What if Mr. MacMichael visits again? Since he's seen it, I think it would be nice if I had a different one to wear."

Her aunt glared at her. "How dare you argue with me, Hannah? I said you don't need a dress." She then turned and left without saying anything else.

In minutes, Tobias came to the room and confiscated the wheelchair. He shook his head at Hannah and whispered, "Sorry, miss. You know I wouldn't do this if'n I weren't told to do it."

"Don't be sorry, Tobias. I know you have to follow orders. She might fire you if you don't do what she says."

That had all taken place over two hours ago, and Hannah had read parts of one of the romance books she kept hidden under her mattress. She pulled out the other one hidden there, but for some reason, she didn't want to read any more. She slipped it back in its hiding place and rubbed her eyes. Oh, how she wished she could change her life! Having supper with Mr. MacMichael last night had shown her how often she wished for something different. He had been so charming, and he was kind and polite to her. And what a thrill it had been to be carried upstairs in his big, strong arms. She'd actually dreamed about him last night. But when she woke up to her real life, she almost wished he hadn't visited. Before she met him she was not happy, but was accepting of her fate. Now, she hated being here as much as she did when she was a little girl. But unfortunately, she figured living here was what her future would always be. She couldn't help it…for the first time in a long time, she cried because she felt sorry for herself.

A light tap sounded on her door and she quickly dried her eyes and thought, *If it's Aunt Verbena she'll have a fit if I'm crying.* But she knew there would be no way to hide her red eyes.

Taking a deep breath she said, "Come in."

Minerva came through the door. "I brought you a little something to eat, Miss Hannah." She sat a tray which contained a glass of milk and a little bread cake on Hannah's writing table.

"Oh, Minerva, that's sweet of you, but I don't want you to get in trouble with Aunt Verbena because of something you did for me. She's in a bad mood today."

"She won't never know I brung you this 'cause she ain't here."

"Really?"

"Yes. Somebody died, and I had to make a cake for her to take to the house. She said she'd have to stay a respectful time and wouldn't be back till supper."

"Did Tobias take her?"

"No, he didn't. We was both surprised when she said she wanted to take her buggy herself." She smiled at Hannah. "Now, dry your pretty little eyes and eat up. I had extra batter, so I made you a special little cake."

"Oh, I'm so excited. You know I'm not allowed to have many sweets and I do love the ones you make so much."

"I know. That's why I made a little extra batter. It's all just for you."

Hannah took the little round cake Minerva handed her and bit into it. With her mouth full, she said, "It's heavenly. I'm so glad you made it for me."

"I know I don't have to ask you not to tell your aunt?" Minerva eyed her.

"You should know I'd never do that."

"That's right, I shouldn't have said nothing." Minerva looked around the room. "I would've brought your chair up, but I was afraid your aunt would punish you more if I did."

"You're right. She would have." Hannah ate more of her cake and accepted the glass of milk Minerva held out to her. "I feel like a princess."

"You should be treated like a princess, but I'm afraid as long as you're in this house you won't be."

Hannah sighed. "I'm afraid you're right, but I can always wish for something to happen to change things for me."

Minerva reached out and patted her shoulder. "Don't you ever give up your wishes, child." She gave Hannah a big smile and patted her shoulder. "Just remember, if and when you ever leave this house, me and Tobias are going to go with you."

"Oh, Minerva. That's such a sweet thing to say."

"Me and him have done talked it over. Ain't no way we'll stay here with you gone. We's couldn't stand it."

Hannah swallowed her last bite of cake and drank the milk. She handed the empty glass to Minerva. "Then let's all agree to wish on the first star we see tonight that we can leave this house together someday soon."

"When he gets back, I'll tell Tobias to let me know when a nice bright star is out and we'll shore wish that very thing on it with you."

"That will be wonderful...but I thought you said he didn't take Aunt Verbena."

"He didn't, but he went somewhere as soon as she left. He didn't tell me when he'd be back, but I'm sure he'll probably beat her home." She picked up the tray. "Now, I better get back in the kitchen and wash this afore your aunt catches me. I'll be back with you some supper later, and if she'll let him, Tobias will bring you your chair."

"Thank you, Minerva. You and Tobias are special, and I love the both of you."

"We love you, too, Miss Hannah." She hurried out the door.

Chapter 5

Tobias Johnson stood in the lobby of the hotel with his hat in his hand. He knew he had to wait until the desk clerk acknowledged him. Though it made him feel less than human, he knew, though he was now free, a Negro man in Savannah, Georgia in this day and age still had to be careful of what he said or did or he could land in jail for looking at somebody crooked. It hadn't been that long since every person of his race had been a slave in this town, and many people thought they still should be.

Finally, the thin man behind the counter glanced at him. "Did you want something?"

Tobias nodded. "Mrs. Verbena Wedington sent me to speak to Mr. Jarrett MacMichael." It was a lie, but he hoped he'd get away with it.

The clerk glared at him. "Mr. MacMichael is in the restaurant having his dinner. Stand outside the door, and when he comes through, I'll tell him you're here. He can come out if he thinks your message is worthwhile."

Tobias bit his lip to push down his temper. "Yes, sir," he muttered through clenched teeth, and went out the door.

He stood against the building and watched the people scurrying by. The few who looked at him acted as if he was invisible, and one or two muttered insulting words. He held his temper and ignored them by ducking his head and staring at his feet.

He was beginning to think the clerk hadn't told MacMichael he was outside when the door opened and Jarrett appeared.

"Tobias, how long have you been waiting?"

"Oh, not too long, sir."

"The clerk said you came in shortly after I went in the restaurant for dinner. Why didn't you come in and join me?"

Tobias had to smile. "I wouldn't be allowed to do that, sir."

"Why not?"

"A Negro isn't allowed in a white man's place of eating here in Georgia, Mr. MacMichael."

"I guess I keep forgetting I'm no longer in Arizona."

"Can I ask you what difference it'd make if you was in Arizona?"

Jarrett looked surprised. "Don't you know that a large percentage of the cowboys in the west are Negroes, Tobias? Most people don't pay any more attention to them than they do anybody else that rides a horse. Of course, there are a few who do, but it's not the normal way folks there react."

"I didn't know they was Negro cowboys, but it sounds like I'd like to live in Arizona."

Jarrett grinned. "Well, I'm sorry you had to wait on me. I wouldn't have stayed so long if I'd known you were here."

"I know you're a busy man, but I want to talk to you about something if you have the time, and will listen to me."

"Sure, I'll listen, and I have all the time in the world, Tobias. Would you like to come up to my room where we can have privacy?"

"If you think it'll be all right fer me to come in there."

"Sure, it will. Come along."

Tobias followed Jarrett into the hotel and up the stairs. He couldn't help noticing the hard looks they were getting from the desk clerk and an overweight woman with a huge hat with what looked like a hundred feathers. He held his head a little higher and followed Jarrett.

Once they reached the room, Jarrett said, "Have a seat. Would you like a drink?"

"I don't want to be no trouble, sir."

"For heaven's sake, relax, Tobias, and I'll pour us a drink. I keep a bottle here because I like a drink or two before I go to sleep." He moved to the table and filled two glasses with a good brand of whiskey. He turned and handed one to Tobias, who was still standing.

Jarrett chuckled. "You can stand for this conversation if you like, but I intend to take a seat where I'll be more comfortable."

When Tobias was seated, he said, "I hope this talk will remain between you and me, Mr. MacMichael?"

"If that's the way you want it, it will."

"I happened to overhear some of the things you said to Mrs. Wedington last night and I hope you won't be offended when I say that I found some of it hard to believe."

Jarrett laughed out loud. "And I thought I'd been convincing."

Tobias dared to smile. "I'm sure Miz Wedington believed every word you said."

"Good, because she was the one I was trying to fool. Now, tell me what you wanted to talk to me about."

"I've been working at the Wedington house ever since before Miss Hannah come to live there. Minerva and me have tried as best we can to look after the young lady and I want to make sure you don't mean her no harm."

"I assure you, Tobias, my reason for coming to the Wedington house is to make sure Miss Hamilton is being well taken care of. I would never cause any hurt to come to the girl."

"Well, sir, you already have."

Jarrett frowned. "What do you mean?"

"Mrs. Wedington got upset this morning and sent me to take Miss Hannah's chair away. That's one way she punishes her. She knows Miss Hannah can't get to the window or anywhere without her wheelchair."

"Did she say why Hannah was being punished?"

"She never tells us, and we don't know unless we happen to overhear. Minerva said she thought it was because Miss Hannah asked for new material to make a dress, in case you visited again."

"She'd punish the girl for that?"

"Oh, Mr. MacMichael, she'd punish Miss Hannah for much less than that. I've known Mrs. Wedington to send her to her room because she smiled wrong."

Jarrett looked as if he was thinking. In a minute, he said, "You trusted me not to tell Mrs. Verbena that you came to see me so I'm going to trust you not to let her or to let Hannah know why I'm really here in town."

"I must tell you that I overheard you tell them you was here to build a hotel, so I think I already knows why you're here."

"No, you don't, Tobias. That was a lie I told to get into the Wedington house. I'm not an important businessman as I pretended to be. I'm actually a detective, but it's true that I'm from Flagstaff, Arizona." He then went on to tell Tobias why he'd come to Savannah, and that his main goal was to check up on Hannah.

"You don't know how glad I am to hear this, Mr. MacMichael. If there's any way me and Minerva can help you, just let us know. We're always trying to make Miss Hannah's life a little easier. When I left, Minerva was going to slip her up a special treat while Mrs. Wedington was gone to a friend's house."

"So, she's not home now?"

"No, but she said she'd be back by supper time."

Jarrett downed his drink, put his glass on the table and stood. "Then I have an idea. Let's go to the livery. I'm going to rent a buggy and take you home."

"Are you sure you want to do that?"

"Yes. I'm very sure."

Tobias didn't argue. He simply drank his drink, placed his glass on the table beside Jarrett's and followed the tall man out the door.

When they left the livery stable in a buggy, Jarrett questioned Tobias about Hannah's early days with her aunt.

"So you're saying that the aunt seemed to enjoy having her in her home, at first."

"Yes, sir. She liked to dress her up and show her off to all her friends as the poor little crippled girl that nobody wanted. Miss Hannah was the sweetest little thing. She seemed to like Mrs. Wedington, and she did everything she could to please her, but you know how little ones are. There is times they act up. It's the way with young'uns, even the crippled ones. When Miss Hannah would act up a little, she was always punished. Me and Minerva tried to cover up for her at times, but most of the time, her aunt would find out."

"What would she do to make her aunt mad enough to punish her?"

"Nothing bad enough to be punished like she was."

"Give me an example."

"I remember one time Minerva cooked some butter beans as one of the vegetables for supper. Miss Hannah tried them, but didn't like the taste. Miz Wedington tried to get her to eat them anyway, but Miss Hannah said she was not gonna eat them. Mrs. Wedington got as mad as an old wet hen. She made Minerva take the little one's plate away and bring a clean one. When she brought the new plate, Mrs. Wedington filled it with butter beans and said that Miss Hannah would eat ever one of them or starve. The little one cried and cried, but her aunt wouldn't give in. And Miss Hannah didn't give in neither. Finally her aunt grabbed her up and took her in the parlor and spanked her good and hard. We heard the licks even in the dining room. Then, for three days, Mrs. Wedington wouldn't let the little girl have anything to eat except butter beans. She might have been about five at the time and I can't 'member Minerva cooking butter beans since."

"Verbena must be an evil woman."

"She is, Mr. MacMichael. She keeps it hid, but she's a devil hiding under all her fine clothes and living in her fancy house."

"What I can't figure out, is why she allows her niece to live there."

"I've wondered the same thing. So has Minerva. We finally decided that somebody knows something on Miz Wedington, and she don't have no choice but to let Miss Hannah stay."

"You're probably right, but who is this person and what do they know?"

"That, I don't know, sir."

"For heaven's sake, Tobias, stop calling me *sir* so often. In fact, it'd make me more comfortable if you'd call me Jarrett."

Tobias stared at him, but didn't say anything.

"I didn't mean to offend you, but I'm not used being called Mr. MacMichael or sir by another man all the time. Just call me Jarrett."

"I don't think I'll be able to do that, sir."

"Well, work on it." He pulled the buggy up at the Wedington house. "Do you think Mrs. Wedington is still out?"

When the front door didn't open, Tobias said, "I guess she ain't back. She would've come running when she saw your buggy."

"Then let's get inside before she shows up."

"I'm not supposed to use the front door."

"Forget that. It's the quickest way in. Let's go."

As they stepped across the threshold, Minerva dropped her dust cloth. "Tobias, you ain't supposed to come in the front door."

"I know, but…"

"I brought him in." Jarrett smiled at her. "I assume the mistress of the house isn't home."

"No, sir, she ain't. Maybe you should come back about…"

"It's all right, Minerva. He's got a plan."

She frowned. "What 'er you talking 'bout?"

Tobias frowned at her. "Just let him talk and tell us both what to do. I'll tell you what it's all about later."

"I don't think it'd be prudent for me to be in Miss Hamilton's room when her aunt returns. Why don't you bring her down, and I'll be in the parlor." Jarrett turned to Minerva. "Would you please serve us some tea? I think that would be what the aunt would want us to have if she were here."

Minerva stared at him.

Tobias headed up the stairs. "Don't just stand there, woman. Do like he says. I said I'll 'splain to you later."

Minerva shook her head and headed out of the entry.

Jarrett opened the door to the formal parlor. He decided this was where he'd talk to Hannah. Her aunt might be mad, but frankly, he didn't care. Now that he had the Johnsons and Lydia on his side, he was about to give Mrs. Verbena Wedington a taste of her own medicine, but he had no intention of involving Hannah until he was ready to tell her what he was up to and he felt sure neither Lydia nor the Johnsons would give him away.

Hannah was surprised when her door opened and Tobias came in. "I'm here to take you downstairs, Miss Hannah."

Hannah frowned. "Why? Has my aunt decided to forgive me?"

"I don't know if she has or not, Miss. All I know is that you're wanted downstairs."

"Let me comb my hair…"

"Miss Hannah, I don't want to rush you, but I don't think you need to tarry."

Hannah knew he was right. Aunt Verbena would be irate if she didn't come immediately. "I'm sorry, Tobias. Let's go."

He picked her up and headed down the steps.

"Where are we going?" She asked when he turned toward the parlor.

"In here."

"But I don't think…" She stopped talking when she saw Jarrett sitting on the settee. Her hands automatically reached to smooth down her hair, and she was conscious of the terrible outfit she had on. The green skirt was so faded it was almost gray, and the yellow shirtwaist was patched on the left sleeve and the pocket on the left side was missing. Why had she put on such terrible clothes this morning? Then she remembered it was washday and this was what she always wore while the laundry was being done. The only other decent thing left in her wardrobe was her one made-over dress, and she tried to save it for special occasions. And if she'd known Mr. MacMichael was here, she'd have insisted Tobias wait until she put it on.

Jarrett looked at her and she knew exactly what he was thinking. She was dressed in rags and her hair was a mess. She knew, too, he felt sorry for her and this, she couldn't abide.

"Hello, Mr. MacMichael." She smoothed her skirt as if it was a satin ball gown when Tobias lowered her to a chair facing the man.

Jarrett smiled at her. "I'm delighted to see you again, Miss Hamilton."

Minerva came in with the tea service and set it on the table beside Hannah. "Would you like to serve the tea, miss?"

"I'm sure Aunt Verbena will want to serve it, Minerva."

"She's not here, Miss Hannah."

Hannah was stunned. "What…then why…" She glanced at Jarrett.

"I requested the tea," he said. "I also asked Tobias to bring you downstairs. There's something I want to discuss with you before your aunt gets home. I thought it would be better to do it down here than in your room. I'm pretty sure she doesn't want me to be up there in your room with you."

"I suppose you're right, but what could you possibly have to discuss with me?"

Jarrett nodded for Minerva to leave and said, "Go ahead and serve the tea, Miss Hamilton and I'll tell you what I want to discuss with you."

Mechanically, she reached for the teapot, hoping she wouldn't spill the liquid or chip one of her aunt's fancy cups in her nervousness.

Jarrett went on. "I had a nice visit with your sister today."

She held a cup of hot tea toward him and her hand began to shake. "You visited Lydia?"

He took the tea before it spilled and thanked her. "Yes. I found her to be a delightful lady. Like Mrs. Wilcox, she's concerned about how your aunt is treating you."

Hannah poured herself a cup, put the pot down and picked up the saucer containing her cup. She stirred sugar into the liquid with her still shaking hand and said, "I've told Lydia again and again that things are going well here. I also told Drina that in a letter. They have no need to be concerned about me."

"Lydia told me your aunt punished you at times by keeping your wheelchair downstairs for the slightest infraction."

Hannah's gaze dropped and she sipped her tea. "Occasionally, she does that."

"And what had you done this time to make her decide to dish out the punishment today?"

"I'm not being pun…"

He interrupted. "Don't lie to me, Hannah. I saw your chair behind the stairs when I came into the house."

She sat her cup on the table because she was afraid she was going to drop it. "It wasn't anything serious. I asked for something and she didn't think I should have. I'm sure she meant to send the chair upstairs before she left the house, but forgot about it."

"Did she go out the front door?"

"I guess she did. She usually does. Tobias usually brings her carriage around to the front and she leaves that way."

"Then she couldn't have forgotten your chair since it's sitting right there in plain sight."

Hannah was getting more nervous, but she tried not to show it. What did this man want, and why was he insisting on saying these things? He was going to get her in trouble, and she didn't want to go the rest of the month without her chair. It was too boring in her room when she didn't have access to it.

She decided to ask him directly. "Mr. MacMichael, why are so interested in what's going on with me? You're here to build a hotel, not to delve into the life I'm living with my Aunt Verbena."

He gave her a smile and she couldn't help the little flip her heart did. "Aaron Wilcox asked me to check on you, so that makes my asking questions about your living conditions part of my business here in Savannah."

She began to wring her hands. "But don't you see? You asking so…"

The door jerked open and Verbena asked in a crisp voice. "What's going on here?"

Jarrett quickly stood and moved to her. "Mrs. Wedington, I'm so glad you arrived home. I was becoming concerned."

Hannah stared at him. Why did he say that? Not once had he mentioned he was concerned about the older woman.

He went on. "Won't you please come over here and sit on the settee with me?"

Verbena looked confused. "Well, I…"

Jarrett led her to the plush settee. "Sit right down, and I'm sure Minerva will bring a cup for you shortly. You look as if you could use a cup of your wonderful tea."

"Well, yes I guess I could. I suppose Hannah ordered the maid to bring it for you."

Before Hannah could answer, he said, "I'm the guilty party. I remembered how good it was when I was here with you and Miss Hannah last evening and I wanted to see you again today. As soon as I arrived, I sent Tobias up to bring Miss Hamilton down. I then asked Minerva to bring the tea, because I thought that was what you'd do if you were here. I hope that was all right."

"I suppose it was." Her aunt still looked flustered.

Minerva entered with a teacup on a small tray. "I saw you arrive, Miz Wedington and thought you'd want to have some tea with Miss Hannah and Mr. MacMichael."

"Yes, I would." She took the cup and reached for the teapot.

Minerva hurried out.

Hannah wasn't sure what was going to happen, but she was sure whatever it was, when her aunt realized her niece was downstairs when she should be in her room, there would be another punishment. Mr. MacMichael's silver tongue might sooth her aunt's feathers for a while, but it wouldn't last. At least, she didn't think it would.

Yet, as she watched the man, he seemed to be a different person than the one who was, only minutes ago, asking her about her life in this house. Now, he didn't act as if she was in the room. He was totally focused on her aunt. Hannah was enthralled at his words and actions, and wondered what he'd say or do next. Whatever he came up with, she was sure both she and Aunt Verbena would be shocked. She was right.

"I'm a man who makes decisions quickly, as you might have guessed, since you're such an intuitive person. When I learned one of my business partners had to cancel the meeting tonight because of some problem at home, I decided I'd come and invite you and your niece out to supper with me. I hope you'll accept, because it's kind of a thank you for the wonderful meal you served me last night."

"Oh, my, that's impossible." Verbena stuttered as she said the words.

"May I ask why, ma'am?" His face contorted in what looked like puzzlement—or was he putting on a performance?

"Well," Verbena stuttered again. "I'm sure Minerva has already prepared supper."

"Couldn't you store it and have it for dinner or supper tomorrow?"

Her aunt seemed to be gathering her wits. "That wouldn't work. It's probably perishable. Besides, Hannah doesn't go out. It's hard for her when she does, and it often proves to be embarrassing when she has to have her chair rolled inside, or worse, to be carried into a restaurant."

Hannah couldn't help staring at her. *How would she know if it would embarrass me to be rolled or carried into a restaurant? I've never been taken to one. I have no idea how I'd react myself.*

Jarrett shook his head and took Verbena's hand. "I'm so sorry if I offended you, gracious lady. I should have known that you couldn't drop everything to accommodate my whims. In Arizona, we are much more informal. If a man wants to be friends with a woman, he simply decides to show his affection for her immediately. I suppose, in Savannah, you rely more on good manners and protocol."

Again, Hannah was shocked. Did this man really like Aunt Verbena, or was he spreading on the charm for some other reason?

Verbena blushed. "Why, Mr. MacMichael, I never ..."

He interrupted. "So you won't think I'm trying to upset you, or that I'm saying anything inappropriate, I think I should explain why I felt such an immediate affinity to you."

"Please do."

"Yesterday, when I arrived, I was so enthralled that I almost grabbed you and hugged your neck when I first saw your lovely face. You may not believe this, but you're so much like my sainted sister. For an instant, I thought Charlotte had come back to life here on earth, though my logical mind told me that's impossible."

"Oh, I'm sorry. I had no idea you'd lost someone so special to you." She patted his hand. "Do you mind telling me what happened to her?"

"I don't mind at all." He took a deep breath. "She and her husband were in

New Orleans visiting his parents. They were strolling along when a small child darted into the busy street in front of them. Being such a caring mother herself, Charlotte ran after the little girl and pulled her to safety." A sad look came into his eyes and he added, "But my sister didn't make it back. A carriage came careening around the corner and ran her down, right there in front of her husband." He bit his lip and looked down at his hands. "She died almost instantly. I don't think I'll ever get over the tragedy." He cringed to think of what Charlotte would do if she knew he'd killed her off just like he did their parents.

"Oh, Mr. MacMichael. I'm so sorry." She actually looked as if she was sympathizing with him. "If seeing me helps with your hurt, I'm glad you came to visit unannounced."

"You're so understanding, and yes, it helps a great deal. It makes me realize what a wonderful woman Charlotte would have grown into." He stood. "I'll go now, and I promise not to bother you again."

Verbena stood, too. "Don't fret about it, please. I hope you'll come by often while you're in Savannah. It does me good to know that my presence helps you cope with your sorrow."

"Thank you so very much. I will come, but I'll try not to be so bold next time." He turned his back to her and took Hannah's hand. "Thank you for talking with me until your aunt arrived home. I hope to see you again soon."

He then did something that made Hannah wonder if this man had told the truth about anything, or even if he had a sister. He winked at her.

Chapter 6

After Jarrett left, Hannah thought she would be in trouble for sure, but he must have really charmed her aunt, because this evening held another surprise for her. Without saying anything to her niece, Verbena called Tobias. When he came into the room, she said, "Bring Hannah's chair into the parlor, then wheel her into the dining room. Since she's already downstairs, she might as well eat her supper in the dining room with me tonight."

During the meal of boiled beef and cabbage, her aunt continually talked about what a nice man Jarrett MacMichael was and how they must always welcome him when he came to the door. Hannah could tell Verbena Wedington was taken with the man.

As for herself, Hannah wasn't sure what to think of him. The wink he gave her behind her aunt's back was probably some sort of signal to her, but she hadn't yet figured out what it was all about. In fact, she was beginning to wonder that maybe this man had met Aaron Wilcox and somehow had learned Verbena was a woman of means. Because of his actions with her aunt, she wouldn't be surprised at anything he did or said. He could very well be trying somehow to con the widow out of some of her money.

Yet, why did he go to visit Lydia? Something was up, and she wanted to know what, but who was she going to ask? Certainly not her aunt. Maybe Tobias would know something when he took her to her room. She would try to ask a few questions of him then. If he was unaware of what was going on, she guessed she'd have to wait until Lydia visited again. Surely, her sister would tell her.

But she didn't get a chance to ask Tobias anything. When the meal was over and he carried her up the steps, her aunt followed. The older woman went to Hannah's wardrobe and looked inside.

Shutting the door, she turned to her niece. "Hannah, I feel sure Mr. MacMichael was shocked at the way you were dressed. Maybe I was too harsh when I said you didn't need to sew a new dress for yourself. I have some extra yardage in my room, and I'm going to give you an early birthday present. I want to see how fast you can sew something that will make you more presentable than you were today. I'm sure he'll visit again soon, and I don't want him to find you dressed this way."

The thought of a new dress made Hannah temporarily forget about Jarrett MacMichael. "Oh, thank you, Aunt Verbena."

"I suppose since you're going to be eighteen soon, you need a new dress."

Before Hannah could thank her again, Verbena followed Tobias out the door.

Hannah stared after them. *What is going on? Aunt Verbena has never given me a birthday present before. Is she so taken with Jarrett that she's beginning to mellow a little?*

"If that's so, I wish he'd visit every day," she muttered aloud.

In a matter of minutes, Tobias returned with the chair. On the seat was a folded length of blue material with tiny white flowers. Hannah couldn't help smiling as she picked it up. "This is beautiful."

"It looks like the same color as your eyes. It'll make you a pretty dress, Miss Hannah."

"Yes, it will. I look forward to having something new to wear." She smiled at him. "Tobias, have you noticed anything different about the way Aunt Verbena is acting this evening?"

He returned the smile. "Yes, miss. I has noticed, and I shore has a feeling that Mr. Jarrett MacMichael had something to do with it."

"Me, too, but why does he continue to flatter her so much? Do you think he's for real, Tobias?"

"Yes, miss, I do." He continued to smile. "Does you mind if I give you a piece of advice?"

"I don't mind at all. Your advice is always good."

"Then, Miss Hannah, I thinks you should be thankful that Mr. Jarrett has come into our lives. He's gonna make everything around here work out for you... and maybe for the rest of us. I'm sure of it. Now, you must believe what he tells you, and only you. Don't you pay no attention to what he says to your aunt. Can you do that?"

She frowned. "I suppose I can, if you think I should."

"I does and it's good you do it. Now, don't forget. Mr. Jarrett has his reasons for what he says. You'll see."

"What in the world are those reasons, Tobias?"

"You'll soon find out, Miss Hannah. Just listen to what I said and remember it when he's talking to your aunt." He turned to the door. "I'll see you tomorrow, miss."

She wanted to ask him another question or two, but didn't get the chance. He'd left the room. She couldn't help wondering what Tobias was talking about and why he trusted Jarrett MacMichael so completely. Did everyone in this house know what was happening, but her? Was he right? Would she soon understand Jarrett MacMichael's actions? To take her mind off of the idea of asking more questions about the handsome and mysterious Jarrett MacMichael, she picked up the material her aunt had sent up to her and smiled. She knew just how she wanted to construct her new dress. She wouldn't waste any time. She'd cut it out tonight. That way, her aunt couldn't change her mind and take the material back.

♥♥♥

Verbena lit the oil lamp sitting on the table by her bed and closed the door to her room. She dropped to the green stuffed chair to think about Hannah's birthday. There were only a few weeks left before the girl would be eighteen.

Shaking her head to change her thoughts, Verbena wondered if she made the right decision by sending the cloth to the child, though she didn't feel she had any other option. Maybe she shouldn't have sent her such a lovely length of material. She had the dress she'd made over this past fall. It was still nice enough for no more socializing than Hannah did, but she did have to admit they were getting a little old. The girl had to have something decent to wear for appearances sake. Verbena was being honest when she said she didn't want Jarrett to ever again see her dressed like she was tonight. The man could go back to Arizona and report to Drina's husband that Verbena wasn't allowing the girl to have decent clothing. If that happened it could cause a lot of trouble. Besides, there might be a time when one of her friends caught Hannah looking as bad as she did tonight. Or even her sister, Lydia could say something. That would be a disaster, too. Verbena decided she'd have to see that the clothes the girl had on tonight disappeared and her niece was never seen in them again.

For the years Hannah had lived in this house, Verbena had been able to keep everyone, including her other nieces from getting close to the truth of why their little sister had had the privilege of living her life in the lovely Wedington home while they lived in poverty with their unscrupulous father. Now, it was much too late to let them start asking questions which could bring to light things best left hidden. Things that could change all their lives.

Lydia and Drina had been young when it happened, and couldn't possibly remember what had taken place. The only ones still living who knew what went on at the time were Burl Hamilton…and her. She knew as long as she was able to continue making the tax payment on his farm and sending him a little money now and then, he wouldn't say a word. As for Hannah, she was only four when she became the ward of her aunt. She knew nothing, not even why she had to leave her sisters and come to live with Verbena. Though Verbena resented having to take the child, it did give her the opportunity to prove to her friends what a good Christian woman she was for taking in the poor crippled girl that nobody else wanted. It also gave her a chance to train Hannah in the way she wanted her to grow up—which was to be seen when her aunt wanted her to show her off to her friends and to occasionally to speak, but only when spoken to.

Tonight, she realized things would have been better if Jarrett MacMichael had never come to Savannah, but she couldn't help being glad he was here. It was the first time a man other than Reginald Phillips had shown her any attention in a long time. Though she knew it was because of Jarrett's departed sister that he was so kind to her, she still enjoyed his company and would always welcome him into her home. Though his showing up without invitation was something she had to get used to, she decided it was something people must not think was an unusual thing to do in the wilds of Arizona. She couldn't expect him to act like the gentlemen did in Savannah.

Verbena stood, moved to her wardrobe and looked at all the lovely dresses Hannah had designed for her. She had to admit that Hannah was truly talented with a needle and thread. Not one of the dresses the girl had made had disappointed her and it always made her feel better to look at them. She knew the clothes had helped her keep up the appearance of the rich widow, because they had brought many compliments from her friends. As she wore them, she knew they fit well and looked good on her. Even Reginald had noticed, and had commented on an outfit or two. She wondered if Jarrett MacMichael had noticed. Though she was probably fifteen or twenty years his senior, she couldn't help liking the attention Jarrett had shown her, even now that she knew about his sister.

She sighed and decided she'd wear the violet organdy the next time he visited. She might even wear it for Reginald one day if she came to the conclusion that being his wife would benefit her. Of course, if they decided to marry, they'd have to cope with Hannah and Calvin in the house for a while…or make sure they were settled in with Hilda. Verbena didn't think there was anything she could do about what would happen to her if Hannah's eighteenth birthday did arrive with those specific stipulations in the agreement that was drawn up and signed by all the interested parties several years ago. Though Burl Hamilton might remember, she was the only one in town who knew what the consequences would be if her niece was still single after her eighteenth birthday. But that wasn't going to happen. She'd take care of it in the next week or so.

Verbena closed her wardrobe door and moved back to her green stuffed chair with a smile on her lips. It was all going to work out the way she wanted it to.

♥♥♥

Lydia said, "Enter," when a hard knock sounded on her office door.

The door opened and Ramon stuck his head inside. "That cowboy is here to see you again."

"Mr. MacMichael?"

"Yes, ma'am. Do you want to see him?"

"Yes, Ramon. Send him in."

The big man stepped aside, and Jarrett entered.

Ramon seemed a little unsure as to what to do. "Do you want me to wait in the hall, Miz Patterson?"

"No, Ramon. Go on back downstairs in case there's any trouble."

Though he looked a little uncertain, he nodded and left.

Lydia turned to Jarrett. "It's nice to see you again. Have a seat."

"Thanks." He removed his hat and placed it on the empty chair he'd used before. "I'm glad you were willing to meet with me again."

"I told you to come by anytime, Jarrett." She smiled and took a chair beside a mahogany table. "But I have to admit, I didn't expect you this soon."

"I had an interesting visit with your sister this evening, and I thought you'd want to know how it came about."

She reached for the crystal whiskey decanter sitting on the table by the lamp and poured two drinks into matching glasses. Holding one out to him she said, "I certainly would."

"Your aunt's butler came to see me today and told me that he thought I should ask some more questions concerning Hannah. I made a quick decision to go to the Wedington house and see what I could find out. Verbena was out, so I sent Tobias upstairs to bring your sister down."

He paused, took a drink, then went on, "Lydia, you wouldn't believe the way Hannah was dressed."

"What do you mean?"

"She was in what I would classify as rags. I've seen women on the western prairie harnessed up to their mules and plowing their gardens or getting ready to do their weekly wash who were dressed better then she was today."

Lydia frowned. "She's not always dressed up fancy when I visit, but she usually says her clothes are in the wash or she didn't want to dress up that day."

"Have you ever checked inside her wardrobe to see how many clothes she has?"

"No. Did you look today?"

"I didn't go up to her room this time. I didn't want to give Verbena any ammunition to use against her, so I sent Tobias."

"I see." Lydia sipped her drink. "Come to think of it, I've taken her a few pieces of material, but I've never seen her wear a dress made from any of them."

"Did you give the cloth directly to her, or to your aunt?"

"Sometimes one and sometimes the other. Why?"

"Just a thought." He took another drink and changed the subject. "I'm beginning to think your aunt has such a tight hold on Hannah that the poor girl is afraid to tell anyone what's really happening in that house."

"Oh, Jarrett, I hope you're wrong. It would break my heart, and Drina's, too, if we learned that all these years Aunt Verbena had been abusing our little sister."

"I don't think she's physically abusing her, but I do think she's been so strict through the years that Hannah is afraid to tell anyone what's going on between them. I've noticed when they're together that Hannah seldom speaks unless you talk directly to her. At least, that's the way it happens when I'm there."

"Is there something we can do to find out what's going on?"

"There's always something that can be done, Lydia. I think the first thing I'm going to do is go visit your father again."

She looked shocked. "You saw Pa?"

"I rode out there the day after I got into town." He grinned. "He wasn't very friendly. In fact, he ran me off, but I'm wondering if he might be able to give me more information than I thought at first. I think I'll give visiting him another try."

Lydia thought a minute. "Pa's a strange man. If he doesn't want you there, it could be dangerous for you to go alone. I think it would help if I went to the farm with you; that is, if you want me to."

He looked interested. "I think you going would probably help a lot."

She finished her drink and put her glass on the table. "I'm busy tomorrow, but why don't you pick me up on Sunday and we'll head out there? Sunday's a pretty slow day around here, and I won't be needed until late in the day."

"Sunday would be fine with me. How about around eight?"

"That's a little early. Pa used to always get drunk on Saturday night and sleep it off on Sunday morning. I doubt his habits have changed. How about ten o'clock? He should be up by then."

"Fine." He stood, sat his empty glass on the table and picked up his hat. "Then I'll see you at ten on Sunday."

♥♥♥

Minerva couldn't sleep. She turned over on the straw mattress and asked, "You awake, Tobias?"

"Yep. I'm having a hard time going to sleep, too."

"What's going on with Miz Wedington? She's sure acting funny since she got home from that wake."

"I noticed she was kind of strange. Miss Hannah thought so, too."

"What'd Miss Hannah say?"

"Jest asked me if I didn't think her aunt was acting different."

Minerva sighed. "She shore was right about that. Did Miz Wedington have a conniption because Miss Hannah was downstairs when she got home?"

"Not at all. You know she had her to the dining room for supper then she had me carry her upstairs like usual. Strange though, she went with me. When we come back downstairs, Miz Wedington told me to take her wheelchair back upstairs, and that surprised me, because she was punishing Miss Hannah by keeping her chair away from her."

"She don't never change her mind 'bout the punishment she hands out."

"I know, but that weren't what surprised me the most."

"What else did she do?"

"She had me wait until she went to her room and get a piece of cloth. She told me to take it to Miss Hannah so the girl could make her a dress."

"My Lord, don't that woman have enough dresses?"

Tobias chuckled. "She didn't send the cloth up for a dress for *her*. She sent it for *Miss Hannah* to make herself one."

"You're lying to me, Tobias."

"No, I'm not. It's the gospel truth."

Minerva shook her head in the dark. "Sometimes, I think that woman is as crazy as they come. If it weren't for Miss Hannah, I'd say you and me needs to move on out of here, but I can't see leaving that girl to Miz Wedington's wiles."

"I agree with you, wife. But you're right, we can't leave Miss Hannah."

"I guess that's best. But since we's free now, it would be nice to go somewhere that we weren't still treated …"

"Don't say it, Minerva. We ain't slaves no more. Miz Wedington pays us to work here. Not much, that's true, but we gets a little money and we have a nice room here in the back."

"Sometimes, I dream a foolish dream that we leave here and get a little place of our own, but I know that's not gonna happen. We ain't got no place to go, anyway."

"I don't know, honey. Jarrett MacMichael said they was a lot of Negro folks in the west. He said they weren't looked down on like we is here. If we ever leave this place, I think we'd go to the west."

"That would be nice. Maybe we could take Miss Hannah with us."

He chuckled. "Now Minerva, that there is a really foolish dream."

Chapter 7

Jarrett noticed that Lydia stiffened when he turned the buggy down the rutted dirt road that led to the farm. He frowned. "Are you all right?"

"Just a little nervous. It isn't easy for me to come out here to see Pa."

"I didn't realize how it would affect you. Maybe I should've come alone."

"No. I offered to come, Jarrett. I know how Pa is. He's as likely to shoot you as to let you come in."

"Has he always been this way?"

"As far back as I can remember." She sighed. "I do remember that Mama loved him, though. The more I thought about it, the more I wondered why."

"I guess people don't always have a choice of who they fall in love with."

She chuckled. "You're right there. I never dreamed I'd fall in love and marry a gambler and a saloon owner. Then I met Bradly Patterson."

He saw that talking seemed to relax her so he asked, "How did you meet your husband, Lydia?"

"It was almost three years ago. Drina and I had been visiting Hannah while Pa went to the saloon as he always did when we were in Savannah. When he didn't come back to pick us up as usual, Aunt Verbena got upset and said it was time for us to leave because Hannah needed rest. Of course that was a lie, but we'd learned a long time ago not to cross Aunt Verbena, because if we did, she always took it out on Hannah. Drina and I figured we'd have to walk back into town, but dear auntie told Tobias to take us to the saloon in her buggy and let us out. Of course, she warned us not to go inside." She laughed. "Do you think we listened to her?"

He chuckled. "Probably not."

"You're right. As soon as Tobias was out of sight, we pushed the door open and went inside. Naturally, we got lots of stares and some whistles, but actually, there were no insults, nor did anyone try to come up to us. That is, except Bradly Patterson, but we soon learned he only approached us to offer help. When we told him we were looking for our father, he called out Pa's name. I remember distinctly that one man hollered back, 'You won't find Burl Hamilton here. He'll be on the other side of town.' At the time, I didn't know what he meant, but I later learned that the saloon we were in was a respectable place that the town's elite male population came to play cards and have a drink. There were no women or prostitution involved." She glanced at him. "Am I getting too long-winded?"

"Not at all. I'm interested. Please, go on."

"Well, as it turned out, Bradly hitched up his buggy and drove Drina and me to a more shady section of Savannah where there were several saloons. He wouldn't let us go inside any of them. We waited in the buggy and he'd go inside and look for Pa. He finally found him in the fourth one. Pa was furious. He said it was embarrassing to him to have his friends know his daughters had come looking for him, so I guess Bradly told everyone we were outside waiting." She took a breath. "Anyway when we got home, Pa was still mad. He decided he'd make us pay for embarrassing him."

"What did he do?"

"He whipped us."

"You're kidding."

"No, I'm not. When he would get that angry, he'd often use his horse whip on us."

"It takes an evil man to do something like that, Lydia."

"I know, but I guess we'd gotten used to it. Anyway, after a couple of weeks, Bradly showed up at our door. I was flattered, but didn't expect anything to come of it. I was wrong. Pa got all upset seeing him there and tried to run him off. When he refused to go, Pa grabbed his whip and ran me in the house. That was the last time Pa hit me. I learned later that Bradly told him he'd kill him if he ever touched me again. Three months later, Bradly asked me to marry him. I was so in love with him by then that I couldn't say no. I did feel guilty, leaving Drina alone with Pa, but she insisted I grab my chance at happiness. After Bradly and I were married, I tried hard to get her to come to work in the saloon with us, but she wouldn't do it. It was then that I found that ad for a mail-order-bride and took it to her. She didn't like the idea at first, but I think the last beating Pa gave her changed her mind, because the next thing I knew she was on her way to Arizona."

"So, I'm guessing it worked out well for the two of you."

"It sure did for me, and from her letters, I think Drina is happy with her cowboy." She smiled at him. "Now that I've poured out my life story to you, tell me something about yourself, Jarrett MacMichael."

"Well, my life certainly hasn't been nearly as interesting as yours. My folks own a medium-sized ranch near Phoenix, Arizona, and I have a brother and a sister. My sister, Charlotte, is the youngest. She's married to a rancher and they have twins; toddlers. They live a few miles from Mom and Dad. My twin brother Everett and I are the oldest. Neither of us is married, and we decided we wanted to do something different from ranching, at least for a while, so we formed MacMichael & MacMichael Detective Agency in Flagstaff. So far, we've been able to make a living, but we're certainly not getting rich." He chuckled. "I guess the Pinkerton agency has something to do with that. That's about all there is to know about the MacMichael family. As I said before, we're not a very interesting bunch."

"You're wrong, Jarrett. Your folks are very interesting to me. It's the kind of family I've always dreamed of. I think my sisters have those same kinds of dreams."

He didn't know how to answer her, so he kept quiet. Jarrett loved his family, but he'd never thought them anything special. Maybe he was wrong. To those whose mother had died and left them with a father like Burl Hamilton, he figured Cyrus and Abagail MacMichael did sound pretty special.

Lydia interrupted his thoughts. "Turn on that road to the left. It's a short cut and will lead us to the farm."

He nodded and turned the buggy. "Are you still wanting to go through with this visit?"

"Yes, Jarrett. Hearing about your family has given me courage. I know I can face Pa today. It wasn't a good life with him, but I know I'm happy now. Someday, I hope Bradly and I have a baby. I want it to have a good home like you had." She sighed. "Do you think that's possible when a couple works in a saloon?"

"Yes, Lydia, I do. I think it's the amount of love you give a child, not the job the parents happen to have, that makes a good family."

"Thank you. I want to believe you mean that and that's what I decided to do." She smiled at him. "Can you make this horse go a little faster? I want to get this visit with Pa behind me."

Jarrett shook the reins over the horse's rump and he sped into a gallop. It wasn't long until the ramshackle farm house came into view.

Verbena entered the house thorough the front door and put her Bible on the table in the formal parlor. She glanced around to see if everything in the room was in its place. Seeing that it was, she left the room and headed upstairs.

Pausing at Hannah's door, she knocked. When Hannah called to her to come in, she pushed the door open and stepped inside. Seeing Hannah working on her new dress, she bit her lip. "Do you think it's proper to be sewing on Sunday?"

"I'm sorry. I was only rushing to get it finished." Hannah put the dress aside. "Did you enjoy the church service this morning?"

"Of course I did. Reverend Calhoun did his usual expert job of spreading the gospel, as I knew he would." She looked around and went on, "Mrs. Calhoun wore the dress you sewed for her, and she said she'd had many compliments on it."

"I'm glad she liked it."

"She wants another one and I told her to come by this week and you'd be glad to make one for her."

"Yes, I'll be happy to."

Verbena nodded. "I know you sometimes come downstairs on Sunday, but I'm expecting company for dinner today and you'll need to stay in your room. I told Tobias when he went to put up the horse and buggy to bring your food up for you."

Hannah nodded.

"Eat everything and someone will come for the dirty dishes. Then, before you start working on your dress again, which I'm sure you will, though it's Sunday, you need to read today's Bible chapters." She took a paper from her pocket and handed it to Hannah. "Here's the list of the chapters that Reverend Calhoun used for his sermon. Be sure to study them carefully, because as usual, I'll ask you some questions tonight to make sure you didn't skip any of the reading."

Hannah took the list. "Yes, ma'am."

Verbena went out the door without saying anything else. She hurried to her room and stepped inside. She put her hat in the its box and placed it on the shelf in her huge wardrobe. Turning to the beveled mirror over her dresser, she smoothed down her hair and started to leave the room, then paused. On impulse she turned and picked up the atomizer on her dresser and sprayed a tiny amount on her throat. The perfume was old, but it still held its expensive smell as well as it did the day Hector had presented it to her on her birthday more than twenty years ago. She wondered what he'd think if he knew she was using it today to make herself attractive for another man. Then, she realized that she didn't care what he'd think. It had taken some years, but now her memories of him didn't influence her actions in any way. In fact, she seldom thought of him at all. Verbena looked in the mirror again and did something she seldom did. She laughed. It wasn't that she wanted to make herself alluring, but she thought it would be interesting to see if Reginald even noticed the fancy smell.

♥♥♥

Jarrett stopped the horse near the front steps and wrapped the reins around the brake stick. Before he could get out of the buggy, Burl Hamilton came out of the house with his shirt half off and a shotgun in his hand.

"Well, well, looky who's here. I see that gambler's done got his fill of you and brung you home. I knowed it'd happen sooner or later." Burl laughed a deep harsh laugh and waved the shotgun toward the buggy where Jarrett and Lydia sat. "Git on in the house and fix me something decent to eat, girl."

"This isn't the gambler, and I'm not here to cook for you, Pa."

He squinted at her. "Then why're you here?"

"We want to ask you some questions."

He spit tobacco on the ground and shook his head. "Then you might as well turn around and git out of here. I ain't got time for no questions."

"Mr. Hamilton," Jarrett said. "It's important that we speak to you."

"Ain't important to me, so git going."

Jarrett wondered how he was going to get through to this man, but before he could speak again, Lydia reached over and put her hand on his arm and whispered, "Let me handle this."

He nodded and she turned back to her father. "Pa, I think we have some trouble, and I need to talk to you about it."

"I ain't got no trouble."

"You may have more trouble than you can handle if you don't talk to us."

He wrinkled his brow. "I don't see how."

"Then, let us come sit on the porch and explain."

He turned and propped his gun against the wall beside the door. "Well, come on, if you're coming. I ain't got all day."

Jarrett didn't think the chairs on the porch looked stable, but he managed to find one he thought was safe enough to sit in. He dusted it with his handkerchief and placed it near the door for Lydia. He leaned against one of the posts that held up the sagging roof.

Burl took one of the rickety chairs and plopped down. He scowled at Jarrett. "Ain't I seen you afore?"

Jarrett thought about lying, but changed his mind. He didn't think there was any reason to hide his identity from this man. "Yep. I was here the other day, but you were too busy to talk with me. Name's Jarrett MacMichael, in case you forgot."

"I never forgot 'cause I never paid any attention to it in the first place." He turned to Lydia. "Now, what is it you want, gal?"

"Pa, I figured out that Aunt Verbena is paying the taxes on this place so you can keep it."

"What if she is? It ain't none of your business."

"Not really, but if something happened to her, you'd not be able to pay those taxes, would you?"

For the first time, he looked scared. "She ain't dead, is she?"

"No, she's not dead, but she's acting mighty peculiar."

"What do you mean?"

"Well, Jarrett here has become friends with her, and he says she's trying to cover up something."

"Yes," Jarrett put in. "We thought you might be able to tell us what she's doing her best to hide from everyone."

"I don't know nothing." He refused to meet Jarrett's eyes.

"Pa, why did you give Hannah to Aunt Verbena?"

He looked agitated. "She weren't no good to us around here. She couldn't walk."

"There had to be more than that. Did Mama want her to be sent to our aunt?"

He jumped up and shoved his chair backward. He grabbed his gun and went storming into the house, slamming the door behind him.

Lydia looked shocked when she turned to Jarrett. "I never expected him to react like that."

"It probably means he knows a lot more than he's willing to tell. I've often found that happens when I'm getting close to the truth, or if I'm not, the person thinks I am."

"Should I go after him?"

"Let's wait a few minutes and see if he comes back." He smiled at her. "I'm sorry if this is getting to be too much for you."

"I'm fine, Jarrett, but I think it's easier to handle some of the worst drunks in the saloon than to handle Pa."

The door opened and they both turned, expecting to see Burl come out. Instead, a rotund negro woman stepped across the threshold. "Do you all want some coffee or something?"

"Who're you?" Lydia managed to spit out.

"I's Lulu."

"What in the world are you doing here, Lulu?"

"I lives here."

Puzzlement covered Lydia's face. "How long have you lived here?"

"For 'bout six months. Ever since his girl run off to marry a cow man in the west. " She stepped back as if she expected Lydia to hit her.

"Why in the world would you want to live here?"

"Mr. Burl needs somebody, and I needs a place to stay. We figured we would make do with each other."

"I see." Lydia looked at Jarett. He shrugged and she turned back to Lulu.

"Do you think he'll come back out here to talk to us?"

"No, miss. Him done gone out the back door with his jug and a handful of shells. He headed to the woods. That's where he goes when he don't want to see nobody. I don't 'spect him to come back till supper time, if he comes then."

"Miss Lulu…" Jarrett started.

"Lordy, young man. You don't needs to call me miss. Just plain Lulu will do fine."

He grinned. "All right, Lulu. Maybe you can help us out."

"If you didn't come out here to run me off, I might try."

"We don't want to run you off, do we Lydia?"

"Not at all. In fact, I'm glad to know somebody's here to look after Pa."

Lulu eyed her. "Is you the one who married the cow man?"

"No. That was my sister."

"So you ain't coming back here to live?"

"No, I'm not, and neither is my sister."

"Now that we have that straight, could we come in and have that coffee you mentioned? I can always talk better with a good cup of coffee."

Lulu returned his grin. "Then foller me, folks."

Chapter 8

The next morning, Jarrett went back to his hotel room after having breakfast in the hotel dining room. He put his hat on the table, took off his coat, and adjusted the gun in the shoulder holster—something he was never without. He then sat at the desk and picked up the pen. Before he did anything else today, he wanted to draft a letter to Aaron Wilcox. Now that he was ready to write, he wasn't sure what he wanted to say.

Could he believe anything Lulu had said yesterday about Burl Hamilton, or was she addled in the head? Yet, she seemed convinced the man talked in his sleep. Did he really admit to her there had been an arrangement between his wife and her sister concerning Hannah's future? If so, what was that agreement, and would Lulu keep her promise to try to find out? Maybe he should've given her more than five dollars as an incentive to try to find out for them; but he hadn't, and now it was too late.

Whatever, he knew he had to continue what he had planned and the first thing on his list this morning was to write that letter to Wilcox.

He placed the pen in the inkwell and began to write. *As of yet, I haven't discovered the entire truth about Hannah Hamilton's plight, but I do think I'm getting close. I have seen the young lady on two separate occasions and I can assure you that she is not being physically mistreated. She is fed regularly and her room, though sparse, is clean and seems to be comfortable. Let me explain how I managed to see her room.*

Jarrett wrote about the time he'd carried Hannah to her room over the protest of her aunt. He then went on to explain how he'd found comrades in Tobias Johnson and Lydia. Going on, he told how he'd visited the Hamilton farm on his own, and with Lydia. He said he felt he was getting close to answers at the farm.

He then wrote, *Let me say that without knowing so, Verbena Hamilton is also a help. She seems to like me, and has invited me into her home as a friend whenever I show up. I intend to keep her thinking I'm only interested in being friends as long as I'm in Savannah on business. I have a feeling she will tell me more than she wants to without knowing she's doing it.*

He ended the letter with, *Tell your wife that her sister misses her and is looking forward to a letter from her. I will have more news soon, and if things start to happen fast, I'll send a wire.*

He closed the letter and sat back. He hoped Aaron would be pleased with the progress and would permit him to stay on the job. He chuckled. *I don't guess it really matters whether he wants to keep paying me or not. I don't intend to leave this town until I get to the bottom of this mess. I want to see Hannah out of that house and somewhere she'll be happy. She's too young and beautiful to waste away shut up in that sparse upstairs bedroom of hers.*

Though he'd been denying it to himself, Jarrett also knew he was attracted to this woman. He had to get over that. After all, he was still immersed in the affair with Felicia Newell. She had been so grateful when he and Everett had finished the job he did for her that the two of them had even bickered about who would win her grateful affections. At this point in the relationship, he was sure he had the advantage over his brother, but things could have changed since he'd been in Georgia. He wouldn't put it past Everett to grace the woman's bed if given the opportunity.

Realizing this, he decided he needed to hurry and finish up this case and get back to Flagstaff. If he didn't, he was sure Everett would make a play for the beautiful raven-haired Felicia, and frankly, though Jarrett had no intention of becoming anything more than a lover to her, he wasn't ready to end the affair.

Standing, he reached for his coat. He intended to go to the court house and see if he could find anything that would tell him there had been an agreement in writing between the Mrs. Wedington and her sister. If so, that could wrap up things here in a hurry. He could then get back to Flagstaff and see if Felicia was still his or if Everett had won her affections while his twin was away working this confusing case.

♥♥♥

Lulu sat a bowl of watery stew on the table in front of Burl and put one for herself across the table from him.

He glared at the bowl. "This all we got to eat tonight?"

"You can't cook something out of nothing. If you want something better, you need sell enough of your brew to buy some supplies, or at least go hunting for a rabbit or a squirrel to stew."

"You ain't worth…"

"Don't start that with me. What do you think *you're* worth?" She looked at him. "Nothing, that's what. You laze around here and drink yer brew till you pass out. No wonder your daughters don't have nothing to do with you."

"Lydia's the only one who's ever been worth a damn. That was, till she married that old gambler."

"I heard the other one took good care of you till she run off to somewhere in the west."

"She was a fool. Won't be long till that cowboy sends her back here. Then,

I won't need you no more, and you'll have to move out, old woman."

"I ain't worried. From what her sister said the other day, she's happy with her gambler and her sister's happy with her cowboy. Ain't neither of them never coming back here, so you might as well shut up and eat."

He slurped some of the stew and frowned. "Tastes like dishwater."

"How'd you know? You ever eat dishwater?"

"Maybe."

Her black face wrinkled with a smile. "Yeah, I bet. What about your other daughter? The crippled one? Do you think she'll ever come back here?"

"No! She better not ever try to come here. I don't count her as a daughter."

"Why? She's your child."

"I said I don't claim her. Her aunt takes care of her."

"Why?"

"She just does, that's all."

Lulu tried again to get him to tell her more. "But there's got to be a reason. It ain't normal for a man to give one of his young'uns away."

"I didn't want her cause she couldn't do nothing. I couldn't take care of her if'n I'd wanted to, 'cause she couldn't walk."

"But why did her aunt want her?"

"She didn't."

Lulu frowned. "Then why's she got her?"

"'Cause that's what her mama wanted."

"Why'd her mama have anything to do with it?"

Burl hit his fist on the table. "I ain't talking about my young'uns no longer. Now, shut up so I can eat the rest of this slop, or I'm gonna back hand you across your mouth to shut it for you."

Lulu decided she'd better drop the subject for now. Maybe she could get him to talk about it again, but she wouldn't press her luck today. She wondered if that MacMichael fellow would think what he paid her was worth her finding out that the girls' mama was somehow involved in all of this. She sure hoped he would. She didn't want to give the money back, because she needed to get a few supplies. She knew Burl didn't have the money to buy any now. He hadn't sold any of his homemade brew in several weeks.

After dropping off his letter at the mail and telegraph office, Jarrett decided to walk to the Wedington house instead of renting or hiring a carriage. It was a nice day and Savannah was a pretty town to walk around in. Besides, walking helped him organize his thoughts. He'd certainly paced the wooden sidewalks of Flagstaff when he needed to think things through on a hard-to-solve case or, at times, his personal life. Sometimes, when Felicia Newell was pushing him to think about marriage, he'd walk for hours trying to decide how to tell her men didn't marry women like her, and he was no exception. He knew he would never marry her. It wasn't that he didn't like Felicia. He did. It was just that Jarrett was not ready to settle down with any one woman, especially one with the loose morals of Miss Newell.

Today, he told himself his visit to the Wedington house had nothing to do with women. It was all business, though in spite of himself, he hoped to get a glimpse of the beautiful Hannah while he was finding out what he wanted to know about Mr. Reginald Phillips, a name that had crept into the conversation from time to time. He was sure he could find out about the man from Mrs. Wedington. He decided he'd also ask her about Hannah, but if the young woman wasn't downstairs, he knew he couldn't press the issue. Tobias had made it clear that Hannah Hamilton was only allowed to spend time in the lower section of the house when her aunt wanted or permitted her to. If he didn't see her this time, he'd make sure he did on his next visit. He certainly wasn't going to go long without coming face-to-face with the beautiful girl.

Heading up the walkway, Jarrett studied the stately Wedington mansion and saw some things he hadn't noticed before. The house needed some work. It looked like the support of one of the balconies on the second floor was rotting around the edge that held up the porch. A brick was missing in the foundation where the front steps were located, and there were a couple of windows with cracked panes. He wondered why he hadn't noticed these things before and decided it was because he usually came by horse and went inside without a good look at the house.

Still, he couldn't help frowning. As particular as Verbena Wedington was with the inside of her house, how could she let the outside deteriorate in this way? He wasn't going to ask her about it today, but he knew he probably would eventually have to. There was something going on here that wasn't right, and he intended to get to the bottom of it before he left Savannah.

Tobias answered the knock on the door and showed Jarrett into the formal parlor. "I'll get Miz Wedington fer you."

As soon as he thanked the butler, he whispered, "Is Hannah downstairs?"

Tobias shook his head and left the room.

In minutes, Verbena entered. "What a surprise, Mr. MacMichael. I had no idea you'd come by this morning."

"Please forgive the intrusion, and I promise not to stay long. I need some advice, and I felt you were the one person I could trust not to steer me wrong."

She smiled. "In that case, do you have time for coffee, Mr. MacMichael?"

He returned her smile. "I'll take the time. The coffee at the hotel doesn't compare to what you serve."

"I'll have Minerva make some fresh. Please, have a seat and I'll be right back." She hurried out of the room.

Jarrett took a seat and using his detective eyes, he looked around the room. Not at the expensive furnishings, but at the little things that most people would never notice. The heavy maroon-colored velvet curtains were trimmed in a thick gold braid, and almost completely hidden were several places where the braid had unraveled and been sewn back together.

He glanced at the marble topped table at the end of the settee and saw a chipped corner on the back, though it was discreetly turned toward the wall. And the Oriental rug facing the fireplace had a damask topped stool sitting on the edge near the hearth. He figured it hid some kind of flaw.

Verbena came back into the room. "The coffee will be here shortly."

He nodded. "Thank you. As I said when I came in, I'm sorry to intrude so early in the day, but I did want to consult you on something, because I have respect for your opinion."

"What a nice thing to say. I'm flattered you would think of me in such a way."

"As a businessman, I think I have an insight into people and what makes them tick. I knew when I first met you that you were an astute woman and you had a lot of admiration and respect in the community."

Verbena actually blushed. "Why, Mr. MacMichael, I don't know what to say."

"You don't have to say a thing. I only have a couple of questions."

"Aren't your business associates able to help you?"

"Oh, yes, but," he paused and lowered his voice. "I'm a little concerned about one of them."

"Oh, my. Really?"

"When I mentioned that I wanted to transfer some of the money I plan to invest in Savannah to a bank here so I could get my hands on it quickly, he acted overeager to get his hands on my money."

"What do you mean?"

"He dropped all plans for the hotel and began telling me about all the great things his bank could do for me."

"I'm so sorry, but sometimes you have to work with greedy people."

"You're so right."

"But how do you think I can help you, Mr. MacMichael?"

"I was sure you'd know a banker and a bank I could trust. Maybe the one who handles your accounts."

Minerva interrupted by bringing in a tray with coffee and a small plate of cakes. She sat it on the table beside her mistress, then left.

Verbena didn't speak until the maid was out of the room. She then poured coffee for them. "If I knew which bank you wanted avoid, I'd not recommend that one."

Jarrett was prepared for that question. "I'm sorry, but we have a confidential agreement and I can't give out anyone's name. But if you mention this bank, I will tell you that I can't use that one."

She nodded. "I certainly understand keeping something to oneself. I know a bank that I think you might like. A friend of mine is the owner and works as the manager there. It's the R. Phillips Bank."

"That puts my mind at ease because that's not the one my associate works for. I don't know how to thank you, Mrs. Wedington. You've been very helpful." He drank his coffee and put the cup on the tray. "I'll go see Mr. Phillips right away."

"Would you like me to write a letter of introduction to Mr. Phillips?"

"I wouldn't think of asking you to do such a thing, Mrs. Wedington. I don't want to be any bother to you."

"It's no bother, Mr. MacMichael. I'd be delighted to do it for you."

"Then I'll owe you, my dear. How about I take you and Miss Hamilton out to supper tonight?"

"I thought I told you Hannah doesn't go out to eat, and I think I explained why."

"I'm so sorry. You did. But I must do something. Do you have any suggestions?"

"Why don't you come back and have supper with us?" She stood.

"Are you sure?"

"Yes, I'm sure. I want to find out how you liked R. Phillips Bank and Mr. Reginald Phillips, personally."

He wasn't going to have to ask where Hannah was. He'd see her tonight for sure. "Then, I'll be happy to come for supper. Thank you for inviting me."

Leaving the Wedington house, he decided he'd rent a horse, after all. He wanted to go to the bank, and then probably back to the saloon to report to Lydia. Besides, he was tired of using a horse and buggy. He wanted to be in the saddle again.

Chapter 9

"Well, well. Tobias, what in the world are you doing coming to my saloon in the middle of the day?"

"Miz Wedington sent me, Miz Lydia."

Lydia looked disgusted. "What does the old bird want now?"

"She said to give you this." He handed her a sealed note.

"What is this?"

"I don't know, ma'am. I can't read, and I wouldn't read your mail if I could."

"I know that, and I'm not mad at you. I'm just stunned that she'd send you to me with a note." Lydia ripped open the envelope. Her face registered anger as she read. Glancing up at Tobias, she almost shouted, "I can't believe this."

He looked alarmed. "I just brought the note, Miz Lydia."

She shook her head. "As I said, I'm not angry with you, Tobias. I just can't believe the nerve of this woman. She wants me to send her some money because she says Hannah's expenses have amounted to more than she can allot for her this month. What extra has she done for my sister, is what I'd like to know."

Tobias didn't say anything and after thinking a minute, Lydia called, "Ramon."

The big man appeared. "Yes, ma'am."

"See that Mr. Tobias, here, gets whatever he wants to drink on the house, then go get my horse and buggy ready." She turned to the butler. "I'm going to my office for a few minutes, then we'll go back to Aunt Verbena's together. I need to talk to that woman about this."

She turned and headed up the stairs.

Ramon turned to Tobias and waved toward the bar. "This way, sir. What would you care for this afternoon?"

"Does you think I could have a beer?"

"Yes, sir. Since you're a friend of Miz Patterson, I'll make sure you get one of the good brand."

By the time Lydia came downstairs and ushered Tobias to her buggy, she'd calmed down. "I'm sorry if I alarmed you, Tobias, but sometimes Aunt Verbena makes me so mad I could scream. I'm bad to overreact when she irks me."

"She can be trying at times."

"Tell me, Tobias. Have there been any unexpected expenses concerning my sister lately?"

"I wouldn't know about that, Miz Lydia."

"Oh, I think you would. You and Minerva are the only people who can see what's really going on in that house." He didn't answer and she went on. "You would tell me if Aunt Verbena was abusing Hannah, wouldn't you?"

"She don't hit her, if that's what you mean, ma'am."

"I'm glad of that, but she doesn't treat her kindly, does she?"

"Most of the time, Miss Hannah stays in her room and does what she wants to. Like reading or sewing. Your aunt don't say much." He sighed. "It's just when Miz Wedington gets upset that she seems to take it out on Miss Hannah."

"What does she do besides make Hannah stay in her room without her chair?" When he kept quiet, she prodded. "Come now, Tobias. Tell me what's going on."

"Well, most of the time she won't let Miss Hannah come down to eat her meals. Me or Minerva has to take them up to her."

"Does that upset Hannah?"

"It don't seem to, but the thing is, Miz Wedington don't always send the good food to Miss Hannah. She'll send her milk and bread or something like that."

Lydia looked around at him. "You mean she starves my sister."

"Oh, no, ma'am. There's food for Miss Hannah, but it's jest sometimes not the fancy stuff Miz Wedington eats." He kind of chuckled. "She'd be mad as a old kicked dog if she knowed me and Minerva ofen slips something special up to Miss Hannah."

"I'm glad you do so, and I want to thank you for it, Tobias."

"It's mostly Minerva who does it. She spoils Miss Hannah ever chance she gets. Sometimes, she knows when Miz Wedington is going to keep the good meal from her and she'll take something to her afore Miz Wedington eats, herself." He grinned. "Many a time, Miss Hannah gets the best piece of roast or chicken and her aunt don't know a thing about it."

"I think that's wonderful. I'm proud of Minerva."

"You ain't gonna tell…"

Lydia patted his arm. "Of course not. I'd never tell Aunt Verbena a thing. I want you and your sweet wife to continue to look after my sister."

"We will, Miz Lydia. We shore will."

♥♥♥

Jarrett sat across the desk from Reginald Phillips. He guessed the man to be in his late fifties, and the type of person who led a soft life. His hands were smooth and he dressed in duds suited for a banker. His graying hair was combed to each side from the middle, and was plastered close to his head by some tonic put on it, probably by a barber. His face was smooth-shaven, and his bluish eyes were bright. To top it all, he was friendly, and his manners were impeccable. But for some reason he couldn't explain, Jarrett didn't trust the man.

"I'm so glad Mrs. Wedington recommended me to you, Mr. MacMichael. I'm sure we can be of service to you in your banking needs."

"I hope so, Mr. Phillips. No longer than I've been in Savannah I've already learned there are people you can trust and those you can't. Fortunately, I met Mrs. Wedington and I find her to be an upstanding person with no agenda of her own. I feel I can rely on her to introduce me to others in town who will be of the same character as she."

"Verbena...I mean, Mrs. Wedington is a wonderful woman. She's not only a dear friend, but she's the one I turn to when I need advice. Friends like that are invaluable."

"I agree completely."

Reginald shuffled some papers on his desk and smiled. "Now, what can I do to help you, Mr. MacMichael?"

"I'll be transferring a large sum of money to Savannah in the near future. Because of Mrs. Wedington's recommendation, I was hoping you'd be the one to take care of my finances for me when the money gets to town."

The banker's eyes lit up. "By all means. I can assure you, your assets will be handled with the best of care and utmost discretion. If you wish, I'll handle the account myself."

"I would appreciate if you would do so. As I said, I'm not sure who to trust and who not to until I've been in town a while longer."

Reginald nodded. "I can promise you, I'll oversee everything to do with your account. You'll not have a thing to worry about."

"I really do thank you for that, Mr. Phillips." Jarrett rubbed his chin as if he was thinking. "Tell me, Mr. Phillips. Do you oversee Mrs. Wedington's account?"

He swallowed. "Absolutely. Nobody touches her money except me. I admit sometimes her account gets muddled, but I do my best to see that it pleases her at the end of every month."

Jarrett raised an eyebrow. "What do you mean, muddled?"

"Oh, it has nothing to do with the bank and the way we do things. It's just that she often takes money from the account and I'm not told about it until later.

It's easier to keep track of things if I see every transaction as it happens."

"Why does she take money without your knowledge?"

"I honestly don't know, Mr. MacMichael. But she draws some out every month or so and I have no idea what she does with it."

"Maybe it's for her unexpected household expenses."

He shook his head. "She has an allowance for that. Even for the emergencies."

"Does she take a lot of money?"

"Sometimes as much as ten or even twenty or thirty dollars." He shook his head. "I shouldn't be talking about such a thing, but I care for Verbena, as I feel you do. I don't want to see her end up with no money since her husband left her wealthy. I'm trying my best to save her fortune for her."

"You seem to be a capable man so I'm sure you'll be able to do it."

"Thank you, Mr. MacMichael. When I visited her the other day we did discuss an issue that could save her some money."

"And that would be?"

Reginald frowned. "I'm not sure I need to say more."

"I'm sorry if you think I'm trying to pry. I'm not. I'm only concerned to see to what lengths you'd go to help me protect my money."

He relaxed. "I see. I will say this much. It has to do with that girl she's had to support all these years. I feel that's a drain on her budget." He turned back to his desk. "Now, let's discuss your account. How much money are you planning to bring into the bank?"

Jarrett decided he'd better not press the issue of Verbena's account any further. He put a thoughtful expression on his face. "I think five or ten thousand would be enough for a start. Of course, when my business partners put up their money, I'll probably have to send for a lot more."

Reginald Phillips almost looked as if he was going to salivate. "That's wonderful. When will you be wiring the money?"

"I'll get in touch with my bank in Flagstaff in the next few days. You should get a draft from them soon." Jarrett stood.

Reginald did the same and held out his hand. "It was wonderful to meet you, Mr. MacMichael. I'm sure our association will be a very productive one."

Jarrett took his hand. "It was my pleasure, Mr. Phillips. I think I'll go tell Mrs. Wedington how pleased I am with her suggestion that I come here. Then, I'll see you in a few days to make sure my money has arrived."

As Jarrett climbed into the saddle on the horse he'd rented earlier, he couldn't help thinking he'd learned a lot more from this talkative banker than he thought he would. Now he knew Verbena Wedington wasn't as wealthy as people thought, and Reginald had eyes on what was left of her inheritance. He also realized there was a plan to do something with Hannah. He wondered what scheme the two of them had thought up. He felt he could probably have pressed the issue with Phillips and found out more, but he didn't want the man to become suspicious. He felt there was still time to learn all the answers.

He turned the horse toward the Wedington mansion. He'd go by and thank Verbena for the introduction to Phillips. Though it was slight, there was a possibility he could find out from her what the two of intended to do for or about Hannah.

He turned the corner to her street and was surprised when a buggy came from the other street and almost ran him down. He pulled up and waved when he recognized Lydia. She came to a stop, too.

Jarrett smiled at her. "You're sure in a hurry."

"I sure am. That aunt of mine has the audacity to send Tobias to bring a note asking for me to send her some money. I'm on the way there to give her a piece of my mind."

"Wait. That might not be a good idea."

"Why not? I gave her fifty dollars a couple of weeks ago. Now, she says Hannah has cost her more and she needs extra money. I'm…"

"Let me explain, Lydia." Jarrett leaned on the saddle horn and looked down at her.

"Please," Tobias interrupted. "I need to get back before Mrs. Wedington wonders why I've been gone so long."

"He's right. It's only a couple of blocks from here. Why don't you go on ahead, Tobias? Lydia and I need to discuss something before we go to the house."

Tobias nodded, jumped from the buggy and hurried down the street.

Lydia glared at him. "I don't think there's anything we need to discuss."

"I disagree. Why don't you pull over to that park on the right and hitch your buggy? I'll follow. I have something interesting to tell you."

She looked as if she was going to argue, but must have changed her mind. She parked her buggy and got out. Jarrett followed her.

They settled on a marble bench under a large oak tree with moss hanging from its branches. After telling Lydia what he learned at the bank, she sat in silence for a minute. When finally she spoke, she said, "I guess you're right. I need to play my cards a little closer to the vest. We need to find out what Phillips and my aunt have planned concerning Hannah. If I go in there angry and making demands on her, Aunt Verbena will just take it out on my sister."

"I think you're right. If we keep checking into things, I'm sure we'll get to the bottom of all this soon. In the meantime, I don't think we should tip Mrs. Wedington off. Also, I think we should keep Hannah in the dark about why I'm here a little longer."

"Why?"

"She's a sweet, gentle soul who tries to keep your aunt placated about things and I'm afraid she might tip her off without meaning to."

Lydia sighed. "You're right. I'm glad you stopped me, Jarrett. I would have gone in there and messed up everything."

He grinned. "I still think you should go. If your aunt wants some money, give her a little, and I'll do my best to find out why she needs anything from you. Though he never said right out, Reginald Phillips indicated she had a nice account at the bank."

"Something doesn't add up."

"Not yet, it doesn't, but it will." Jarrett stood. "Why don't you go on to your aunt's and I'll come a few minutes behind you? Be careful, though. We can't afford to let her know we've ever met."

"You're right. She'd get suspicious. I'll make sure she never suspects when she introduces us."

"Good. Now, I'll walk you back to your buggy and I'll see you at the Wedington house shortly."

♥♥♥

"Hello, Aunt Verbena," Lydia said when Minerva showed her into the informal parlor.

Verbena looked shocked as she glanced up from the book she was reading. "Lydia, I'm surprised to see you."

"Your note sounded urgent. I thought I'd better come by to see if everything was all right."

"Oh, it wasn't urgent, dear." She seemed a little nervous. "I just had some unexpected expenses this month and thought you could help me out a little."

Lydia ignored her statement. "Where's Hannah? I'm surprised she's not in here with you."

"She's in her room…"

"She's not being punished, is she?" Lydia interrupted her.

"No. Of course not. It was her decision to stay in her room. She's finishing up a new dress for herself."

"I see." Lydia took a seat on one of the pull up chairs without being invited. "Then, tell me. Why are you running short on money this month? I gave you some not long ago."

Verbena frowned. "I had to buy some extra things for your sister, dear."

"Like what?"

The aunt hesitated. "Well, the material and supplies to make her a new dress for one thing."

"I see. What else?"

Before she could answer, there was the sound of the brass knocker on the front door.

Verbena frowned. "Oh, my. Who could that be?"

Tobias came in from the back and rushed to the door. "I'll get it, ma'am."

Verbena looked even more perplexed when Jarrett MacMichael walked in. "Dear Mrs. Wedington, I had no idea you had company. I shouldn't have barged in."

"No. No. It's perfectly all right." She glanced at Lydia as if she was wondering what to do. Finally, she added, "This is Lydia Patterson. Jarrett MacMichael, Lydia."

Jarett took Lydia's hand. "I'm delighted to meet you, Miss Patterson."

"It's Mrs. Patterson, sir. And I'm glad to meet you, too."

He turned back to Verbena. "And where is that delightful niece of yours?"

"She's upstairs. I'll have Tobias bring her down, if you like." Verbena started out of the room, but paused at the door and called her butler.

"So, you've met my sister, Hannah, Mr. MacMichael?" Lydia cocked an eye at him, hoping she was fooling her aunt.

"Is Hannah your sister?" Jarrett had a surprised look on his face.

Lydia smiled and wondered how he accomplished the look. This man was a good actor. "Yes, she is my youngest sister."

"I have met her. She's a delightful young lady."

"I can't disagree with that. Hannah has always been a special person."

Tobias appeared at the door and Verbena whispered something to him. Lydia couldn't hear what, but in an instant, he turned and headed back to the kitchen.

"Maybe I should explain why I came by, Mrs. Wedington. I went to the bank you recommended and had a long, interesting talk with Reginald Phillips. He thinks very highly of you."

Verbena smiled. "Mr. Phillips is a nice man. I'm glad you got on so well."

"I'm sure I'll enjoy doing business with him."

Tobias appeared again and headed up the stairs. Minerva was following him.

Lydia frowned. She couldn't help wondering what that was all about.

Jarrett and her aunt continued to discuss Reginald Phillips and the merits of his bank and Lydia watched the stairs. In a matter of minutes, Tobias appeared with Hannah. Minerva followed with the wheelchair, but that wasn't what caught her attention. It was the dress Hannah was wearing. It was made of the material Lydia remembered bringing to her several months ago. Actually, she'd left it with her aunt to give to Hannah. She had forgotten the whole thing until she saw it again. Now, she wondered if this was the new dress her sister designed. If so, what right did Aunt Verbena have to say she had to buy cloth for Hannah?

Though Lydia wanted to lambast her aunt in front of everyone, she decided the best thing to do at the moment was to keep quiet. She'd reckon with the old lady later.

As the three from upstairs entered the room, Jarrett stood and smiled at Hannah. "Hello, there. It's wonderful to see you again."

"Thank you." She spied Lydia. "Hello to you, too, sister."

Minerva pushed the wheelchair beside Lydia and Tobias sat her in it. Hannah reached out and took Lydia's hand. "What's going on? Did you arrive with Mr. MacMichael?"

"No, honey. I only met him a few minutes ago when Aunt Verbena introduced us." Lydia squeezed her hand. "You look awfully pretty. Is that the new dress you were sewing?"

Hannah grinned. "Yes. Do you like it?"

"Very much so. The color is perfect for you." She wanted to add that she bought it because it was the same blue as Hannah's eyes, but she didn't.

"I thought it would look good on her." Verbena seemed to force a smile.

After a few minutes of small talk, Lydia excused herself and said she had to get back to work. She left, hoping Jarrett could find out something about what her aunt was up to. She now knew the woman was stealing from Hannah. *At least, I know she's pilfered the dress material I brought for my sister. If she'll take something so insignificant as a length of cloth, what else is she capable of stealing?*

Chapter 10

Lulu looked up when the back door slammed. "Well, well, look who's a 'come dragging in."

He ignored her remark. "I'm hungry. Where's dinner."

She frowned at him and continued peeling the apple she was holding. "I ain't cooked no dinner. You weren't here for supper last night or fer breakfast this morning. I had to give your food to the dogs."

"Well, get up off your lazy butt and cook something for me."

"Why should I?"

He walked over to where she sat at the table and slapped the apple out of her hand. "I said I was hungry."

"Alright, alright." She stood. "I'll warm up the taters."

"I want something 'sides taters."

"I'll fry some of that deer you killed sometime back. I found a little bit that had been left in the cellar when I was down there yesterday. You need to kill another one so we can have a little meat now and again."

"Stop your complaining and start cooking whatever you got. I'm hungry."

"So you said." She put an iron frying pan on the old cook stove. "Where you been, Burl?"

"Ain't none of your business."

"If 'n I have to do your cooking I needs to know when you're not gonna be here."

"I'm here when I'm here." He plopped down in the chair she vacated. "Give me a cup of coffee while I wait."

She sat a chipped mug full of re-heated strong coffee in front of him. "Here. And I don't want to hear nothing about it not being fit to drink."

"Anybody been around here while I was gone?"

"If you mean your daughter and that good-looking man who come with her, no, they ain't been back."

"I don't mean them. Was they somebody else that come?"

"Old man Jones come by to see if you had extra brew for sale. I told him to come back. He said he would, and I hopes he does. We's need some money."

"That old drunk'll come back in a day or two. He won't go long without his whiskey. Anybody else?"

Lulu turned the meat over in the pan. "No. Who you expecting anyway?"

"I ain't expecting nobody."

"Then quit asking about people coming around." She wondered if she should ask him any more questions, but before she made up her mind, he spoke.

"You like staying here, don't you, old gal?"

She whirled around. "Why you asking that? You ain't gonna make me leave are you?"

"No, I ain't asking you to leave, but if'n the wrong person shows up here, you and me could both be looking for another place to stay."

She frowned. "Who's that wrong person?"

"You don't need to know. Jest keep your eyes open. Don't let nobody sneak in here that I don't know about."

"Don't worry yourself, Burl. I'll tell you 'bout anybody who comes around."

"Good. Now, you got that meat done?"

"It'll be done in a minute. Want some taters with it?"

"Might as well." He picked up his coffee and took a long drink.

Lulu poured the potatoes in a pan with some onions and salted and peppered them. As she stirred the concoction, she made up her mind that the next time he left for the woods she'd start searching this place. There had to be something around to give her a clue about what was going on. She might even find something that MacMichael man would give her another five dollars for.

Soon, the food was ready. She made a plate for him, then decided since she'd lost her apple, she might as well eat, too. She made a second plate for herself and sat in the chair opposite him. Though she knew it would be the perfect time to pursue the questions with him, she didn't know how to start the conversation. They ate the meal in silence.

♥♥♥

The next morning, Jarrett decided his first stop would be the newspaper office. He walked through the front door and the smell of ink and paper accosted his nose. A man wearing a long white apron and with his sleeves rolled up looked over his wire rimmed glasses. He had a big, friendly smile on his face.

"Hello, there, mister. How can I help you?"

"I'm Jarrett MacMichael. I'm in Savannah on business, and I'd like to check some of your back issues to see how businesses have grown in the area in the past several years."

"Well, I'm Al, the typesetter, but the editor is out right now, so I guess that means I'm in charge. I don't see any reason why you can't look at all the old papers you want to."

"I appreciate that, Al."

"Then follow me. I'll show you where we keep them stored. The shelves are labeled by the years."

"That's great."

"I'd stay and help you, but I've got to finish up the set up for this week's paper."

"I'll be fine. Thank you."

"You're welcome and if you need any help, just yell."

"I'll do that, and thank you again."

In a matter of minutes, Jarrett sat at a small table in the back room of the newspaper office with a stack of old papers. He busied himself looking through copies of old editions containing the stories and announcements about the deaths of Ella Carlton Hamilton and Hector Wedington. There was nothing unusual about Mrs. Hamilton's death. She had been sick for some time, then she contracted a fever and died after a few days. She left three daughters, a husband and a sister. No one else was mentioned in the obituary.

On the other hand, Wedington was mentioned in several stories other than his death. He was a prominent businessman and had influenced many of the happenings in the town, and even on the state level. Other than his political and business dealings, there were stories of his personal life. His marriage to Verbena Carlton not only had a half-page story, but there were several photographs of the couple at their lavish reception. He couldn't help noticing Verbena was a lovely woman in her younger years. Other papers showed the couple at different charity events and social gatherings. It was when he found the write up of Hector Wedington's accident that his interest was pricked. According to the story, the maid, Minerva Johnson, heard a loud crash and came running into the entry to find her boss crumpled at the bottom of the stairs. A scream brought Mrs. Wedington and the butler, Tobias Johnson. Tobias went for the doctor. Mrs. Wedington's sister, Ella Hamilton, who was visiting, extended her stay to be with her sister and to help with her brother-in-law's care. Though he was unconscious for several days, Mr. Wedington seemed to be improving. Then, after a restless night, he died in his sleep and was discovered by his wife the next morning.

There was nothing unusual there. Jarrett then turned to the obituary, and after the first reading, his instincts began to niggle at him. He read the announcement again. It said Hector Wedington died in the early morning in his wife's arms instead saying she found him dead.

He knew reporters often embellished stories and it could simply mean the writer thought it sounded better to say the man died in his wife's arms. Or, it could mean the first story writer didn't bother to find out Verbena was with him when he died. It was too bad Verbena's sister wasn't here to ask. But there was someone he could question. He was sure Minerva and Tobias could shed some light on the story and would more than likely be willing to talk to him about it.

Jotting down some notes, Jarrett folded the old papers and stood. Back in the front office, he thanked Al and hurried out of the newspaper office. Now, all he had to do was think of a reason to visit at the Wedington house, and while there, manage to talk with the Johnsons without Verbena getting suspicious.

She'd invited him to lunch on Sunday. Maybe he'd go early. Verbena would surely be at church, and this would be the best time to talk with the help alone.

♥♥♥

There was a knock on the bedroom door and Hannah stuffed the book she was reading for the fourth time under her mattress. Putting her hands in her lap, she said, "Come in."

Verbena stepped into the room. She had an envelope in her hand. "Tobias picked this up for you when he was in town this morning. It looks like your sister, Drina has finally written you a letter. It also looks like it's taken a long time for the letter to get here."

Hannah's eyes grew wide with excitement and she reached out her hand. "Oh, I can't wait to read it. I'm so glad to hear from her."

"Calm down, Hannah. I think you should probably read this letter without thinking your sister is perfect. She could be just saying things to make you dissatisfied with your life here."

"What do you mean?"

"Well, you know you have a good home with me, and I do my best to see that you have what you need. I'm trying to look out for your future so you won't get strange notions in your head."

Hannah frowned. "I don't understand."

"Just remember what I said." Verbena handed her the letter, whirled around, and left the room.

For a few minutes, Hannah stared at the door and wondered what her aunt was trying to tell her. It was confusing. Shaking her head, she put Verbena's peculiar actions out of her mind and looked at the letter in her hand. She recognized Drina's delicate script, but the letter was smudged and looked as if it had been mishandled.

Turning it over, she gazed at the back of the envelope. Though there was no way to prove it, she couldn't help wondering if the letter had been opened and resealed.

Sighing, she opened the envelope and slid the letter out and began to read.

My dear sister Hannah,

I hope this letter finds you well. I am fine, except I miss you and Lydia more than I imagined that I would. I hope things work out so we can see each other again in the future.

Since I promised to write you as soon as I could to let you know how things were going in Arizona, I decided to do it today.

The handsome Aaron Wilcox and I were married on the day I arrived. I wore the beautiful dress you made me and everyone thought I looked lovely. Mr. Wilcox has a big ranch and the house is larger than I ever dreamed it would be. Believe it or not, there is a housekeeper who does most of the cooking and the cleaning. At first, I was a little taken aback by her because she's an Indian, but we have become good friends and she is very accommodating of me. Her name is Beulah Longfellow. Also, one of the older men on the ranch has become a friend. He is originally from Galveston and had been to Savannah when he was working as a sailor. His name is Seymour Andrews, but everyone calls him Salty because of his time at sea. He's the kind of man we always wished our father had been.

You can't imagine how different the area is out here. There are some trees, but not as many, or few, as close together as those in Georgia. A lot of the land is barren with only stubby grass and bushes. The mountains are different, too. The nearest town to the ranch is Hatchet Springs. It's nothing like Savannah. It's such a small place that it wouldn't even be called a town in Georgia. I've only been there once since my marriage, but the people seem nice.

Please write me as soon as you can. I worry about you and your circumstances. I do wish things had been different so I could have brought you with me to Arizona. Please tell Aunt Verbena that I am glad I came west, and when you see Lydia, give her my love and tell her I'll write her later.

Your loving sister forever,

Drina

Hannah let the letter drop to her lap. It wasn't a bad letter, but it was confusing. It sounded as if it was written shortly after Drina arrived in Arizona. Could this be the answer to the letter Lydia said she would write Drina and explain that Hannah hadn't heard from their middle sister since she went west? No that wasn't possible. There had to be another answer.

And why hadn't Drina said more about her husband? She only mentioned that he was handsome. There was no mention of whether they liked each other or not, or if they hated each other on sight. She didn't say she was happy to be married to the man, or that she might one day fall in love with him. But maybe it wasn't all bad for Drina in Arizona. She did say to tell Aunt Verbena she was glad she decided to go west.

She then picked up the letter and looked at it again. The date Drina had jotted in the top corner jumped out at her. The letter had been written almost five months ago. Either the mail was awfully slow or this letter had arrived…and it had been kept from her.

Hannah bit her lip. Because of the letter's condition, she was sure it was the latter reason. She was sure of something else, too. From now on, she was going to have Minerva or Tobias mail her letters if she didn't see Lydia to have her do it.

♥♥♥

On Sunday before Verbena left for church she knocked on Hannah's door. "Come in."

She pushed open the door. "I just wanted to remind you that Mr. MacMichael is coming for dinner at one. Make sure to put on your new dress. I don't want you to look like a ragamuffin when he sees you this time."

"Yes, ma'am."

"I also told Tobias to bring you down a little early. I want you to be downstairs before my company gets here. I don't want him thinking I make you stay in your room all the time."

Again, Hannah said, "Yes, ma'am."

Verbena nodded and closed the door. Smoothing her dress as she went down the stairs, she muttered. "I've got to have another new dress. This is the third time I've worn this one to church. I can't have my friends thinking I'm wearing old clothes. I'll manage somehow to get some material this week. Maybe something rose-colored this time. I've always thought rose looked good on me."

Tobias was waiting at the bottom of the steps. "Your carriage is ready, Miz Wedington. Shall I drive you to church?"

"Not today, Tobias. I'll drive myself. I want you here to bring Hannah down about twelve, or a few minutes after. I may be a little late, because Reverend Calhoun asked that the ladies on the decorating committee stay after the service."

"Yes, Miz Wedington. I'll bring her down."

"I'll be here in time to greet Mr. MacMichael when he arrives at one. Make sure Minerva knows he's coming so she'll prepare the special meal."

"I will, ma'am."

Verbena nodded and went out the front door. Tobias followed to help her into her buggy. After she was seated, she shook the reins over the horse's rump and drove off without saying anything else to her butler.

Though Verbena thought Tobias and Minerva were good servants, she never felt the need to thank them for anything they did for her. After all, she paid them what she thought was a decent wage, so there was no need for informality between them. She'd tried to teach this to Hannah, but the young girl insisted on saying 'thank you' and 'please' to the couple. Finally, Verbena had given up trying to change the girl's habit. After all, she never left the house anymore, so nobody heard the remarks she made to the couple and wouldn't think she was being too familiar with the servants.

When she pulled the buggy to a stop near the hitching rail at church, Verbena noticed Reginald Phillips was already parked in his usual spot under the old gnarled oak tree. As she sat there, it crossed her mind that she could invite him to lunch, but she immediately rejected the idea. Hannah would be there and she wasn't sure he wouldn't bring up something about the girl getting married in front of everyone. Especially Jarrett MacMichael. He'd already said he knew Drina's husband. She couldn't have him telling tales to Hannah's sister or to the cowboy she married.

So engrossed was she in her thoughts, Verbena didn't notice the couple behind her until a female voice said, "Good morning, Mrs. Wedington."

She whirled around to see Hilda Sawyer and her brother, Calvin walking toward her. "Good morning, to you, too." She smiled at them.

"I can help you a down from your buggy, Mrs. Wedington."

"Why thank you, Calvin. That's quite gentlemanly of you." She held out her hand to him and he took it. When Verbena was on the ground, he crooked his arm for her to take. She did.

"Hilda tells me I should always be a gentleman around old women."

Hilda blushed and punched her brother with her elbow, but Verbena wasn't offended. Like everyone else, she knew how muddled Calvin's brain was. He was so childish he didn't often think before he spoke.

"Why'd you punch me, Hilda?"

"Never mind."

He shrugged and continued to hold Verbena's arm as they walked forward.

Following them, Hilda said, "How's your niece, Mrs. Wedington?"

"She's fine. As I've told you before, I'd like to bring her to church, but I've about given up trying to get her to come. She's just too embarrassed with her crippled foot."

"Don't see why," Calvin said. "I'm sure nobody will make fun of her, but if they do, she can just ignore them. That's what Hilda tells me to do when people say mean things about me."

"Hilda is right. You should always be proud of yourself, no matter what anyone says."

He grinned. "I like you, Mrs. Wedington. You're always nice to me."

"I'm glad. Just for that, I'll invite you and your sister to come by the house next week. I'm sure you might like to see if you could persuade my niece, Hannah, to come to church, and I have some things to discuss with your sister."

"Can we go see her today, Hilda?"

"No, Calvin. We must wait until we're invited."

"I'm sorry I can't invite you today, but I'm having company for lunch. Why don't you come the first of the week?" Verbena felt the marriage to Calvin was the divine the answer to her problem of getting Hannah married. She was almost positive Hilda felt the same way about Calvin. But she did need to talk to Hilda privately about it since time was getting close. She already knew Hilda would be happy to rid herself of such a burden as her brother. Most important of all, Hilda hadn't said a word about Verbena paying her anything to cement the marriage.

They reached the church door. "Do you want me to help you to your seat, Miz Wedington?"

"I think I can make it, Calvin."

"Okay. Hilda and me always sit in the back 'cause sometimes, I can't sit still and she takes me out."

"I understand."

"If the preacher wouldn't talk so long, I could be still."

"Calvin, Mrs. Wedington needs to get to her seat."

"Okay. Go on and sit down. I know you sit in the front and it takes an old person a long time to walk down the aisle."

"Thank you, Calvin." She turned and added, "I'll look forward to you coming to visit me next week, Hilda. There are some things I'd like to discuss with you concerning my niece and your brother. Maybe he and Hannah could become friends."

"Thank you, Mrs. Wedington. I'll look forward to the visit, too."

As she went down the aisle to her pew, Verbena was delighted with the way the plan had fallen into place today. Nothing could be better for her than getting Hannah married to this slow-thinking man. She knew that with his problems, Calvin would never complain about a wife who couldn't walk like a normal man would. She just hoped Hilda wouldn't nix the idea when she thought it through, but again, she didn't think that would happen. Before she even came up with the plans for the marriage, she remembered Hilda dropping some hints at Bible study meetings that she wished there was something she could do for Calvin and his future. At the time, Verbena read between the words and figured Hilda was looking for a way to get rid of her brother. Now, both women thought the nuptials were a good idea.

Verbena still had these thoughts on her mind when Reginald Phillips walked up, smiled and slid into the second row pew beside her. She returned his smile. Things were going to work out as they should. If she was careful, she could even bring Reginald in on her plan. She was sure he'd like the idea as much as she was beginning to.

Chapter 11

Jarrett arrived at the Wedington mansion an hour before time for Verbena to return from church. Tobias looked surprised when he opened the front door. "We didn't expect you this soon, Mr. MacMichael. Minerva ain't got dinner ready yet."

"I didn't think she would have, Tobias, but I have a special reason for coming early."

"Shall I go get Miss Hannah so she can entertain you till Miz Wedington gets home?"

"Not yet. I actually want to talk with you and Minerva."

"Well, sir, she's purty busy."

"I understand. I'll come into the kitchen to talk with you."

Tobias looked puzzled. "Are you shore?"

Jarrett nodded. "I'm sure. Lead the way."

A confused Tobias led Jarrett through the house to the kitchen where Minerva was alternating stirring in a pot and turning something in a cast iron frying pan.

"Minerva, Mr. MacMichael is here."

Without turning around she said, "He's too early."

"I know, but…"

"I guess you better go get Miss Hannah and put them in the parlor. I'll get them something to drink in a minute."

"You don't understand, Minerva. He's here in the kitchen."

"What?" She whirled around with the wooden spoon in her hand. It looked like some kind of tomato sauce that dripped from it. She grabbed a dishtowel and wrapped it around the spoon.

Jarrett smiled at her. "Hello, Minerva."

"Hello, sir."

"As I told Tobias, I came to dinner early because I want to talk to the two of you when nobody can hear what I'm saying."

Tobias nodded and Minerva frowned.

Jarrett went on, "If it's not too much trouble, could I get a cup of coffee and I'll sit here at your work table and tell you what's on my mind. That way, you can go on with your cooking."

"I appreciate that, sir. Miz Wedington will be mad at me if'n I don't have dinner ready when she gets home." She took a cup from the shelf near the stove and poured coffee for him, then put it on the table in front of where he sat. "It might be a little strong. I admit, it's left over from breakfast."

"Remember, I'm from the west. I like my coffee stronger than I've been finding in Georgia." When she picked up the cream pitcher, he waved it away. "I drink it black, Minerva, but thank you."

She sat the pitcher down. "If'n you don't mind, sir, I need Tobias to start shelling these peas so I can start them cooking."

"I don't mind at all. He can sit here at the table with me to do the job. That way, both of you can hear me."

"Are your shore you don't mind me setting with you?" Tobias raised an eyebrow.

"I'm sure. Now, grab your peas and have a seat."

As soon as Tobias was seated, Jarrett said, "I went to the newspaper office Friday and looked up some things. There were two reports on Hector Wedington's death, but they didn't agree with each other."

Jarrett didn't miss the quick glance that passed between Tobias and his wife, but neither of them said anything. He decided to drop the idea of questioning them about the death notice. Instead he said, "I understand you heard Mr. Wedington fall, Minerva."

"Yes, sir, I's did. I's a gittin' ready to put breakfast on the table. I'd took out the bread and was wrapping it in a towel the way Mr. Wedington liked it. He always told me he didn't want me serving him no cold bread." She checked a pot then turned back to him. "It was a awful racket. I put the bread on the counter and went a runnin' to see what was going on. Miz Wedington must of heard it, too 'cause when I got to the bottom of the steps, she come to the top. She screamed and come a runnin' down the stairs. Tobias must've been in the downstairs somewhere 'cause he had got there about the same time she did. Miz Hamilton was a-visitin' and she come runnin', too. Miz Wedington told Tobias to go get the doctor. Miss Hannah, who was a baby at the time, started screaming, and Miz Hamilton had to go back to the room to take care of her. Me and Miz Wedington kind of straightened his body and she said we needed to put a blanket on him. I don't know why she wanted that, but I run and got one out of the closet downstairs."

"Did he say anything, Minerva?"

"Not a word. He was out cold. When the doctor got here, Tobias helped him get Mr. Wedington upstairs to his room."

Jarrett's brow wrinkled. "His room? Didn't the Wedingtons share a room?"

Again, the glance between the Johnsons. Minerva spoke first. "They each had their own room. His was the big one upstairs, and hers is here on the first floor. I thought she might use the big one up there after he passed, but she says the one down here is more convenient. She still uses it."

Jarrett took a drink of coffee. "If her room was down here, what was she doing upstairs?"

"I wouldn't know that, sir." Minerva turned back to the stove and didn't add anything else.

"Was Hannah living here at the time?"

"No, sir. Her mother was still alive. Miss Hannah didn't come here to live until Mr. Wedington had been dead for a few years," Tobias said.

"I see." He finished his coffee. "Now, about the two reports of his death. One said Verbena found him dead in the morning. The other said he died in her arms. Which of these accounts is the real one?"

Tobias looked at his wife. "I think we ought to tell him what it is we suspicion, Minerva."

Minerva wiped her brow with the corner of her apron. "I guess you's right. Go on and tell him. You're better at explaining things than me."

"Now, Mr. Jarrett, there ain't no way Minerva and me really knows what happened, but we did have some thoughts about what went on. We didn't think things were right that morning. We don't know why Miz Wedington was upstairs afore Mr. Wedington fell. She didn't go up there much, and when Minerva asked her why she was up there, she got so mad she told us that if we dared to question what she did in her own house again we could go looking for new jobs. We didn't ask her no more questions."

Minerva interrupted. "I only ask her that one 'cause I thought I might be able to help her do something up there. After she yelled at me, I didn't say no more 'bout it, but I did wonder."

Tobias continued his story. "While I was gone for the doctor, I don't know what went on, but Minerva said Miz Wedington sent her to get a blanket."

"When I got back with it, Miz Wedington was at the top of the steps. She was bent over and picking up something from the floor. I don't know what."

Jarrett rubbed his chin. "So, while her husband was lying at the foot of the stairs, she was up there getting something off the floor."

"Yes, sir."

"Did you see what she picked up?"

Minerva shook her head. "No, sir. I didn't ask 'cause I was afeared to."

Tobias went on. "When I come back with the doctor, we got him up to his room. Miz Wedington follered us. We'd no more than put him on the bed when she turned and told me to go tell Minerva to make sure breakfast was done, then she closed the door."

Jarrett frowned again. "So, her husband was in bed unconscious, and she wanted to eat?"

"I thought it was a strange, too, but I went and told Minerva to get the food ready. Since Miz. Hamilton was visiting here, I figured that might be why she wanted the food fixed."

Minerva took up the story. "After a while, her and the doctor and Miz Hamilton come down and eat breakfast in the dining room. I was surprised Miz Wedington could eat so much when I heard the doctor tell her Mr. Wedington might not ever wake up."

"So, she knew her husband might die?"

"She had to know. I heard the doctor tell her."

Jarrett nodded and took out his pocket watch. "It's getting close to time for Verbena to get home. I'll think over what you folks have said and we'll talk again, but maybe you should finish getting dinner ready before she arrives. I'll go up to get Hannah and bring her down to the parlor."

"Do you need me to go get her, Mr. Jarrett?"

"No, thank you, Tobias, but when you finish helping Minerva, you can go bring Hannah's wheelchair down."

Hannah put the last pin in her hair and hoped it would meet with Aunt Verbena's approval. Before her aunt had left for church she'd come to Hannah's room and told her to make herself presentable for the Sunday dinner meal. She said they were having company, and she didn't want her niece to embarrass her.

Verbena had frowned when she'd added, "And put your hair up in the back. I don't want it flowing down your back. Only loose women wear their hair that way. A respectable lady always wears hers neatly up. Also, wear your new dress. Not the usual faded ones you often wear."

Hannah heard footsteps in the hall. She bit her lip. *Oh, no. Aunt Verbena came home early today and has sent Tobias for me. I hope I look good enough to please her.*

"Come in, Tobias," she said, in answer to the knock.

The door open and she almost gasped when she saw Jarrett MacMichael standing there. "Hello, Hannah."

She lifted her hand to her throat and her heart began to pound. "Hello, Mr. MacMichael."

"I think I asked you to call me Jarrett. If I didn't, I'm asking you now."

"All right, Mr.—I mean, Jarrett."

"That's better. I've come to take you downstairs. I hope you don't mind."

She couldn't let him know she was thrilled he was going to carry her down. She smiled. "I'm surprised Aunt Verbena sent you for me instead of Tobias."

"She didn't. I came on my own." He moved into the room and swept her into his arms. "By the way, you look very pretty today."

She blushed. "Thank you, Mr…I mean, Jarrett."

"You're welcome." He looked down at her in his arms and winked. She blushed again.

When they entered the formal parlor, she looked around. "Where's Aunt Verbena?"

"She hasn't come from church yet. I arrived early and decided you needed to come down to entertain me." He still had her in his arms. "Where would you like to sit until Tobias goes for your chair?"

"It doesn't matter."

"Then until you decide, I'll stand here and hold you in my arms, which I don't mind at all." He winked at her again. "Of course, that only goes until your aunt gets home and yells at the both of us."

Hannah couldn't help a small giggle. "Then I guess you'd better put me on the settee."

"Oh, heck," he said as he walked to the settee and sat her down. "I was hoping you'd wait until she got here so we could see what Verbena had to say when she saw us."

"You probably wouldn't want to hear or see her reaction."

"Think she'd punish us?"

"Not you, but she sure would me."

"What do you think she'd do?"

Hannah shrugged. "Probably make me stay in my room a week without my wheelchair. That's her favorite punishment for me."

"So I've heard." He smiled at her. "Haven't you ever tried crutches, Hannah?"

"Aunt Verbena wouldn't let me."

"Why not?"

"She said they'd make too much noise."

Jarrett shook his head and took the chair facing across the tea table in front of the settee. "You look so pretty, I think I'll sit here so I can look at you."

Hannah dropped her head. "You shouldn't say such things, Jarrett."

"Why not? You're a beautiful young woman, and any man in his right mind would enjoy looking at you."

She shook her head and wouldn't look up at him.

He leaned across the table and touched her hand. "I'm sorry if I embarrassed you, Hannah."

"It's just that I'm not used to anyone talking to me the way you do."

He took his hand off hers. "Again, I'm sorry. I'll try to be more careful about what I say."

Hannah was afraid she'd offended him. "Oh, please, Jarrett. I don't mind what you say. You just must understand that I've never been around many men. Aunt Verbena doesn't usually let me come downstairs when her male guests visit unless it's the preacher, and sometimes, she doesn't let me visit with him."

"Does she have a lot of male guests?"

"Oh, no. Mostly the preacher, and then there's the banker. He visits often, but I've only seen him a couple of times. I'm not sure why she doesn't want me to be here when he comes." She looked up and smiled at him. "I don't know why she lets me down when you're here, either, but for some reason, she doesn't seem to mind me being down here when you come."

"It might be because I always ask about you if you're not downstairs."

"Or, it might be because you know my sister's husband. I'm sure Aunt Verbena doesn't want to upset him, for some reason."

"Probably because he's a rich man and she thinks he'll be sending you money."

She frowned. "Why would you say that?"

"Just a hunch." He smiled at her.

Hannah was a little confused. Why would Jarrett say such a thing? Though she'd had the same idea herself, she didn't think it could be a real possibility. "I hope you're wrong."

"Me, too." He changed the subject and a serious look crossed his face. "Hannah, I want to ask you something, and I want you to be honest with me."

"I always try to be honest."

"I thought you would." He leaned across the table and took her hand again. "I want you to close your eyes and think back to when you were little girl."

"Why?"

"Please, Hannah, just do it."

She nodded and closed her eyes. At least, she thought, with her eyes closed, Jarrett couldn't see how his holding her hand was affecting her.

Jarrett went on. "Do you remember your mother taking care of you when you were little?"

She shook her head. "Not really. Drina and Lydia used to tell me stories, but as to actual memories, I don't have any of my own. I'm sorry."

"There's nothing to be sorry about." He squeezed her hand. "Let's try this.

Think back as far as you can and tell me what you can remember."

She let her mind drift backward. "I remember riding in a carriage. It was a pretty spring day and I had on a pink dress. I was eating a peppermint stick and some dribbled on my pretty dress. It made Aunt Verbena mad and I cried."

"Why did you cry? Did she spank you or something?"

"I don't know. That's all I remember about that day."

"That's fine. Now, see if you can remember another day."

She thought a minute, then said, "One day, Pa brought Lydia and Drina to see me. We were playing on the veranda and were having a good time. Then we heard Pa yelling at Aunt Verbena. I don't know what he was saying, but Lydia said she thought they were arguing about some papers. I didn't care. I just wanted to play with my sisters, but after they quit yelling at each other, he came and made Lydia and Drina leave. I cried, and Aunt Verbena told me if I didn't get quiet I wouldn't get any supper that night." She shook her head. "That's all I remember about it, and I don't want to think about my childhood anymore."

Again, Jarrett squeezed her hand, then let it go. "You don't have to, but you did a good job. Now, I just want you to tell me one more thing."

"What's that?"

"Tell me the worst thing your aunt has done to you in the last year or so."

"Why do you want to know about that?"

"Please, humor me."

Hannah took a deep breath. "I think the worst thing, to me, would be the fact that she kept Drina's letters from me, or at least I think she did. The date of the one she gave me showed Drina had written it almost five months ago. It wouldn't take that long for it to get here from Arizona, would it?"

"I don't think so." He looked at her and his face became serious again. "Have you written Drina?"

"I wrote her three times and I gave the letters to Aunt Verbena to mail. Lydia said Drina wrote and said she hadn't heard from me, so now I'm wondering if my aunt mailed them. I gave Lydia the last one I wrote to mail for me."

He nodded. "I can understand why that would upset you. From now on, if you can't get your letters to Lydia, give them to Tobias or Minerva and they'll see that I get them. I'll be sure they're mailed for you. Also, I'll talk to Tobias and tell him when he picks up the mail to make sure anything with your name on it goes to you, not your aunt."

"But I don't think Tobias can read."

"I'll teach him to read your name."

Hannah couldn't understand why he was being so good to her, but she was glad. He was as nice as she thought he was. It was too bad she was a cripple. He might … *Stop it*, she chided herself silently. *There's no use to think such thoughts. No matter how wonderful I think he is, he'd never want a crippled woman on his hands. I need to get wishes about it being different out of my mind, because I'll always be a cripple.*

"Another thing, Hannah," his voice interrupted her thoughts, "when your aunt gets home, I'll have to make her think I'm giving her all my attention. Please don't think I don't enjoy talking to and being with you, because I do. Verbena is just the type to keep you upstairs when I visit if I don't make her believe she's the only reason I come here, but you and I will know better."

"Do you really mean that?"

"Of course I do, and I want to make sure that your aunt doesn't punish you because I show you attention."

"I understand, Jarrett. She definitely would punish me if she thought I was trying to get your attention."

"I'm glad you understand, because I want us to have more of these private talks."

She nodded, because she was thrilled at the thought of being alone with him again. She didn't get to say anything further, because Verbena walked through the door. "My goodness, you're here already, Mr. MacMichael."

He stood and walked to her. Taking her hand he said, "Now, my good lady, I think our friendship is at the point we agreed to use first names."

"You're right. I'm glad you beat me home, Jarrett. I hope you haven't been waiting long."

"Not at all. Your niece has kept me company."

Verbena glanced at Hannah. "I'm glad Tobias brought her down. I'd hate to think you sat here bored waiting for me."

Tobias wheeled Hannah's chair in. "Here you go, Miss Hannah."

"I'm glad you brought that down as soon as you brought my niece, Tobias. She's more comfortable in her wheelchair than she in on the settee."

Hannah noticed that Tobias glanced at Jarrett, but he only muttered, "Yes, ma'am." He pushed the chair close to the table, then quickly left.

"Well, my goodness. He didn't even help her into the chair." She moved to the door. "I'll call him back."

"Oh, don't bother, Verbena. I'll put her in her chair."

Before Verbena could protest, Jarrett swept Hannah up in his arms and moved to the wheelchair. He sat her down, and with his back turned to Verbena, he smiled and winked at Hannah.

She tried not to blush, but she couldn't stop it. "Thank you," she managed to mutter.

Minerva appeared at the door. "Dinner is ready, Miz Wedington."

"Good. I'm guessing that Mr. MacMichael is hungry."

"You're so right." He moved to her and offered his arm. "May I escort you, dear lady?"

She took his arm and almost giggled. "I'd be delighted."

Hannah looked at Minerva and whispered, "I guess that means you get to push me to the dining room."

Minerva chuckled and moved behind the chair. "I 'pose you're right, Miss Hannah."

They followed Jarrett and Verbena into the dining room without saying anything else.

♥♥♥

After Jarrett left the house and Hannah had been taken to her room, Verbena sat at the desk in what used to be Hector Wedington's office and wondered when she'd decided she'd waited long enough to get Hannah married off to Calvin Sawyer. It had happened the moment she began to suspect her niece was having impure thoughts about Jarrett as they sat right there at the dining room table eating Sunday dinner. She guessed she'd first started suspecting her niece of having more than a casual interest in Jarrett when she saw the way the girl couldn't seem to keep her eyes from wandering to the handsome man's face. She also remembered that she would sneak glances at him the other time he'd visited. Verbena knew she was no expert on romance, but today she had no doubt Hannah was having these indecent thoughts about Jarrett MacMichael. This was something Verbena couldn't abide. If he found out, it not only would make her niece look foolish, it'd be a bad reflection on her, as well. Therefore, she had to put a stop to it before it went any further. The solution couldn't wait, and the best way she knew to solve the problem was to get Hannah married. And married in the next few days. That way, as a married women, the silly girl wouldn't dare have another man on her mind. Especially a virile and handsome man like Jarrett MacMichael. He'd never be interested in a cripple.

I don't know how or why the mindless little fool got such a notion in her head in the first place. I don't care how much she admires him; she should realize there's no way a man like Jarrett would ever be interested in a crippled girl like her, even if she was pretty. If he found out she was swooning over him, he'd be so embarrassed he'd never come around again. He could never return such feelings to a woman like Hannah. He needed a woman who could walk at his side and go dancing with him so he could show her off. He needed one who'd be able to provide a lovely home and give him children. Hannah should be smart enough to realize she isn't capable of any of this. When it comes to a man, she is much more suited to Calvin than she is to Jarrett. That's why I intend for her to become Mrs. Calvin Sawyer in the next few days. Now, all I have to do is recruit Hilda and maybe Reginald to help me make this happen before the little idiot can make a fool of herself and ruin all our reputations. Or before she can refuse to do what I tell her she has to do, in case she realizes she can make her own decisions when she reaches her eighteenth birthday.

Chapter 12

On Wednesday, Reginald Phillips was expected to come visit Verbena and stay for supper. Of course, Hannah was banned to her room. Tobias carried her up about five, and told her Minerva would make sure she had a good plate of food for her meal.

"Tell Minerva not to rush. I'm used to being sent up here, Tobias. I'll be fine."

He thought about those words as he headed back to the kitchen. *Poor child. I wish there was something me and Minerva could do to make things easier for her. It just ain't right, the way Miz Wedington treats her.*

When he entered the kitchen, Minerva turned from checking the chicken and dumplings Verbena had requested. "Did you get Miss Hannah settled?"

"I did. I told her you'd send some good food up to her later."

"I will, too." She shook her head. "I don't understand it Tobias. Why can't the girl eat with her aunt when this man comes? She eat down here on Sunday when Mr. MacMichael was here."

"I don't know why she can't come down this time, but we'll see she don't miss getting something good to eat. Why don't you go ahead and fix her a plate and I'll slip it up to her?"

"At least I can do that." Minerva reached for the dishes and began filling them.

"I guess you better hold up on fixing it now. I hear the door knocker. I guess I have to go let Miz Wedington's guest in."

"See if she wants me to bring some of that tea she keeps back for special times. I already made it 'cause I's sure she'd want it. While I'm serving her, you can run this up to Miss Hannah."

"That, I'll do." He reached over and patted her shoulder.

Minerva grinned, but didn't say anything else.

After showing Reginald Phillips into the formal parlor, Tobias informed Minerva that, yes, Miz Wedington did want the tea. He then slipped up the back stairs with the tray holding Hannah's food. He grinned when he saw the extra-large piece of pie Minerva had sent the girl for dessert.

When he returned to the kitchen, Minerva wasn't there. With nothing else to do, he went into the dining room and began taking the good dishes from the china cabinet. He was almost finished setting the table when Minerva walked through the door.

She smiled at him. "I appreciate your help."

"Don't have nothing else to do. By the way, Miss Hannah said to thank you for the food. She begun eating it right away."

"She's always so polite and thankful. She shore didn't get that from her aunt."

He placed the last fork beside the fine china plate and followed his wife into the kitchen. "You look upset about something, woman. What's wrong?"

"I guess it ain't nothing, but I heard Miz Wedington say something about finding a husband."

"Lord, don't tell me she planning on getting married."

"I don't think the husband she was talking about was for her."

Tobias frowned. "Then who was it for?"

"I swear I thought I heard her say something about Miss Hannah, but she quit talking as soon as I got in there with the teapot."

"Lord, woman. You don't think she's a trying to marry off that sweet girl, do you?"

"I don't know, Tobias, but I think we better try to hear some of what they say when they come in the dining room to eat. If'n we stay close to the door, we can understand them and they'll never know we're listening."

He nodded. "You're right. We'll have to be careful, but we'll do that."

♥♥♥

Standing behind the dining room door, Tobias almost felt Minerva's cringe when Reginald reached for Verbena's hand and said, "I'm delighted that you decided to make one of my very favorite dishes for supper, my dear."

"I would have done something more fancy, but I remembered once hearing you say that you'd love to have some good chicken and dumplings."

"I'm impressed you remembered, and they look wonderful."

"I hope they'll be to your liking."

Hearing Minerva heading for the door, Tobias stepped back. He knew she'd be frustrated, and he didn't want her slamming the door against his nose.

"Did you hear what they said?" she whispered as the door closed behind her. "She almost said she cooked the meal. I'm the one who stood over the hot stove to make shore them dumplings was just right. It's almost like we's still slaves."

"I know how you feel, Minerva, but that's how things is," he whispered back.

"I know you's right, but it still galls me sometimes. If it weren't for Miss

101

Hannah, I'd jest wish we could work somewhere else instead of for that woman."

"We've talked about this before, but it probably wouldn't make no difference. I think anybody who can afford to pay us would be as bad or maybe even worse than she is. Besides, most of them think we's still slaves."

She sighed. "I guess you's right, but it gets hard to take sometimes."

"Do you want me to help you serve anything?"

"I got ever thing in there for the time being. Just watch and make sure she has her glass and he has his cup full. She's drinking tea, but he wanted coffee."

"Shh."

"What is it?"

"He said something about Miss Hannah."

Minerva moved to the door.

The voices coming from the dining room were clear. Verbena said, "Don't worry, Reginald. The servants won't hear a word we say. They're probably in the kitchen gobbling down some of the food. They think I don't know they help themselves to what belongs to me."

Tobias shook his head, but said nothing. He wanted to hear everything their boss and her guest said about Hannah.

"I suppose you're right. I've found that most of the freed Negroes in Savannah don't understand much of what white people are talking about most of the time, anyway."

"That's true. Even if they happened to hear a word here and there, they'd never figure out what it's all about."

Minerva made a face at Tobias. He wanted to laugh, but he knew he better not.

Reginald's voice went on. "So, you think you know a man who will be willing to marry your niece?"

"Yes, I do."

"Do you think he'll refuse when he finds out she's a cripple?"

"Not at all. If he doesn't realize Hannah is his only chance to marry, his sister will point it out to him." She laughed. "When I tell you who he is, you're going to agree with me."

"Then don't keep me in any further suspense, Verbena. Tell me who the intended is."

"Calvin Sawyer."

The pair in the kitchen heard an eating utensil clatter to the table and Tobias wondered if one of the diners dropped it or threw it.

"You must be kidding, Verbena. Calvin Sawyer may be a grown man, but he has the mind of a little boy."

"Think about it, Reginald. I admit Calvin is slow, but where are we going to find a normal man who'd be willing to marry a cripple? I don't know one, do you?"

"No, I don't, but will Calvin's sister let him get married?"

"I think she'd be delighted, because she'd think he was getting out of her house. Stacy Wilson asked Hilda to marry him last year, but he found out her brother came along with the deal and he refused to marry her as long as Calvin was living with her. At the time, she refused to put him in an institution because her parents' will says all their assets go to his caregiver. She fills that role now, but if she sent him away, the assets would go with him. I understand it's quite a large sum."

"I see why she'd want to keep him with her."

"But if he marries, his wife would have to look after him. Then maybe she can rekindle the romance with Stacy."

"But where would they live?"

"They'd have to live with her so she could still get the money."

"Then Mr. Wilson would still refuse to marry her."

"I said he'd have to live with her, but I didn't say she couldn't believe he'd be leaving."

"I don't know what you're saying, Verbena."

"I'm saying I'll let her think they'll be living here with me. Only when they're married will I let her know she'll lose the money if they move out of her house."

Reginald laughed. "My dear, you are devious. I see what you're getting at. This will solve all of your problems, too. By marrying her off, you won't have the responsibility of your niece any longer. Then, you could concentrate on your own life."

"I would love to be able to do that. Don't you think I've come up with a good plan to accomplish it?" Her voice sounded whiney and Tobias made a face at Minerva.

"It's a wonderful plan, my dear, Verbena. Now, it seems like we've got to get your niece to agree to marry this boy. Do you think she'll balk at the idea?"

"Why should she? She has to do everything I say until she turns eighteen. Besides, I think she's smart enough to know no other man will ever want her."

"But does she want to get married?"

"Doesn't every woman?"

"Yes, but if she refuses…"

"I guarantee she won't refuse. She'll be married before she ever knows what's happening."

"How are you going to pull that off?"

"Don't let it bother you, Reginald. I have my ways to make people close to me do what I want them to do." She let out a little laugh. "Now, let's talk about something else. I'm sure Minerva will be in here soon with dessert, and even if she'd too dumb to understand, I don't want her to hear me talking about Hannah. She and Tobias think a lot of the girl."

"I understand."

Tobias leaned over and whispered to Minerva, "I'd like to murder that woman."

"So would I, but what can we do?"

"Don't worry. Now we know what's going on, we can do something about it."

"Do you have any idea what we can do?"

"We'll talk about it later. Now, why don't I go clean off that table for you and then you can serve dessert before she starts yelling for you?"

Minerva stared at Tobias for a second, then nodded and turned to the kitchen table and started cutting slices of the apple pie she'd made.

He couldn't help noticing the slices were much smaller than the one she sent to Hannah. He smiled and watched her to be sure she was going to be all right to serve the food without giving away the fact they'd eavesdropped. When he saw she was fine, he went into the dining room and began clearing the table. He had the urge to throw the bowl containing the remaining dumplings on Verbena's head, but he moved methodically and didn't let her see any of the emotion he felt.

She chatted away about something going on at their church and ignored him. Her actions didn't surprise him. Though it made him angry inside, he was used to being ignored in this household by his mistress unless she wanted him to do something extra for her. He knew his wife felt the same way.

♥♥♥

The next day, Jarrett had lunch in the hotel dining room, then returned to his hotel room. He now sat at the small table in the corner and picked up the half-glass of bourbon sitting at his elbow. He took a gulp, set it down, and turned to the notes he'd made after his second visit to the newspaper and the trip this morning to the courthouse. His suspicious nature had made him go back and search through old papers again yesterday, and his intuition sent him to the courthouse today. Now, he was glad he did both. Not only did he suspect that there was a question about the way Hector Wedington died, but he was now suspicious about what had happened to Hannah's father after his wife died.

Newspaper accounts portrayed Burl Hamilton as a prosperous farmer at one time. Then, when he lost his wife, the man was arrested several times for different crimes—public drunkenness, fighting, and once for stealing a bottle of whiskey. Every time his bail was paid by Verbena Wedington. The latest arrest was only six months ago. This time, he'd grabbed a woman on the street and tried to kiss her. Again, Verbena paid his bail, and according to what she told the judge, Hamilton was not only a little touched in the head, but he was so drunk he didn't know what he was doing. She insisted when he sobered up, he wouldn't even remember what he'd done. Jarrett figured this incident happened after Drina moved to Arizona to marry Aaron Wilcox, but he couldn't help wondering why Lydia wasn't informed of the arrest, or if she was, why hadn't she said something about it when he was questioning her about her father. She obviously disliked the man, so he didn't think it would be like her to hide any of her father's disreputable actions.

But most puzzling of all was the connection between Verbena Wedington and Burl Hamilton. They were as different as any two people Jarrett had ever known. He couldn't fathom the two of them having any sort of relationship, yet they must have. Why else would she always pay his bail when he was in trouble? If he was a close relative, he might somehow understand, but they had no actual blood ties. It was her sister who was married to him, not her. Not many sisters-in-law would support him the way he had led his life for years. A life even his daughters couldn't contend with. And certainly, a life entirely different from the one Verbena Wedington led. Yet, there had to be some reason why she'd support him the way she had through the years.

Turning to his notes on the Hamilton farm, Jarrett saw Burl had inherited it from his father upon the elder Hamilton's death. It seemed that when he brought his bride to the homestead, it was a prosperous place. Even after their daughter, Lydia, was born, the Hamiltons seemed to be a respected and productive part of the community. It was when Drina came into the world that things began to slide. Burl Hamilton had his first run-in with the law when his wife was still bedridden, but somehow, she managed to pay his bail and things went smoothly for a while.

Then, Hannah was born with the withered foot. Her father couldn't accept a child with such a deformity, and decided she had to start walking someday or he would get rid of her. When she didn't learn to walk, he started drinking and gambling. His wife died when Hannah was almost two years old, and he quit caring about anything except his drink, and at times, gambling. The three Hamilton sisters were pretty much on their own.

Jarrett sat back, picked up his bourbon glass, took a swallow and looked at his notes. He was surprised he'd been able to piece all this information together from the news stories and the court records he'd found. One thing still bothered him. Why hadn't Verbena stepped in and helped the family when their troubles first began? Her interference only started showing up when Hannah was about three years old, and lasted until she took the child to live with her when Hannah turned four. It didn't make a lot of sense to him. There had to be an explanation, and he wasn't going to give up until he found out what it was.

A knock on the door stopped him. He was surprised to see Minerva Johnson standing there. She looked frightened, and when she didn't speak, he said, "Mrs. Johnson, please come in."

She stepped into the room, but was still silent.

"Is there something I can help you with?" Jarrett looked at her.

Finally, she said, "Tobias made me come."

"Come and sit down and tell me why Tobias sent you."

Minerva sat on the chair he indicated. "I ain't never been in a hotel room before."

Jarrett smiled, hoping to help her relax. He knew better than to hurry her. She was nervous enough. "Would you like something to drink? Water maybe?"

"No, sir. I'm fine." She looked around the room. "I was afraid somebody would try to stop me from coming up here, but they didn't pay no attention to me. I guess they thought I was a maid or something."

"How did you know which room to come to?"

"Tobias told me."

"I see."

She started to get up. "If you'll tell me where that water is, I might get me a drink after all."

"Sit still, Minerva. I'll get it for you." He moved to the table where a pitcher and a glass sat. He filled it and handed it to her.

"Thank you, sir."

He sat in the chair facing her. "Do you feel like telling me why you're here now?"

"There's something going on and me and Tobias don't know what to do about it. He said you'd know."

"Why didn't Tobias come to see me?"

"Mrs. Wedington done got him working in her flower garden. I needed a few supplies, so Tobias said I had to come tell you."

"What is it you need to tell me?"

"Mr. Reginald Phillips come to see Miz Wedington yesterday. I served them tea and some cookies." Minerva took a deep breath. "I know I ain't 'pose to, but I listened to some of their talk."

"Did they say something I need to know about?"

"Me and Tobias thought you ought'a know. I heard Miz Wedington tell Mr. Phillips she was gonna make Miss Hannah marry somebody named Calvin."

Shocked and suddenly furious at the thought of Hannah marrying some other man, Jarrett blurted, "You're kidding."

"No, sir, I's not." Now that Minerva had started talking, she didn't seem able to stop. "She even told him the man was soft in the head and wouldn't fight marrying Miss Hannah. Mr. Phillips said that would be all right since no normal man would ever marry a crippled girl."

Jarrett bit his lip to keep from cursing. He couldn't believe what he was hearing. He didn't say anything, and Minerva went on, "They's settled on a plan for her to marry the man Miz Wedington's done gone and picked out, even if Miss Hannah don't want to marry him."

"I don't think her aunt has to pick out a man for Hannah. She's a beautiful girl. I'm sure a lot of fellows would like to marry her." Jarrett was actually grinding his teeth he was so angry.

"That's probably true, but if'n Miz Wedington has her way 'bout it, she'll be the one picking out the husband, not Miss Hannah. Me and Tobias don't want that sweet girl to be forced to marry some old addled boy, and we want you to help us keep Miz Wedington from making her do it."

Jarrett's voice had a determined ring in it when he said, "Mrs. Wedington *is not* going to make Hannah get married if she doesn't want to. I'll see to that."

Minerva's black face broke into a big grin. "We knowed you'd help her. You're a good man, Mr. MacMichael. We knowed that all the time. Thank you, sir. Thank you."

"You don't have to thank me, Minerva. I like Miss Hannah, too."

"We knows you do."

"What did you say the man's name was that Mrs. Wedington wanted Hannah to marry?"

"His name's Calvin Sawyer."

"I'll check this fellow out."

She grinned again. "We thought you might not like the notion of her marrying him. That's another reason I come. Me and Tobias thinks it'd be a good idee if you'd be the one to marry Miss Hannah."

Jarrett could only stare at Minerva. He was too shaken to answer her.

"Would you do it, Mr. MacMichael? Would you marry Miss Hannah?"

He came out of his shock. "That's not going to happen. I'm too old for

Hannah."

"No, you ain't. Lots of older men marry up with young pretty women. 'Sides, Miss Hannah will be eighteen years old soon."

"I thought she was only about sixteen."

"No, sir. She'll be eighteen soon."

Jarrett couldn't help liking the fact that Hannah was a young woman and not a child, but he still couldn't consider marrying her even if she did make his heart race when he looked at her. After all, he was thirty. That would make him twelve years older than Hannah. Though not a vast difference, he felt it wouldn't be right to tie a beautiful young girl on the verge of womanhood to someone his age. Finally, he said, "I don't think I'll be marrying her, Minerva, but let me guarantee you that Miss Hannah will not marry anybody she doesn't want to."

"I wish you'd think about it, but if'n you don't want to marry her, then there's nothing I can do about it and I guess that's 'bout all I got to say 'cept we's counting on you to stop Mrs. Wedington from carrying out her evil plan." She stood. "Now, I guess I better get my supplies and get back, afore Miz Wedington wonders where I be."

He took Minerva's arm. "I'll walk downstairs with you. I don't want anyone trying to stop you in the lobby."

"Thank you, sir."

When they reached the street, Jarrett watched Minerva head toward the market. Before she was out of sight, he realized because of her news he was going to have to rearrange his day. Minerva was right about one thing. He had to stop this foolish notion of Verbena's to marry Hannah off to some slow-thinking man. The thought of that made him not only angry, but sick as well. That wonderful young woman wasn't going to be forced to marry anybody she didn't want to marry. Though he wouldn't let the thought completely form in his mind, deep down he knew if Hannah married anybody, it was going to be him.

♥♥♥

The next day, Reverend Cedric Calhoun's wife was having the Bible study group meeting and had invited the women to stay afterward for the midday meal. Excited to be a part of this group, Verbena, dressed in the newest creation Hannah had made for her, slapped the reins over the back of the horse pulling her buggy and headed down the street. She was a little late, but that was the way planned it. She wanted to make an entrance, because she was sure all the women there would be envious when they saw she was wearing such a distinctive frock. Verbena enjoyed it when her lovely clothes made her the center of attention in this special group.

Turning the horse at the next corner, she screamed when a man darted from behind a roadside bush and took hold of the horse's bridle. Grabbing the whip beside her, she tried to hit him, but he jerked the whip out of her hand.

"Stop that, you damn fool woman."

Verbena gasped when she recognized the voice. "What are you trying to do?"

"I have to talk to you."

"You have nothing to say I want to hear, Burl Hamilton."

"Oh, I think you'll want to hear this." He moved to the side of the buggy and climbed in beside her.

She jerked her body around and slapped at his shoulder. "Get out of my buggy, you filthy beast. You smell horrible."

A deep, grotesque laugh escaped his throat and he grabbed the hand she was still trying to hit him with. "Well, my dear Verbena, you're going to have to put up with my horrible smell for the time being."

"What do you want with me, you swine?"

"Thought you'd get away with it, didn't you?"

She frowned. "Get away with what?"

"You know damn good and well what I'm talking about."

"No, Burl. I don't know."

"Don't hand me that, you greedy bitch." He twisted her arm. "Now, why'd you do it?"

Perplexed, Verbena stared at him. "Do what?"

He twisted a little harder, but didn't say anything.

"Please, Burl. I don't know what you mean." Pain shot through her arm and a tear slid down her cheek. What did this crazy fool want with her? Had he somehow found out that she planned for Hannah to get married? But how? Nobody knew except Hilda and now, Reginald. If Burl had found out, why did he care anyway? He didn't even own up to the fact that Hannah was his child.

He twisted again and she let out another little scream. "You better make it right and you better do it today." His voice left no doubt that he expected her to do whatever it was he needed.

"Tell me what you want me to do, Burl and I'll do it. I'll do it today, if that's what you want."

"If'n you don't, I'll pull out them papers and head straight to the sheriff."

She gasped. "You wouldn't."

"Oh, yes I would. Now, don't tarry. Go take care of it." He twisted her arm one more time then jumped out of the buggy without another word.

"Wait, Burl. What am I supposed to do?"

He didn't hear her because he'd disappeared behind the hedge surrounding the house on the corner.

Chapter 13

"Why in the world would Aunt Verbena do this?" Lydia's face showed complete confusion as she looked at the notes Jarrett handed her about the arrests. "I've always thought she hated my pa."

"Maybe she does."

She frowned. "Then why would she pay all these bail bills for him?"

"That's what I'm trying to find out. I don't think it's because of the goodness of her heart."

Lydia sneered. "There's no way she'd do that. Aunt Verbena always has a reason for doing what she does, but it's not because of her goodness."

"And you didn't know anything about it?"

"No, Jarrett. I had no idea, and just like you, I'm completely confused by it."

Jarrett believed her. "Do you think Hannah would know anything about it?"

"No." Her voice was sharp. "I'm sure she doesn't know a thing, and I don't think you should upset her by asking."

Jarrett nodded, but didn't comment. He wasn't sure whether he'd say anything to Hannah or not. He changed the subject. "Do you have any idea who else would know?"

She shook her head. "Not unless it would be somebody at the courthouse where she paid the bail."

"The more I look into this situation, the more strange questions I find. Questions that can't seem to be answered."

"Do you think this has anything to do with Hannah?"

He raised an eyebrow. "I don't know, Lydia, but I figure anything that goes on in your aunt's house affects Hannah one way or the other."

"You're probably right about that." She handed him the paper he'd showed her. "What are you going to do now?"

"I need to talk with your aunt, but I know I have to be careful there. I don't want her to catch on that I'm investigating her. I also think I should go to your father's farm again. I gave Lulu a little money to watch him and see if he seemed to be hiding anything. I don't know if she'll be successful, but it's the only way I could think of to try to find out what's happening at the farm."

"From what I can tell Tobias and Minerva are devoted to Hannah. Have you asked them to watch Aunt Verbena?"

"I haven't had to. They're doing it already."

"Good. As long as they're there I don't think anything will happen to my sister."

"From the way she acts, Verbena has never noticed how intuitive Tobias and Minerva are. She thinks of them almost as slaves though she has to pay them. She has no idea they see and hear more of what goes on in that house than she'd ever guess."

Lydia was quiet a moment, then she asked, "Jarrett, when you get to the bottom of all this, what's going to happen to my sister?"

"Don't worry. Your sister will be fine. I'll see to that."

She nodded. "I have no recourse but to trust you."

"You can, Lydia."

Before she could answer, the door burst open and a tall, handsome blond-headed man walked in. "Well, look here. I go out of town for a few days and come home to find my wife entertaining a man in my office."

Jarrett was glad the man was smiling when he said it.

"Bradly, you're home." Lydia jumped from her chair and threw her arms around the man's neck. "I'm so glad you're back. I missed you so much."

He kissed her quickly. "I missed you, too, sweetheart. Besides entertaining men in my office, what else have you been up to in my absence?"

"You'd be surprised." She poked his belly and turned. "I want to introduce you to Jarrett MacMichael. He's here to investigate Aunt Verbena. Jarrett, this is my husband, Bradly Patterson."

Jarrett stood and offered his hand.

Bradly took it. "Why in the world are you investigating Lydia's aunt?"

"Have a seat, darling and we'll tell you all about it." Lydia guided him to the chair beside hers.

"Maybe I should go." Jarrett was still standing.

"Wait until we explain things to Bradly." She turned back to her husband. "Would you like a drink, honey?"

"Yes. I've had a long day."

"I'll pour you one, and then we'll get started." She filled a crystal glass and handed it to him. "Jarrett, tell Bradly how Drina's husband hired you to come here to check on Hannah."

Though Jarrett wasn't too sure he should tell Bradly Patterson all about his visit to Savannah, Lydia had left him no alternative. He launched into his story.

When he finished, Bradly asked, "Is there any way I can help you with this?"

"I'm not sure, but maybe you can. Let me think about it." He stood. "Now I think it's time for me to get out of here. I'm sure you and your wife have things to talk about and you don't need anyone here to interfere."

"It was good to meet you, Jarrett. We'll talk again."

Jarrett nodded and left the office. Maybe Bradly was right. There was a possibility he could help. After all, a man who worked in a saloon was privy to all types of information that a man on the street wasn't.

♥♥♥

Tobias opened the front door and Verbena walked in. Surprise showed on his face. "Miz Wedington, you're back early."

She only nodded and walked past him. "Go take care of the horse and buggy, Tobias."

"Yes, ma'am."

On still-trembling legs, Verbena made it to her room and closed the door. Throwing her purse and her hat on the bed, she collapsed in the stuffed chair beside the window and tried to make her hands stop shaking.

Why in the world did Burl accost her the way he did? Right out in the open street where anybody could've seen them together. The last thing she ever wanted was to have people see her with this disreputable man. It would be the ruination of her if her friends thought she had anything to do with a man like Burl Hamilton, even if he was Hannah's father. He should know better than to come to her the way he did. The man must be going crazy.

What did he want anyway? It was as if she'd done something or failed to do something for him. But what could it be? She was caring for Hannah as she was supposed to do. She was paying his monthly tax bills. She was...

Oh, good heavens! She sat straight up. *I haven't been to the court house in two months to pay those taxes. So much has happened that I forgot all about them. No wonder he was so irate. They must have threatened to foreclose on the farm. How could I have been so forgetful? Still, the fool could've come to me at night. Not in broad daylight where anyone could see us together.*

Sitting up, she moved to her dressing table and began straightening her mussed hair. She stood, replaced her hat and picked up her purse. Leaving her room she went into the kitchen as her butler came in the back door.

"Tobias, get my horse and buggy ready. I need to go out for a while."

"But I just put them away." He looked totally confused.

"I pay you to work for me, not to question me when I ask you to do something. I expect you do what I tell you when I tell you to do it, not to argue with me. Now, get my horse and buggy ready. I need it."

Still looking confused, he shook his head, turned and went out the way he came in.

Verbena turned to Minerva. "Honestly, sometimes I wonder if your man has all his senses."

Minerva nodded at the woman and without answering, turned to the stove.

Jarrett decided he'd go to the bank and check on the money he'd promised to transfer there. It was a good excuse to see if he could get more information out of Reginald Phillips about the Wedington estate. As he came down the street, he was surprised to see Reginald walking Verbena to her buggy. He wondered why she was here, but he guessed she had some business that had to do with her money. He slowed down until she pulled away. He wasn't in the mood for trying to be the perfect gentleman with her today. That would come later.

He reined his horse up to the hitching post at the corner and climbed out of the saddle.

Reginald looked at him. "Mr. MacMichael, how good to see you."

Jarrett nodded. "Wasn't that Mrs. Wedington I saw leaving?"

"Yes, it was. She came by to get some of her money. Honestly, I don't know why she thinks she has to help everyone she knows. At the rate she's going, she's going to spend the entire fortune Hector Wedington left her. I can't figure what that woman does with all the cash she takes out of this bank."

"She's a nice lady and I'm sure she has her reasons. I'm just sorry I missed getting to speak to her today."

"I'm sure she'll be sorry, too. She thinks a lot of you." He turned toward the door. "Is there something I can help you with today, Mr. MacMichael?"

"I hope so." Jarrett followed the man through the door and into his small office off to the left of the lobby.

"Have a seat." He indicated the chair in front of his desk.

Jarrett took the chair. "Before you sit, Mr. Phillips, would you check and see if the money I had wired here has arrived? Sometimes, my bank in Flagstaff is a little slow."

"I'll be right back." Phillips slipped out the door.

Jarrett glanced at the folder on Reginald's desk and wondered if it belonged to Verbena. Glancing at the door, he reached for it. It was her file, and what he saw inside shocked him, but before he could read the details he heard footsteps outside the door. He shoved the file back to the center of the desk and busied himself looking out the small window.

"Well, Mr. MacMichael, I'm sorry to tell you," Reginald said as he came back into the office, "we haven't received any money as of yet."

Jarrett shook his head. "I might have known they'd drag their feet. I suppose I need to wire them again. I just wish they were as efficient back home as you are here."

Reginald grinned. "I do my best."

"I'm glad Mrs. Wedington referred me here. She seems pleased with the way you handle her affairs."

"I try. As I said, she's spending too much money."

"Women often do that." Jarrett knew his sister, Charlotte, would hit him in the head with whatever she could get her hands on if she heard him say that, but right now the important thing was to win Reginald's trust. "What Verbena Wedington needs is some man to marry her and take over her finances."

Reginald blushed slightly. "That is a possibility."

Jarrett noticed. "Oh, my. Did I stumble upon a romance?"

"Of course not." The banker began stacking the papers on his desk.

"You're not married are you, Mr. Phillips?"

"Well, no...but..."

"But what?"

"There are some obstacles that have to be overcome before Mrs. Wedington will be able to take another husband."

"Oh?"

"I'm sorry, Mr. MacMichael, I've said too much." He gave Jarrett his professional smile. "Now that you know your money hasn't arrived, is there anything else I can help you with?"

"I guess not." Jarrett stood. "As I said, I'll wire my Flagstaff bank again and see if I can get them to hurry up the transfer."

"I think that's a good idea." Reginald stood and offered his hand. "I'm glad you came in today."

"I'm sorry if I offended you, speaking of Mrs. Wedington." Jarrett pumped the hand. "It's just that I think a lot of the woman and I would like to see some good man take on the responsibility of looking after her. I don't think any woman who would make as good a wife as I'm sure she would, should be left alone."

"I agree with you, and I assure you, there's no offense taken. I just don't feel exactly comfortable talking about my private life."

"I understand. I guess in the west, we're more open to discuss such things."

"That must be true. Just be assured that Mrs. Wedington will be taken care of." He walked Jarrett to the door. "Drop in anytime. I'm sure we'll receive your money soon."

"Thank you, Mr. Phillips."

Jarrett walked to his horse, though he wanted to run. He needed to get to the courthouse to check out the new information he'd learned at the bank. If he hurried, he might even catch Verbena Wedington there. If so, he'd drop a few hints and see what her reaction would be.

♥♥♥

Hannah sat at the window looking at the beautiful sunshine glimmering on the flower beds and wishing she could walk down the stairs and out into the lovely day. The thought of the crutches Jarrett had mentioned crossed her mind. If she had a pair, she could at least go out to the veranda occasionally. Today she could hear a bird singing somewhere in the yard. Probably in one of the huge trees that graced the lawn. If she could open the window, she was sure she could figure out just which limb he sat on. But that wasn't going to happen. She'd had Tobias open the window a few years ago so she could get fresh air, but it had made Aunt Verbena furious.

"I'll not have birds and flies and bees and all kinds of insects flying into my house."

"I'll keep my door closed, Aunt Verbena. That way, nothing can get into the rest of the house," Hannah had explained.

"Don't be silly, girl. You don't want them in your room, either."

"I don't mind."

Her aunt had turned and glared at her. "I'm trying to stay calm, Hannah, but you're trying my patience. Now, drop the subject before I have to punish you. You're not to open this window ever again."

Hannah had said no more, but her aunt had punished her anyway. She'd made the girl stay in her room for three days without her wheelchair and hadn't allowed her to have any desserts. Though unbeknownst to Verbena, Minerva had slipped Hannah a piece of cake, some cookies, and a piece of pie.

That wasn't the end of the matter, either. A week later, Aunt Verbena had sent Tobias up to nail the window shut. It remained nailed to this day.

There was a knock on the door, bringing her out of her memory. "Come in." She turned her head as the door opened.

"I brung you something to eat, Miss Hannah. Me and Minerva was afraid you was a-getting hungry."

"I'm fine, Tobias, but thank you. Please put it over there on the table like you usually do."

He moved toward the table. "Minerva thought you might like a little before dinner. She sent you three pieces."

Hannah couldn't help laughing. "If Minerva keeps feeding me this way, I'll get so heavy it'll hurt your back when you carry me downstairs."

"Oh, no. I don't think that'll happen. I's purty strong." He set the tray on the small table Hannah used as her desk and to keep her sewing supplies in.

"What's going on with Aunt Verbena today, Tobias?"

"What do you mean, Miss?"

"She told me she had a Bible study meeting and she was staying for dinner with the preacher's wife. I saw her leave, but it was only a short while when she came racing down the street in her buggy. She practically ran into the house. You came out and took the horse to the stable. She couldn't have had time to go to the meeting."

"I don't know about that, but yes, I put the horse and buggy away when she come rushing in."

"Then you noticed what a hurry she was in?"

"Yes, but she didn't say nothing."

"Of course she wouldn't, and I thought she'd probably got mad at somebody or something and walked out of the meeting. Then, in a short while, I saw you bring the buggy back around again and Aunt Verbena got in it and rode off a second time. It was confusing."

"It confused me, too, Miss Hannah. I'd no more'n got in from putting the horse and buggy in the stable than she come and told me to hitch it up again."

"Well, I guess unless she decides to tell us, we won't know what she's up to."

"I's agree, and you knows she's not gonna tell us nothing, Miss Hannah." He turned to go. "Is there anything else I can get fer you?"

"No thank you, Tobias."

"Then me or Minerva one'll be back up here in a while to get the dishes."

"Maybe Aunt Verbena will be home by then and will let you bring me downstairs."

"She just might do that."

"Of course, that'll never take place if she's upset about whatever happened at her Bible study meeting."

"You're right about that, so's I guess we'll have to see how she feels when she gets home." He smiled at Hannah and closed the door behind him.

She rolled her wheelchair to the table and looked at the delicious food Minerva had sent. She couldn't help smiling. Even if her own aunt didn't care enough about her to see she had what a young woman needed, Minerva and Tobias took good care of her. They were wonderful, and it upset her when her aunt didn't treat them kindly. She only hoped they wouldn't get mad and quit their jobs. That is, unless they took her with them when they left. She knew it would be a wonderful thing if the three of them could leave this house together.

♥♥♥

Verbena came out of the courthouse as Jarrett reined his horse up beside a hitching post. She looked so intent on getting into her buggy that she didn't notice him. He watched as she turned the horse and headed down the street at a fast clip.

He frowned. Why was she headed in the opposite direction of her house? And what was so important that she felt she had to rush?

Shaking his head, Jarrett hurried into the courthouse. He was glad to see the talkative young man he'd met earlier at the desk inside.

"Why, hello, Mr. MacMichael. What can I help you with today?"

"Morning, Albert." He was glad he remembered the man's name. "Did I happen to see a friend of mine leave here?"

"Who's your friend?"

"Verbena Wedington."

"Oh, my goodness, yes. I'm glad we got our business done in a hurry with her and she went on her way today. She usually spends as much as an hour harassing everybody in the office."

"Oh?"

"Yeah. Most of the time she'll only deal with the mayor or another top town official, but today, she paid me the back taxes and flew out of here like somebody was on her tail."

Jarrett smiled. "That's strange. Most people aren't that anxious to pay their taxes."

"Oh, the taxes weren't hers. She pays the taxes on a farm out of town. Been doing it for years. Don't see why, though. Everyone who has seen it says the place is so rundown, it's not worth what she pays for the owner to keep it."

"She's not the owner?"

"No, Mr. MacMichael. The farm belongs to a Burl Hamilton."

"Why doesn't he come in and pay his own taxes?"

Albert shrugged. "Who knows? The only time anybody has ever seen him is when they go out to the place and threaten to foreclose and run him off."

"But he's still on the farm."

"Yeah, and I guess he always will be. The few times the farm has come close to foreclosure, Mrs. Wedington comes in and pays the bill, but most of the time, she's prompt with the payments and it doesn't get that far."

"Albert!" A sharp voice came from a portly man walking into the room.

"Why are you gossiping about a customer?"

Albert ducked his head. "Sorry, sir."

"Can I help you, sir?" the man asked.

As usual, Jarrett thought quickly. "No, thank you. I just thought a friend of mine might be here, but she wasn't. I wanted to take her for coffee."

"I see." The man nodded and turned to Albert. "I suggest you get back to work, and watch what you say."

"Yes, sir."

Figuring his presence wasn't required since Albert was about to get a talking to from his superior, Jarrett excused himself and headed out the door. He felt sorry that he'd been the cause of the man getting into trouble, but was pleased Albert had given him a lot of facts without realizing it. At least Jarrett knew he hadn't pried the information from the talkative clerk. The man volunteered everything.

Jarrett's mind was racing as he mounted his horse. *Why in the name of heaven did Verbena Wedington pay Burl Hamilton's taxes? Did she actually own the farm? If so, why did she let it get so rundown? Why hadn't she run him off and hired somebody to tend the place as it should be tended?* After considering this for a few minutes, Jarrett shook his head. *That can't be the reason. There's something else. Something nobody knows, or won't admit to if they do know. Whatever it is, I've got to get to the bottom of it, because I have a feeling when I do, it will answer a lot of questions I have about the woman... and also about Hannah.*

He figured he knew where Verbena was headed, and it wasn't long until her buggy came in sight. Slowing his horse, he decided it was best if she didn't know he was following her. Of course, he didn't think she'd notice, since she seemed intent on getting to her destination.

Woods blanketed the side yard of the Hamilton farm and offered Jarrett a good cover to watch the happenings. He reined his horse to a stop beside a huge oak tree, which gave him a perfect view of the place. He watched Verbena pull her buggy to a stop in front of the ramshackle cabin and jump down, screaming Burl's name.

Lulu came out with a dishtowel in her hand. "Who is you?"

"I might ask you the same question. Who are you, and what are you doing here?"

"I's Lulu and I's live here and takes care of Burl."

"I might have known he'd pick up somebody to do his work after Drina left. As bad as he is, I'm surprised he chose someone like you."

When Lulu stuck her nose in the air, Jarrett had to smile. *Good for you,*

Lulu.

"Ain't none of you's business, as I can tell." Lulu's voice raised two octaves.

Verbena shook her head and rolled her eyes, but only asked, "Where's Burl?"

"He ain't here."

"I can see that. Where is he?"

"I don't know. He took a jug and headed to the woods."

Jarrett raised an eyebrow and glanced around. He hoped Burl hadn't chosen these woods to come to with his jug.

Verbena waved an arm in his directions. "Those woods?"

"No. He goes down yonder way towards the creek." Lulu pointed to an area beside the dilapidated barn.

"When will he be back?"

"I don't know. Sometimes, he stays a long time, even overnight when he wants to. Then, sometimes, he won't be gone long." She frowned. "What'a you want him fer, anyhow?"

"That's none of your business."

"You can wait for him if'n you want to, Missy. Jest take a seat here on the porch. I got work to do." Lulu turned and went back into the house.

Verbena looked stunned, but she seemed to gather herself together. She walked to the door and shouted, "Tell Burl the taxes are paid."

Lulu reappeared at the door. "Say what?"

"I said to tell him the taxes are paid." Verbena turned to her buggy, but changed her mind and looked back at Lulu. "Also, tell him if he ever comes to town and bothers me again I'll have him shot."

With that, she turned the buggy around, and used the whip on the horse. She didn't look to the right or the left as she left the yard. Jarrett couldn't help smiling as he muttered, "Boy, that woman is mad."

He sobered when his thoughts changed. *I sure hope she doesn't take it out on Hannah. I guess I'd better go by her house and check when I get back to town and make sure she doesn't. I might also get an idea what she's up to about the marriage plans Minerva told me about.*

As it always did when he thought of the marriage, Jarrett began to get angry. Maybe he shouldn't go to Verbena's house this mad.

Chapter 14

Minerva turned from the stove when Tobias walked in. "Did you find Mr. MacMichael?"

"They said he'd left the hotel early and hadn't come back. I waited around a while, but when he didn't show up I thought I better come on back here. Maybe I can go see him later today."

"I feels like we needs to get to him, Tobias. It's no telling what Miz Wedington will do next. She shore acted strange today."

"I know. I wonder where she is now. Do you know?"

Minerva chuckled. "Does you really think she'd tell me?"

Tobias came to her and patted her back. "No, wife, I don't guess she would."

They heard the front door slam.

"Oh, no, I bet she's home again." Tobias went out of the kitchen and hurried to the front hall.

"There you are." Verbena's voice was sharp. "Does Minerva have anything hot I can eat? I haven't had dinner, and I'm hungry."

"I think she does, Miz Wedington. I'll go bring Miss Hannah down."

"No. Go take care of my horse." She marched toward the kitchen.

Feeling an anger he knew he couldn't show, Tobias watched as she marched through the dining room and flung open the kitchen door. Without asking if there was any food, she demanded, "Fix me a plate, Minerva. I'll be in the dining room."

Minerva nodded. "Yes, ma'am."

Tobias shook his head and turned to the door. He was glad he and Minerva had the foresight to see that Miss Hannah had gotten her dinner. The poor girl would have to go without if they hadn't seen she was fed.

Thirty minutes later, he came into the house through the kitchen. In case Verbena was still in the dining room, he whispered to his wife, "Did you get her fed?"

"She gobbled it down then said she was going to her room and she wasn't to be disturbed." She shook her head. "Somethin's goin' on, Tobias. I'm not shore what, but it's worrying me."

"Maybe I should slip off and see if I can find Mr. MacMichael again."

"I don't know. She might want you to do something for her." Minerva looked at her husband. "You's look likes you's worrying, too. Set down and I'll git you a cup of coffee. I knows you can use it."

"I shore can." He took a seat at the kitchen table. "Why don't you git yourself one and set yourself down with me? We can hear Miz Wedington if she hollers."

"I thinks I will. I's tired, too. I done the wash this morning and cleaned her room and I's still got to cook supper."

"Didn't she jest eat?"

"She did. She even cleaned her plate." Minerva giggled. "Then she tells me she don't want to overeat because she'd ruin her supper. I knowed by that I had to cook."

"I don't guess I'll have to do nothing else. I'll help you, Minerva."

She put two cups of coffee on the table and took a seat. "Thank you, Tobias. You's a good husband."

♥♥♥

Later that afternoon, the buggy stopped in front of the Wedington mansion and Hilda Sawyer turned to her brother. "Now, you know you have to act nice when we get inside, don't you, Calvin?"

He wiggled. "I was nice when we came before."

"I know. It's just that I want you to know how to act when you come here to live."

"Can I live here now?"

"Not yet. We're here for a visit, and you have to be on your best behavior. You can't tell Miz Wedington I told you anything about living here."

"I won't."

"Good."

"Will I get to meet the crippled girl this time? She was asleep when I was here before."

"I think you might, and if you do, you know you have to be especially nice to Hannah."

"She can't walk. Everybody says so."

"It doesn't matter whether she can walk or not. You have to be her friend. She needs somebody who will be nice to her."

"I will. Do you think she'd want to play with my toy gun?"

"I don't know, Calvin. I'm not sure how smart she is."

"I bet she's not as smart as me."

"I hope not," Hilda muttered.

"What'd you say?"

"Nothing important. Just do the things I told you to do, and everything will be fine."

"I will, Hilda. I want to live here. There's a pretty yard. I could get a dog and we could have fun running around." He looked at his sister. "Do you think Hannah would want a dog?"

"Maybe she would."

"Good. Then we could play with the dogs. I'd like to have a dog."

Ignoring him, Hilda wrapped the reins around the brake stick and got out of the buggy. "Come on, Calvin. Let's go pay a call on Mrs. Wedington."

"But I want to ask Hannah if she wants a dog."

"Don't start or I'll make you stay in the buggy."

He pursed his lips, but said nothing further.

Hilda took a deep breath. This wasn't going to be easy, but if they could pull it off, it would be the perfect answer for all of them. At first, when Verbena hinted that they should try to get Calvin and Hannah together, she thought the woman was crazy, but the more she thought about it, the better she liked the idea. She'd be rid of the brother who had been a millstone around her neck ever since her parents died, and Mrs. Wedington could take care of the rest. Then, she could have a normal life of her own with the man she'd loved forever. She knew he didn't love her enough to have Calvin in the house, but with Calvin gone, he would surely change his mind. She took a deep breath and clanged the brass knocker on the front door.

A tall black man opened the door. "Yes, ma'am?"

"I'm Miss Sawyer. My brother and I are here to call on Mrs. Wedington. Please announce us."

Tobias stood aside and indicated a room on his left. "Please step inside the parlor and I'll tell Mrs. Wedington you're here."

After Tobias left, Calvin whispered to Hilda, "Is Hannah colored black like that man?"

"No, Calvin. He's Mrs. Wedington's butler."

"What's a butler?"

"A man servant who answers the door and does other things around the house."

"Why don't we have a colored black butler to answer our door?"

"Because we don't have the money to pay one. Now, sit down on one of those chairs, but be careful. We don't want to break anything."

He sat. "I'm glad Hannah isn't colored black. I don't think I'd want to play with ..."

"Shh."

Verbena appeared at the door. "Why, Hilda Sawyer and Calvin, what an honor to have you call on me today."

"I hope you don't mind my dropping by unannounced, but when you didn't show up for Bible study, I was concerned. I wanted to make sure you weren't sick."

"Oh, no, I'm not sick. I'm fine. There was a family emergency that I had to take care of. I've already written Mrs. Calhoun a note with my apology. I was going to have my butler deliver it this afternoon."

"Hilda and I don't have a butler."

She patted her brother's arm and smiled at the older woman. "Mrs. Wedington knows that, Calvin." She turned back to Verbena. "I'm so glad it wasn't your health. Of course, I'm sorry you had a family problem."

"It worked out fine." She returned her guest's smile. "Would you like some tea?"

"I want some beer. I don't like tea," Calvin said.

Hilda looked stricken. "Calvin, that's not polite. Miz Verbena doesn't serve nice men beer."

"It's fine, Hilda." Verbena turned to Calvin. "I'll make sure you get a glass of good cold milk. Would that be all right?"

"I guess so. Hilda makes me drink milk."

"It's good for you, you know."

He nodded and smiled at her. "Does the crippled girl want a dog?"

Verbena looked confused. "What?"

"Please excuse him, Mrs. Wedington. He has the idea that because he wants a dog everyone he meets should want one."

"Well, Calvin, I don't know whether Hannah would like a dog or not. Would you like to ask her?"

"Yes. Where is she?" He started to stand. "Do I need to wake her up?"

"No. You sit still and I'll have her brought down." Verbena stood. "I'll be back shortly."

Hilda leaned toward her brother and whispered, "What's the matter with you today, Calvin? Can't you please stop talking about a dog and just listen to what Mrs. Wedington and I are saying? You don't want me to get mad at you, do you?"

Calvin's mouth puckered and he looked as if he might cry. "I didn't mean to make you mad, Hilda."

"I'm not mad yet, Calvin. I just want you to be quiet and let me do the talking."

He nodded. "After I ask Hannah if she wants a dog, I won't say anything else."

Hilda reached out and patted his arm again. "That's a good boy. Now, put a smile on your face. Mrs. Wedington and Hannah should be in here shortly."

♥♥♥

Hannah looked up when her aunt walked into her room. "Put on your new dress and comb your hair, Hannah. We have company."

"Is it Mr. MacMichael?"

Verbena frowned. "No. They're friends of mine from church. They want to meet you."

"Really?" Hannah was confused. Usually, when Verbena's church friends visited, she was exiled to her room.

"Yes, really. These are special friends. Hilda Sawyer and her brother Calvin." She took a deep breath. "You'll find Calvin a little different."

"What's the matter with him?"

"He's a fine young man, but he's a little slow. People make fun of him sometimes and he just needs someone to be kind to him. I'm sure when you get to know him, you'll like him."

"I'll be kind to him, Aunt Verbena. I know what it's like to be different."

The older woman nodded. "I was sure you'd be nice to him, my dear. Now, get ready and I'll send Tobias up for you."

When her aunt left, Hannah moved to her wardrobe and pulled out her new dress. She was still a little confused about why her aunt wanted her to come downstairs and meet these people, but she wasn't going to argue about it. She'd been in her room all day and she was anxious to get out, even if she did have to help entertain strangers.

I just wish it had been Jarrett MacMichael visiting instead of these people, ran through her mind, but she brushed the thought away. She'd told herself she couldn't think such thoughts about Jarrett, even if no one had a clue she'd entertained them in the first place.

By the time she dressed Tobias arrived to carry her downstairs.

"Who are these people, Tobias?" Hannah asked.

"I don't know, miss, but I want you to do one thing."

"What's that?"

"Be careful what you say to them people down there."

Hannah frowned. "Why, Tobias? Don't you trust them?"

"Can't say as I do. Jest heed what I say 'cause you don't needs to trust them, either."

Though she had no idea what he was talking about, she nodded and said, "I'm sure you have your reason for warning me, and I trust you. I'll be careful."

By this time, they reached the parlor. Verbena said, "Put Hannah there in that chair beside Calvin, Tobias."

"I'll go back for her chair."

"Yes, do. We might want to take her into the garden for a walk."

Stunned, Hannah stared at her. It had been ages since she'd been allowed to go into the garden. Though she'd been wishing for a trip outside, what was so special about today that her aunt would suggest it?

Verbena made quick introductions, because Minerva entered with the tea and a glass of milk for Calvin. There was also a plate of sugar cookies on the tray. Before she had finished pouring the tea for the women, he had finished the entire glass of milk and set the empty glass back on the tray.

Wiping his mouth, he said, "It wasn't as good as beer, but it was good."

"I'm glad you liked it, Calvin." Verbena took the cup Minerva handed her. "Just pour the tea for my guest and Hannah. We'll put sugar or whatever we like in it."

"Yes, ma'am." She served Hilda and Hannah, then backed out of the room.

"I'm glad you could join us, Hannah." Hilda smiled at her. "Your aunt speaks so highly of you."

Tobias's words echoed in her ear, especially because Calvin kept gawking at her. Be careful, he'd said. She nodded at the woman and muttered, "I was happy to come down." She picked up the sugar bowl and put a small amount into her tea and began to stir it.

"Of course, I'm proud of Hannah. She copes so well with her plight."

Before anyone else could speak, Calvin leaned toward Hannah and blurted, "Do you want a dog?"

Hannah jumped, and leaned backward almost spilling her tea.

Hilda touched her brother's arm. "Calvin, calm down."

"But I want to know if she wants a dog." He puckered his lips as if he was going to cry.

"I'm sure Hannah will tell you if she wants a dog or not." Verbena glared at her niece. "Won't you, dear?"

"Of course." She sipped her tea as she thought about her words. "I think a dog would be nice, Calvin, but dogs like to run around in the yard and be active. As you may know, I'd be unable to run around with it because I can't walk."

He grinned at her. "I know you can't walk, but you wouldn't have to worry I'd run around in the yard with your dog for you."

"That'd be nice of you."

"Ah, it wouldn't be any trouble. I'd have my dog to go with, too. They can play when I move in."

Verbena's voice interrupted him. "Oh, my! Look what I did." She had spilled hot tea in her lap.

"Are you all right, Aunt Verbena?" Hannah was almost sure she saw her aunt deliberately spill the tea.

The aunt was frantically dabbing the wet tea spot on her dress with her napkin. "I think I burned my leg a little, but I'll be fine."

Calvin looked at her and frowned. "What made you drop it?"

"Calvin, that isn't polite." Hilda chided him. "I'm sure it was an accident. Why don't you have one of those delicious cookies on the tray?"

"I like cookies, but I don't have any more milk to drink."

"When Tobias comes in with Hannah's chair, I'll have him bring you another glass of milk."

Hannah sipped her tea and watched the group in the room. Why had her aunt sent for her to join them? Hilda had hardly said a word to her, Calvin was in his own world, and her aunt was the strangest of all. Hannah knew she'd watched as Verbena had deliberately tipped her tea cup for some odd reason. What was that all about? In fact, what was this whole gathering about? It made no sense, but she knew she'd continue to be careful about what she said and did.

Tobias entered with Hannah's chair and helped her into it.

Calvin watched and his eyes grew big. Before anyone could say anything to stop him, he blurted, "Why can't you walk?"

"Calvin!" his sister said. "You're being very rude."

"Well, I want to know."

Ignoring Calvin, Verbena said, "Tobias, bring Mr. Sawyer another glass of milk."

"Yes, ma'am."

"Hilda, I want to get a colored black man who we can tell what to do and he'll do it."

"Calvin!"

He wrinkled his forehead. "Don't fuss at me, Hilda."

"I'm not fussing, but you're going to have to be quiet."

He dropped his head. "I forgot."

Verbena took a deep breath. "After you drink your milk and eat some cookies, would you like to go out and see what's around the back terrace?"

"What's out there?"

"Flowers and benches and a little pond."

He grinned. "I like ponds. Is there any fish in it?"

"No, but you can go look at the yard where you can chase Hannah's dog if she gets one."

"I'd like to do that." He grabbed two cookies and crammed them in his mouth.

In a matter of minutes, Tobias returned with the milk.

Again, Calvin drank it without stopping. "Now I'm ready to go see where me and the dog will play."

Hannah sipped her tea when her aunt looked at her and gave her a slight smile. Surely, the woman wouldn't ask her to go out on the veranda with this strange and somewhat muddled man.

But her aunt did just that. "Maybe you'd like to push Hannah's chair out there with you. She likes to sit outside sometimes."

"I don't think..." Hannah started to protest.

Calvin interrupted, "I don't know how to roll that thing she's sitting in."

"If you want to see where you and the dog can play, you'll have to do it." Verbena looked perplexed. "There's nothing to it. Simply stand behind her and push the chair."

"You can do it, Calvin," his sister encouraged. "Just try and see what happens."

"I do want to see where I can play."

"But..." Hannah started to speak again.

"Give Calvin a chance, Hannah." Verbena's voice was sharp. "He's our guest."

She said nothing else as Calvin moved behind her chair. He grabbed the back and began to push forward. He ran her directly into the tea table and knocked one of Verbena's fancy cups to the floor, shattering it and spilling the tea left in it.

"I'm sorry," he muttered and jerked the chair backward and around, making Hannah grab the side to keep her balance. He then headed for the doorway in an almost-run.

Hannah wanted to scream, 'Slow down,' but she didn't get a chance. Before she could speak, her chair slammed into the side of the door facing causing her to pitch forward. The side of her face smashed into the door jamb and blood gushed from her nose. She felt herself twist as she fell from her chair to floor. She sensed a searing hot pain shoot all the way to her shoulder. She tried not to, but she was sure she was going to pass out.

Hilda jumped up and took Calvin's arm. "Now look what you've done!" Her voice was harsh. "You're going to ruin everything."

"I didn't mean to do it," Calvin cried.

"Are you all right, Hannah?" Verbena asked as she looked down at her niece without touching her.

Hannah heard her aunt, but was so stunned she couldn't answer.

"Did I kill her?" Calvin asked.

"Of course not." Verbena frowned at him. "Why don't you pick her up and put her back in her chair?"

He grabbed Hilda's hand. "I don't want to touch her. She's bleeding."

"Oh, my." Verbena sighed. "I guess you'd better help get her up, whether you want to or not, Calvin."

"No. I killed her."

Hannah wanted to say she wasn't dead. She was only hurting, but her mouth didn't work.

"I'm sure she isn't dead." Verbena's voice was firm.

"I don't touch dead people, do I, Hilda?"

Oh, please don't let him touch me. I think he might really kill me if he comes near me again.

Before Hilda could answer her brother, Tobias came into the entry. "I heard a crash, Miz Wedington. Is ever body—"

"Hannah fell out of her chair. She should have held on tighter."

Tobias bristled. "Well, we can't just let her lay there in the floor, Miz Wedington. She's hurt. I'll get her to her room and then go for the doctor."

"I killed her," Calvin began to whimper.

"Be quiet, Calvin," Hilda said. "I don't think you killed her."

"I'm not sure she's even hurt bad enough to need a doctor," Verbena said.

Tobias ignored all of them. He swept Hannah up in his arms and headed up the stairs.

Though her arm throbbed and there was blood running from her nose, Hannah recognized Tobias's voice and felt his strong arms lift her from the floor. Relief flooded through her. She knew she'd be safe, now.

Chapter 15

Tobias stood behind the dining room door where Mrs. Wedington nor her guests could see him. He wished he'd been able to find Jarrett MacMichael yesterday or this morning, but the hotel clerk again told him Mr. MacMichael was out and he didn't know when he'd be back. Now, he had to see if he could find out on his own what was happening. He wanted to know what the doctor said and he intended to listen, whether it was right to do so or not. He heard the stairs squeak and he knew the doctor was coming down to speak to a waiting Mrs. Wedington.

"Well, how is she, Doctor Goddard?" Verbena asked when the doctor reached the bottom step.

"She needs rest for the bump on her head, which is going to require that she stay in bed at least for a couple of days, but the good news is that her nose isn't broken. The information is not so good about her right arm. It has a deep cut below the elbow. We'll have to bandage it and you must make sure she doesn't let it hang down for about a week. It goes without saying, she won't be able to use it for a few days."

Verbena lifted and eyebrow. "Will she be able to sew?"

Tobias shook his head. How could Miz Wedington think about Hannah's sewing when the poor girl was in pain and needed care? He knew it would have to be up to him and Minerva to see that the girl was taken care of.

"Not unless she can sew with her left hand," the doctor said. "I'm sure her arm is also going to be painful. I'll leave some laudanum for later. I wouldn't give it to her until you see she's coherent. Probably by tomorrow. I know the pain will be hard for her to bear, but you don't want her to be in such a state that she doesn't know what's happening around her."

"Would it be dangerous to give it to her tonight if she's in pain she thinks she can't stand?"

"I don't think it would kill her, but it would only render her so confused she wouldn't understand what was going on. As I said, later would be better. I recommend you wait a day before giving it to her. By then, don't be afraid to keep her sedated for a day or two. Afterward, she should be able to stand the pain without medication."

"I appreciate that, Doctor Goddard. I'll see that she is well taken care of."

"I'm sure you will, Mrs. Wedington." He smiled at her. "You know you can call me any time you need my services."

"I do know that." She walked beside him to the front door as she dropped the laudanum into her skirt pocket. "Thank you so much for coming so quickly."

"You're so welcome, dear lady. Let me know if you need me to come back."

"I will." She closed the door behind him and moved back to the parlor door. "Did you hear what he said, Hilda?"

"Yes. I'm so sorry this happened."

"I didn't mean to kill her," Calvin said in a flat voice.

"She's not dead, Calvin. She'll be fine in a few days."

"Can she walk then?"

"No. She won't be able to walk, but she'll be able to sit in her chair again."

"Will she show me the yard then?"

"I'm sure she will." Verbena looked at Hilda. "This could be a blessing. I'm not sure I could make Hannah bend to my wishes if she's in her right mind, but with this…" She held up the bottle, grinned, and slipped it back into her pocket.

"What do you mean?" Hilda sounded interested.

"Well, I'll give her a dose of the medicine tonight and then one in the morning. Why don't you and Calvin come back about three tomorrow afternoon? I'll get the preacher here before then and convince him that marrying your brother and my niece is for their own good."

"Do you mean—"

"Why not, Hilda? This is a blessing for us. It's the best time I know to make sure Hannah does what I wish. Once they're married, there's nothing she or anybody else can do about it. I know it's not the kind of marriage Hannah wishes she could have, but she'll never have a normal one. Marrying Calvin is better than nothing. After all, Calvin is a nice boy. He'll have fun if I give him a dog as a wedding present."

"I want a dog."

Hilda came out into the entry leading her brother. "You are a genius, Mrs. Wedington."

"Don't you think this is the answer for all of us?"

"Yes, I do." She headed for the door. "Come along, Calvin. We need to go home now."

"But I want to see the where I'm going to play."

"You can see the yard tomorrow." Verbena moved to the door with them.

"Will the crippled girl show me then?"

"I'm not sure she'll be able to, but somebody will take you out to see it."

"Then I'm ready to go home, Hilda."

It was all Tobias could do not to run into the entry and grab the bottle from Verbena, but he knew if he moved, they might hear him and know he was eavesdropping on their conversation. He had to stay quiet until the guests were gone

Verbena closed the front door after they exited and moved to the bottom of the stairs. She paused, took the laudanum out of her pocket and looked at it. A sinister smile crossed her face as she began climbing the stairs.

Her actions made Tobias realize he had to move fast. He rushed to the kitchen. "Minerva go to Miss Hannah's room and make sure Miz Wedington don't give her niece any medicine."

"What are you talking about?"

"The doctor gave her a bottle of something, but told her not to give it to Miss Hannah for a couple of days. She's heading up there to give it to her right now."

"How do you know?"

"I heared her say she was going to give it to her. Now, go on. We ain't got much time."

"What can I do to stop her?"

"I don't know, but you can think of something. Go, before she gives the girl the stuff."

"But…"

"Don't argue with me, woman. She could kill Miss Hannah." He moved to the back door.

"Where are you going?"

"To get Mr. Jarrett!"

"Why?"

"I don't have time to tell you everything now. I'll tells you when I get back. Just make sure Miz Wedington don't give none of that medicine to Miss Hannah."

Before she could say anything else, he went out the door. He knew Minerva would head to Miss Hannah's room wondering what she would say to Miz Wedington. He also knew she realized she had to stop the woman somehow from giving medicine to the girl. He had made that clear, even if he didn't tell her why. His wife trusted him, and he knew he could count on her to do everything he asked her to do.

♥♥♥

With a feeling of relief and satisfaction, Jarrett threw the papers he was studying down on the desk in his hotel room. It had been right there in front of him all the time, but was masked by the wording in the legal documents. Though it wasn't obvious, his sharp mind had found the answer he'd been searching for. He'd finally seen what linked all this mess together. He only needed confirmation from an actual party to the agreement, and he knew there was only one person he could get the final answer from. He stood, grabbed his hat and headed out the door.

His first inclination was to go by and ask Lydia to accompany him, but in the same moment, he changed his mind. The woman's husband had just returned from a long trip and he was sure Lydia wanted to spend her time with her man, not going to her father's farm with a detective. Besides, though Bradly Patterson had been cordial when they met, Jarrett had a feeling the man wasn't overly pleased to find his wife with another man when he arrived home.

He could do this alone, anyway. He knew exactly how to do it. There was one thing Burl Hamilton understood and Jarrett had the wherewithal to make it happen. Today, he would finally put an end to all this cloak and dagger business and return to Flagstaff where he belonged. Savannah was a nice city, but he missed the open spaces of the west. It was time to lay his cards on the table and end this job. It was also time for Mrs. Verbena Wedington to get her comeuppance, and for sweet Hannah Hamilton to receive her freedom.

On the horseback ride to the farm, Jarrett's thoughts drifted to Hannah, and couldn't help the smile that spread across his mouth. He clearly remembered coming to town thinking she was a small child who needed to be cared for, but she turned out not to be a child at all. She was a lovely young woman, whose beauty almost took his breath away on their first meeting. As if that hadn't been enough, when he swept her into his arms and carried her to her room, he was shocked at how good it felt to hold her slender body next to his chest. As he'd climbed those stairs, he remembered he wanted her room to be a long way off so he wouldn't have to put her down.

After that incident, he'd made excuses to be with her every chance he got. And the time they'd spent in the parlor alone had left him feeling things he'd never felt for a woman before.

But he knew he had to quash those feelings for the beautiful girl. Not because she couldn't walk. He knew if she was allowed to try, she'd be able to get around fine on crutches. A man who loved her wouldn't mind that.

It wasn't even because she was so young. Eighteen was a woman in every sense of the word, and according to one of those papers he'd found, she would be eighteen in a few days. Then, nobody could say she wasn't a grown woman. Though having been closed up in that house for years, she was naïve in many ways, but she was also smart. Smarter than some married women with children that he knew back in Arizona. She certainly was wise enough to know how to adjust to the rules and regulations her aunt imposed, and as far as he could tell, she never seemed to complain about it.

The reason he knew he couldn't allow those feelings to get inside him had nothing to do with Hannah. It had everything to do with the beautiful lady he was having an affair with back in Flagstaff. Was she that important to him, or was she just a woman he enjoyed sleeping with?

Jarrett let a frown cross his forehead. In his heart, he knew Felicia Newell wasn't the type of woman most men would want as a wife. She was the type they liked until the right woman came along. Though at times Felicia seemed to care lot about him, she'd never led him to believe he was the only man she could fall in love with. There had even been times when she seemed to prefer his twin brother. Jarrett was well aware of the fact that when he returned home, he could find that Felicia had become Everett's mistress instead of his.

At that moment, he felt an unusual sensation, and it shocked him. It was in that moment he realized he didn't much care if the beautiful Miss Newell had chosen his brother or some other man to fill her bed. Why this didn't bother him, he wasn't sure.

Before he could figure it out, the farm house came into his line of vision. He took a deep breath and shoved all thoughts of women from his mind. It was time to concentrate on what lay ahead of him, and the best way to pull it off.

As he reined up in the front yard, the same two old hound dogs that he'd seen before came out from under the front and barked at him. In a matter of seconds, Burl Hamilton shoved the front door open and came onto the front door with his shotgun in his hand.

He moved to the edge of the porch and spit tobacco toward the horse. Giving Jarrett a frown, his voice came out in a growl. "What the hell are you doing back here?"

"I need to talk to you, Mr. Hamilton."

He raised the gun and pointed it at Jarrett's chest. "I told you last time, I ain't got nothing to say to you."

"I think you might change your mind this time."

"Ain't no way. Turn that horse around and git out of here."

"As I said, when you see how much money is involved, you might change your mind."

Burl frowned. "Did you say money?"

"I did." Jarrett dismounted. "Would you like to discuss it now?"

"How much money?"

"Enough."

Burl hesitated for a minute, then turned toward the door. "Come on in. We'll talk in the house."

Jarrett would have preferred talking on the porch, but he didn't have a choice, now. He had the man interested, and he didn't want to jeopardize his chance of getting the final answer here. He followed Burl into the house, and as it was the first time he'd been inside this house, he was surprised to see the combined kitchen and living area neat and clean. He figured this was because of the woman coming in the back door with a basket of wild berries on her arm.

"What's going on?" She glanced at Jarrett.

"We got some business to discuss," Burl said. "Git us a cup of coffee."

Lulu nodded, sat the basket down and moved to the stove.

"Set down there and we'll have that talk." Burl commanded, and propped his gun against the wall by the door.

Jarrett nodded a hello to Lulu and pulled out a caned-back chair.

"I don't remember your name." Burl took the chair across the table.

"It's Jarrett MacMichael."

"All right, MacMichael, tell me about this money you're talking about."

"First, let me tell you who I am." When Burl said nothing, Jarrett went on. "I'm a detective from Arizona. Your son-in-law hired me to come here to check on your daughter, Hannah."

Burl looked puzzled. "What son-in-law?"

"Drina's husband."

"The cowboy she run off to marry?"

"That's him."

"Why would he hire you?"

"Because his wife was concerned about her sister."

"Don't see why. She's fine. Has been since she started living in that fancy house with Verbena."

Lulu interrupted by setting two mugs of coffee on the table. One in front of each man.

"Thank you, Lulu. Why don't you get yourself a cup and join us?"

She grinned. "Why, Mr. MacMichael, I'd be happy to do that."

Burl frowned. "She ain't got no business setting down."

"I'd like to have a witness to what I'm about to say to you, Mr. Hamilton."

"Then quit messing around and set down, woman, so he can tell me about the money."

Lulu poured herself a cup of coffee and sat.

"Mr. Hamilton, I've done a lot of digging in the records at the newspaper office and at the courthouse and I've found some interesting facts. I've discovered that there was a document drawn up between you, your wife, and her sister, Verbena, after Hannah was born."

"Why'd you drag that up?"

"Because it's important that I see a copy of that agreement."

"Ain't no way you're gonna do that."

Jarrett changed the subject. "I understand Verbena Wedington pays the taxes on this farm for you."

"So, what if she does?"

"I also understand if they're not paid, you'll lose the place."

"Ain't no danger of that. She ain't gonna fail to pay 'em. I had to go see her about it the other day. "

Jarrett didn't indicate he knew about that transaction. "There's always a chance of something happening, Mr. Hamilton."

"Why'd you say that?"

"You know how life is. You can be well and fine one day and the next day they're building your coffin." He saw Burl was listening intently. "Verbena Wedington seems to be in good health, but you never know. She's not a young woman."

"Is she sick or something?"

"Not that I know of, but I'm a man who looks at all angles. I can't help wondering what would happen to you if she was no longer here to pay your taxes and your bails when you get arrested."

He frowned and took a big drink of coffee. "I ain't never thought of it like that."

"Of course, you and Lulu might have some money put back that I don't know about."

Lulu laughed. "We ain't got no money put nowhere, Mr. MacMichael. All the money we got is what Burl gets from selling some of his brew. That don't hardly buy what we eat."

Burl looked at her. "If 'n I lose this place, I won't have nowhere to go and you won't neither, old woman."

Jarrett kept his voice calm. "I may have the answer for you, Mr. Hamilton."

Burl gave him a suspicious look. "What can you do about it?"

"I can see that you get enough money so you never have to depend on Verbena Wedington again."

"Why would you do that?"

"Oh, I don't plan on handing you the money for nothing, but I think you have something I'm willing to pay for." Jarrett sat back, took a drink of coffee to give Burl time to think about what it was the detective could want.

Hamilton tuned his head to the side and seemed to think a minute. Finally, he said, "You ain't talking about buying my brew, are you?"

"No, I'm not."

Lulu broke into the conversation. "You know he don't want none of your nasty ole brew, Burl."

"Shut-up, Lulu. This is man talk." She didn't say anything else and Burl turned back to Jarrett. "How do I know you got the money?"

"I guess you just have to trust me."

"Don't know if I can do that."

"Then, I guess you don't want the money."

"I didn't say that." Burl frowned. "How much money are we talking about?"

Jarrett raised an eyebrow. "More than this place looks like it's worth."

Burl still had his frown. "Are you saying you want to buy my place?"

Jarrett shook his head. "I have no need of this farm. As far as I'm concerned you can stay here for the rest of your life, because I'll be heading back to Arizona soon."

"How soon?"

"If I get the information I want from you, I'll be gone in a few days."

"Give him the paper, Burl."

His eyes narrowed. "How'd you know there was a paper?"

"I done told Mr. MacMichael you talk in your sleep. He's a good man. You can trust him to give you the money."

"I don't talk in my sleep."

"Yes, you does." Lulu gave him a knowing look. "You done told me you had a paper and it's somewhere in the barn. I was gonna tell Mr. MacMichael about it. I figured he'd want to know."

"You're right, Lulu. I do want to know, and I appreciate the fact that you were going to tell me about it." Jarrett smiled at her. "I'll even give you a little money for telling me this."

"You's don't have to do that."

"But I want to. I like to help people who help me."

She gave him a wide grin, but Burl frowned.

"If 'n I sell this paper to you, how do I know old sour-puss Verbena won't come looking for me for breaking my word?"

"I have a feeling Verbena will have so much on her mind that she'll never give you a thought."

Burl slammed his coffee mug to the table and glared at Jarrett. "All right, it's time you told me how much money you're talking about."

"How much do you want?"

"I'd have to have at least a thousand dollars for that paper you want."

A look of complete disbelief spread across Burl's face when Jarrett said, "That sounds reasonable to me."

Chapter 16

Minerva looked at the tray of breakfast food Tobias had in his hand. It hadn't been touched. "Tobias, do you think she give the medicine to Miss Hannah this morning?"

"I don't know, but I bet she did. When I took the tray you fixed her for dinner and found this, I knowed she hadn't eat nothing."

"Was she still asleep?"

"Yes." Tobias frowned and lowered his voice. "It wouldn't surprise me if Miz Wedington slipped up there and give her some of that stuff after we went to bed last night."

"I stayed as long as I could when I went up there. I gathered the new dress she got the blood on and the sheets and cleaned some in the room. Miz Wedington left while I was there, but she could've gone back."

"It'd be like her to do it."

"That woman's a snake, Tobias. We can't let her get away with her evil plan to marry Miss Hannah to that man. He's no more than a big boy in his head."

"I know, but I didn't have no luck finding Mr. MacMichael yesterday. As I told you, I tried to find Miz Lydia at her saloon, but her and her husband had gone somewhere. I didn't think I could tell nobody else who worked there what I wanted with her."

"You right 'bout that. If'n Miz Wedington knowed we was trying to spoil her plans she'd probably fire us on the spot."

"Then I guess we'd…shh…I think I hear somebody coming."

Minerva picked up the tray he'd sat down and began dumping the food in the scrap bucket as Verbena came into the kitchen.

"Minerva, did you wash and dry Hannah's new dress?"

"Yes, ma'am. I got all the blood out, and it's good as new."

"Then I need you to go to Hannah's room and dress her in that dress. Also comb and fix her hair. I know her nose is swollen, but that can't be helped. Make her look as pretty as you can."

Tobias looked up. "I was just in Miss Hannah's room and she was sound asleep, Miz Wedington."

"I know. You two will have to make sure she wakes up shortly. At least make sure she's awake enough to sit up." Verbena took a deep breath and turned back to Minerva. "After you finish with Hannah, make sure the formal parlor is cleaned by one o'clock."

"Yes, ma'am."

She ignored Minerva and turned her attention back to Tobias. "You're to go bring Hannah down at two-thirty and put her in the informal parlor. If she isn't awake by then, try to wake her as much as you can. I'm expecting the preacher at one o'clock and I'll receive him in the formal room."

"Yes, ma'am."

Minerva looked at her boss. "Shall I make tea and cookies for the guest?"

"Yes, but don't serve it until I tell you to. The preacher and I have some business to take care of first."

"Yes, ma'am," Minerva said again, but there was no enthusiasm in her voice.

Verbena looked at the watch pinned to the breast of her purple dress. It was the last garment Hannah had designed for her aunt, and Verbena was especially fond of it. "It's almost noon. I'll have my dinner in the dining room, then you can go take care of Hannah." Without waiting for an answer, she turned and marched out of the room.

"Oh, Tobias. She's up to something."

"And I thinks I know what it is." He moved to the door and grabbed his hat. "If she asks for me, tell her I had to go get something for you to make the cookies."

"Where're you going?"

"I'm gonna try to find Mr. Jarrett. I just hope I do find him this time."

"What if you don't, Tobias?"

"I don't know, Minerva. We'll think of something else. Now, try to keep positive. I'll do the best I can."

"Tobias…"

"We don't have time to keep talking. I gotta hurry."

She bit her lip and nodded as she watched him go out the door.

♥♥♥

The feeling of a job well done settled on Jarrett as he rode the rented horse back out of Burl Hamilton's yard and headed toward town. Though he thought he'd get Burl Hamilton to eventually take his offer, he was almost shocked at how quickly the man went to the barn and returned with a small wooden box, sat in on the table and said, "Now, let me see the money."

Jarrett was no fool. His reply had been, "Let me see what you have in the box first."

Without hesitation, Burl broke the lock and pulled out yellowed piece of paper. "I'm sure this is what you want."

"May I check it over?"

Burl eyed him. "If you see what you want to know on this paper, how do I know you'll pay me?"

"Just show me the bottom where the signatures are."

Burl turned to the second page and held it so Jarrett could see where the document had been signed. He pointed out where Ella Hamilton, Burl Hamilton, Verbena Worthington and Barnaby Phillips had all written their names. That was the Phillips man Verbena had said took care of her business until his death. Without reading the form, Jarrett knew this had to be the proof he needed.

After looking over the signatures, Jarrett nodded and reached in his pocket. He pulled out a roll of paper bills and watched Burl's eyes grow big and almost glassy. "I think you said a thousand dollars would satisfy your needs."

Burl nodded and Lulu gasped.

Jarrett slowly counted the money and dropped the bills one at a time until there was a thousand dollars on the table. "I figure this closes our deal."

Putting the paper back into the box, Burl shoved it to Jarrett. He then grabbed the money and said, "It shore does."

Jarrett nodded and turned to Lulu. "I think you should get a little something, too." He handed her fifty dollars.

Tears came into her eyes. "Oh, thank you, Mr. MacMichael. I ain't never had this much money at one time in my whole life."

Jarrett winked at her and stood. "Buy yourself something special."

Burl was counting his money and ignoring them.

"I'll sees you to the door." Lulu stood.

"Thank you, ma'am."

He bid the woman good-by, put the box in his saddle bag and climbed on his horse. Burl Hamilton didn't say anything else to anyone. Jarrett knew he was still counting the money.

Now that he was out of sight of the farm house, Jarrett was tempted to stop, open the box and satisfy his curiosity about the information it contained. But he knew he'd better wait until he got back to the hotel so he could coordinate his findings with the documents he'd already collected from the courthouse and the newspaper. After all, he could be there in half-an-hour or so. He could wait until then.

♥♥♥

Reverend Cedric Calhoun sipped the tea and studied Verbena Wedington.

Was the woman serious? Was she asking him to marry her niece to the slow witted, addled-brained Calvin Sawyer? Why in the world would she want such a thing to happen to the girl? No longer than he'd been the preacher at their church, he knew Calvin was in no condition to marry any woman. He might be a man in looks and size, but he had the mind of a child. Everyone knew that after their first meeting with him.

On the other hand, he'd never actually met Mrs. Wedington's niece. Maybe she was as simple minded at Calvin. It could be that Verbena thought they'd be playmates for each other. That maybe they would be good for each other.

Then, he remembered his wife had met the niece and he distinctly recalled Bessie saying, "Cedric, you wouldn't believe how talented that young woman is. Not only can she sew beautiful clothes, but she's articulate in her speech and manners. Mrs. Wedington can be proud of how she's raised her delightful niece."

He replayed the rest of their conversation. "If this is all true, why doesn't she come to church with her aunt?"

"I suppose it's because she can't walk. It would be hard for Mrs. Wedington to handle getting her here and back home without someone to help her."

"Then I suppose I could make arrangements for someone to help transport the girl to church and back home."

He knew he'd fully intended to discuss this idea with Mrs. Wedington, but there had been so much work in the past few weeks it had slipped his mind. Now, here he was being asked to marry the young lady to Calvin Sawyer. He wasn't sure he could be persuaded to do this no matter how much Verbena pushed him to do so.

Verbena's voice broke into his thoughts. "Would you like more tea, Reverend Calhoun?"

"That would be nice. This is a delicious tea."

Verbena grinned. "Thank you. I keep a supply to serve to my special guests."

"Then, I'm glad you consider me special."

"Of course I do. I think you're the best preacher we've had at our church in a long time. Your insight into the gospels is remarkable. I've learned so much under your teaching."

He couldn't help feeling proud, though he knew pride was a sin. He'd asked for forgiveness for it later. After all, he was human, and it always pleased him when one of his church members complimented him on his Bible knowledge and his teaching. "Thank you, Mrs. Wedington. You're very kind."

She smiled. "Now, shall we get back to the subject at hand? I'm sure you agree with me that this is the perfect solution for my poor crippled niece. She wants to get married so badly, but she's wise enough to know no normal man would ever marry her. She likes Calvin and he likes her. I think they'd be good for each other."

"I'm sure there are other men out there who would overlook her handicap."

"Think about it, Reverend. Would you?"

"Well," he stammered. "I'm a married man, but if I wasn't, you must realize my work requires that the woman I married be able to get around and entertain church members, work in the church and support me in many different ways. That would be hard for someone who can't walk."

"See what I mean? If a preacher can't accept her, who can?"

Cedric thought a minute. "How about a businessman?"

Verbena shook her head. "A businessman needs a woman who can serve as a hostess for his friends and can entertain his associates' wives. If she can't walk, she would make all these people uncomfortable when they were around her. That would certainly hurt her husband's business."

He sipped his tea and didn't answer.

"So Reverend Calhoun, do you understand why I want to do this for my dear niece? She wants to get married, and since no normal man is going to have her, the best I can do for her is to marry her to Calvin Sawyer. He has turned into a handsome man, as you well know, and at least he's a sweet boy. I'm sure he'll entertain Hannah with his cute actions. Also, he'll be around when she feels lonely. I've already promised him a dog so they can sit in the garden and play with it. Hannah loves being outside, and I'm sure she'll like that."

Cedric looked at her but didn't answer right away. Was she right? Was marrying her niece to this boy with a man's body the right thing to do? Would the young woman be happy to have someone in her life, even if his mentality was much lower than hers? He felt he had to stall Mrs. Wedington. "Let me think about this for a bit. You might be right, but I want to be sure we're not rushing things. I wouldn't want to make a mistake and have your dear niece tied to Calvin if she didn't want to be his wife."

Verbena bit her lip. "If you feel you must."

"I do, Mrs. Wedington. You know marriage is a serious and holy commitment and I don't want to make a mistake linking these two souls together for the rest of their lives if I don't feel it's the right thing to do."

"Would it make you feel better to discuss this with Calvin's sister?"

"Yes, I think it would." He nodded. "That's a good idea."

"She and Calvin will be here at three." She looked at her watch. "It's one-thirty now. That gives you an hour-and-a-half to think it over."

He placed his teacup on the table. "I want to pray about this. I'm going to the church where I won't be disturbed. I will return at three, and after my prayers, I may be able to give you my decision without talking to Miss Sawyer."

She stood and walked him to the door. He could tell by her demeanor that she wasn't pleased with his decision to leave, but he couldn't help it. Though she was a faithful member and contributor to the church, he had to feel performing this wedding was the right thing to do before he could, in good conscious, marry them. He didn't want to do anything wrong against Hannah or against Calvin Sawyer, for that matter.

He took her hand at the door. "My dear Mrs. Wedington, I'm sure I'll be able to get the right leading for what we're supposed to do after my prayers. I don't like to make decisions like this without consulting the Almighty."

"Could you tell me what you are feeling about the situation at this moment, Reverend?"

"For some reason, I tend to think you may be right. This could be the only answer for your lonely niece and for Calvin Sawyer. As you said, she would have someone to be with her in her loneliness even if theirs wouldn't be a normal marriage. He'd also have a companion he liked."

Verbena smiled. "I'm glad you see it my way. I'll look for you at three and we'll have everything ready for the ceremony." She then added, "If that is what you feel you're led to do."

He nodded, donned his hat and went out.

♥♥♥

Verbena fumed inside. She wanted to slam the door behind him, but controlled her anger and closed it gently. That didn't keep her from cursing the preacher under her breath. She'd expected him to go along with her plans without bringing up such things as he did and deciding he had to pray about the situation.

Why did he do this to me? I had it all planned out perfectly. All he had to do was his job—marry Hannah and Calvin. Now, I'm going to have to wait to see what his prayers lead him to do. She frowned and marched up the stairs. *I've got to make sure Hannah is still so drugged she can't object to the nuptials. If she says a word, it'd be like him to refuse to perform the ceremony, and I can't let that happen. Even if he gets the idea that he doesn't want to do it, I think with Hilda's help, we'll be able to convince him. We have to. Hannah's going to be eighteen day after tomorrow. If she reaches that day without being married, I stand to lose everything. I can't let that happen. I just can't.*

Pushing open Hannah's door, Verbena stepped inside. She noticed the newest dress was draped over the back of the chair. Beside it were a white cotton chemise, stockings and a clean satin shoe. Petticoats lay across the wheelchair. She nodded and smiled to herself. At least Minerva was planning to carry out the order to get Hannah dressed. She was sure Tobias would perform his part and get the girl downstairs when the time came.

Turning to the bed, she looked at her niece. Verbena had to admit Hannah was a lovely young woman. Of all three Hamilton sisters, Hannah was the most like her mother. Though Verbena had been an attractive young woman, Ella had been the beautiful sister. And Hannah was so like her mother in other ways. She was sweet and kind and seemed to love everyone she met. And when Hannah was a child, she had often been a delight to her aunt. But there'd been times when the young child would rebel, as Ella did when she married Burl Hamilton over her whole family's protests. At the times Hannah acted up, she'd have to be punished to bring her back in line. For an instant, Verbena felt a trickle of remorse ripple through her body. After all, this was her niece, the young woman who designed and constructed all the lovely dresses Verbena wore to show off to her friends. What if Hannah refused to do her sewing when she realized her aunt had forced her into a terrible marriage?

It also crossed Verbena's mind that she was sentencing the girl to a life with a man most people considered an idiot. They'd be considered a cripple and an idiot. What would become of the two of them? Hilda certainly wouldn't want them in her home, and Verbena had no intention of letting them live with her. She sighed. Maybe after the wedding she could ship them off to Arizona to live with Drina. If not, there was always Lydia's saloon. It wouldn't be ideal, but it would be a place for Hannah to spend the rest of her married life. What Drina or Lydia did about Calvin wasn't her problem. She really didn't care what became of the man after he fulfilled his purpose in this plan.

Shaking herself to clear her head, Verbena moved to the bed and placed her hand on Hannah's forehead. "Wake up, Hannah. We're going to have company in a little while."

Hannah didn't move.

Again, Verbena spoke. "You have to wake up. This is your wedding day, my child. You don't want to be late for your own wedding, do you?"

Hannah rolled her head, but still didn't open her eyes.

Verbena frowned and muttered, "I wonder if I gave you too much laudanum."

She began to wonder, too, if she'd messed up the plan herself by over-drugging Hannah. She knew Hannah didn't have to be aware of all that was going on today. In fact, it was actually better that she wasn't. But she did have to be awake enough to sit in her chair without falling out. Since he already had doubts about this marriage, there was no way Reverend Calhoun would officiate a ceremony with the girl unconscious.

She decided she'd send Minerva up and have her work with the girl. She'd probably be able to wake her up. Negroes might be freed from slavery, but they still had ways of working roots and spells that civilized white people had no knowledge of. Verbena was sure of that.

When she reached the kitchen, she found Minerva icing a cake and Tobias heading out the door. Verbena frowned. "Where are you going?"

He turned around and without missing a beat he said, "I was going to check on some plants I put in the yard the other day."

"That can wait." She turned to Minerva. "As soon as you finish that cake, go to Hannah's room and wake her up and get her dressed. The preacher will be back at three and I have other company coming then, too."

"Yes, ma'am."

"Tobias, you can help her. I know you have ways to do things that I don't. You have to make sure Hannah is downstairs and able to sit up in her chair before the guests arrive."

He nodded but didn't say anything.

"Now, don't let me down. This is important to me. I can't have anything going wrong this afternoon." She turned and walked out of the kitchen.

Chapter 17

Tobias held his finger to his lip as he eased across the room and watched Verbena go through the dining room, then head down the hall. He turned to Minerva. "I've got to go find Mr. Jarrett."

"What will she do if you don't get back in time to do what she wants?"

"I've gotta take that chance. You knows what'll happen to Miss Hannah if I don't find him this time."

Minerva bit her lip. "Tobias, does you think we could slip Miss Hannah outta the house and hide her from her aunt?"

Tobias frowned. "What are you talking about?"

"Well, if'n you don't find Mr. Jarrett, is we going to stand by and let her marry Miss Hannah up with that crazy man who is really a child?"

"I don't know how we can stop her, but I'll think of something." He turned toward the door. "Now, you finish your cake and go to Miss Hannah. Makes sure she's dressed, in case we does have to do something drastic."

"I will."

"Say a prayer, woman. I think I might need one."

"I's been doing that all day without stopping, Tobias."

He gave her a quick peck on the cheek. "You's a good woman, Minerva." He then went out the back door. He knew he was taking a chance of getting fired from his job, but at the moment, he didn't care. He went to the stable and saddled Verbena's horse and headed toward Jarrett's hotel. He was petitioning God every step of the way that Jarrett would be there, because if he didn't find MacMichael this time, he didn't know what he'd do.

Did Minerva have the right idea? Should they slip Miss Hannah out of the house? If they did, where would they go? They didn't know many people in town and those they were acquainted with were like themselves, servants to the rich. Those people wouldn't have anywhere they could hide a crippled white girl. Besides, if they were caught, he had no doubt but what he and Minerva would both be hung for the deed. He was willing to take the chance for himself, but he wouldn't let something like that happen to Minerva.

Arriving at the hotel, Tobias hitched the horse to a post and went inside the lobby with his hat in his hand. There was no customers at the check-in desk so he approached it. The man behind the counter glanced at him, but continued to look at the book before him. It wasn't the desk clerk that Jarrett had been informed that Tobias was to be sent to him or told where he was every time the

Negro showed up. Tobias realized this man didn't know him so he stepped back and waited without saying anything.

Finally, the man looked up at him and snapped, "What do you want, darkie?"

"I need to speak to Mr. Jarrett MacMichael, sir."

The clerk frowned. "Is Mr. MacMichael expecting you?"

"Yes, sir."

The man snorted. "I know that's a lie. Why can't you people ever tell the truth?"

Tobias wanted to shout at the man, but he kept his voice low and respectful. "Miz Verbena Wedington sent me with a message for Mr. MacMichael, sir."

"Mr. MacMichael didn't say nothing about expecting a message. Now go along with you and stop bothering me."

"Sir…"

The man looked directly at Tobias. "Do you want me to have you thrown out on the street?"

"No, sir, but I really needs to see Mr. MacMichael."

"Well, you're not going to." The man looked around the lobby as if he was searching for someone.

Tobias knew he had lost the argument. He backed away and went out the door with his head hanging down. Now, what was he going to do?

♥♥♥

As Jarrett descended the hotel lobby stairs, he thought he recognized Tobias going out the door. He frowned and turned to the desk. "Who was that Negro man who was just in here?"

"Nobody important, Mr. MacMichael. I got rid of him 'cause I knew you wouldn't want to be bothered."

"What do you mean?"

"Oh, he had some story about a message for you, but I knew it was a lie. You'd be surprised at how many of these darkies try to take a message to somebody important just to rob them, or something like that."

"Did that man have a message for me?"

"He said he did, but as I said, I got rid of him."

Jarrett couldn't help himself. He reached across the desk and grabbed the startled man by the collar. "Listen here, and listen good. I don't care what color a person's skin is. When somebody comes to this desk with a message for me, you'd better get in touch with me immediately. If you don't, you're going to be sorry. Do you understand?"

Fear filled the man's eyes. "But it was a Negro. They can't be trusted."

Jarrett shoved the man backward. "You fool. I'll deal with you later." He turned and strode out of the hotel where he saw Tobias climbing on a horse.

In a loud voice he yelled, "Tobias!"

The man turned, and the frown on his face turned into a big grin. "Mr. Jarrett. I'm glad I finally found you."

Jarrett could tell the man was glad to see him. "What's going on, Tobias?"

"Oh, sir, you ain't gonna believe it. We needs you to come to the house right away. You's got to stop a wedding."

"What in the world are you talking about?"

"Miz Verbena is gonna marry Miss Hannah off to that idiot man Minerva told you about. You've got to stop her."

Jarrett looked around and saw the benches on the side yard of the hotel. "Let's go over there were we can talk in private, Tobias. You need to explain this to me."

"I ain't suppose to set on them benches. They's for white people."

"I don't give a damn who they're for. Come on."

Tobias followed him.

After they were seated, Jarrett said, "Now, start at the beginning and tell me what this is all about, Tobias."

"Minerva told you that Miz Verbena has decided that Miss Hannah needs to get married and she's picked out this man who don't have a good mind to marry her."

"Yes, but I didn't think it was taking place this soon."

"We didn't think so neither, but it is. She wants them to get married today. The man's sister is helping her and she's got the preacher coming at three o'clock to marry them. I heard them plan the whole thing two days ago."

"Maybe Hannah wants to marry this man." Jarrett didn't want to admit to himself that this thought made him angry, but it did. How could Hannah want to marry a man whose mind was weak?

"No sir, she don't want to marry him. She don't know nothing about it."

"How can she not know?"

"After she fell out of her chair..."

Jarrett's eyes widened. "Is she hurt?"

"Yes, sir. She's got a bump on her head and a hurt arm."

Jarrett was getting more confused. "Why didn't you come tell me?"

"I tried to find you, but I couldn't."

"Well, go on. You said she didn't know anything about this marriage."

"No, sir, she don't. Miz Wedington give her some medicine. The doctor left it for her, but told Miz Wedington not to give it to Miss Hannah right away. She did anyway."

"I'm totally confused, Tobias."

"I'm sorry I'm not explaining it no better, but you need to come to the house to stop this evil woman from forcing Miss Hannah to marry this man."

"When is this wedding supposed to take place?"

"At three o'clock."

Though Jarrett still wasn't clear on what was happening, he knew he had to do something. He looked at his watch and quickly stood. "It's two-thirty. Let's go to the livery so I can rent a horse."

♥♥♥

Minerva's nerves were about to get the best of her, but she knew she couldn't break down now. She'd used the cool, damp cloth to wash Hannah's face several times. Finally, the young woman opened her eyes and muttered something.

"It's alright, Sugar. You jest need to wake up a bit. You've got to fight what's about to happen to you."

Hannah frowned, but wasn't coherent when she mumbled something the maid didn't understand.

Minerva sat her on the side of the bed and knew the girl wanted to lay back down, but she took hold of her shoulders. "Miss Hannah, I's got to get you dressed. Miz Wedington will be mad if I don't."

"She's always mad about something," Hannah muttered. This time her words were understandable.

"She shore is, but we's don't want to rile her today. We got to get away from her afore she messes up your life."

Hannah frowned. "What's happening?"

"I's not shore, but we need to get your clothes on you so we can get you downstairs."

"Where's Tobias?"

"I don't know. I hopes he gets back soon." Minerva had Hannah's underclothes on her and she picked up the dress. "Now, let's get this over your head. Be careful, and don't hurt your arm."

The door opened and Verbena swept in. "Do you have her dressed yet?"

"We're finishing up now, Miz Wedington."

Hannah nodded and opened her eyes. "What's going on, Aunt Verbena?"

Verbena ignored her. "Where's Tobias? It's two-thirty and he needs to get

Hannah downstairs right away. My guests will be here anytime, now."

"He'll be here, ma'am."

"He'd better be."

There was the sound of knocking on the front door. "For heaven's sake it must be the Sawyers. They're early. Hurry up with her and fix her hair, Minerva. Then bring her downstairs."

"Yes, ma'am."

Hannah lay back on the bed.

Verbena grabbed her good arm. "Get up from there. You can sleep after the ceremony."

"I want to sleep."

The knocking on the door grew louder.

"If something goes wrong today, you and Tobias will be sorry, Minerva. I'm holding you responsible." With that, she hurried out the door.

"Oh, Miss Hannah, what are we gonna do?"

Hannah looked at Minerva and smiled. "Let's take a nap."

"I wish we's could, but we gotta do what Miz Wedington says. I's got to get you downstairs." She put the last touches on Hannah's hair, then turned. "Now, you wait here while I takes your wheelchair downstairs then I'll come back and get you."

Minerva hurried down with the wheelchair and put it in the parlor. Hurrying back upstairs, she found Hannah had fallen back on the bed and gone to sleep again.

Moving to her, Minerva raised her to a sitting position. "Honey child, you got to come with me. Your aunt wants you downstairs now."

"I don't want to go."

"I don't want to take you, but with Tobias gone, I don't know nothing else to do, but does what she says for me to do."

Though she struggled, Minerva managed to get her arms around Hannah. As she helped the girl down the back stairs, she wondered if she should've tried to carry Hannah. As it was, she prayed she wouldn't fall or let the young woman stumble and pull them both down.

♥♥♥

Verbena seated Hilda and Calvin in the formal parlor. In an almost-whisper Verbena said, "Hilda, I thought I could convince the preacher, but he has his doubts about doing this. I need you to help me persuade him."

Hilda looked disappointed. "I'll do what I can, Mrs. Wedington. I so hope he'll relent. This is important to me."

"It is to me, too." She motioned them to chairs. "Have you told Calvin anything?"

"I hear you talking about me." Calvin butted in. "I don't like for people to talk about me."

"We're not saying anything bad, brother. We're just talking about the program. Take a seat over there and the program will start soon."

"Hilda said I had a part in the program." He grinned. "All I got to say is, 'I do' when the preacher asks me a question."

"That's correct, Calvin. Your sister told you the right words to say."

"Where's the crippled girl? Hilda said she had a part, too."

"She'll be here in a little while." Verbena smiled at him. "Would you like some milk and cookies while you wait?"

"Yes, ma'am. I like cookies."

There was a knock on the door. Verbena shook her head. "My butler is nowhere to be found. I guess I'd better get that. It's probably the preacher."

As she went into the entry hall, Verbena glanced into the informal parlor. She was relieved to see Minerva getting Hannah arranged in her chair. Though the girl's head was drooping, the maid was coaxing her to wake up. She started to tell Minerva to get the door, then changed her mind. It would be better to let her stay with Hannah.

Opening the front door, Verbena plastered on a smile. "Reverend, welcome back."

"I finished my supplications to God and have His leading. I decided to come back a little early. I decided I wanted to talk with the young people before making my final decision about their marriage."

Verbena bit her lip to keep from asking how he was being led. Nodding, she said, "Come into the parlor. Calvin and his sister are there. I'm sure he'd like to talk with you."

"How about your niece?"

"She'll be there shortly." She turned so he would follow her.

"Hello, Reverend Calhoun." Hilda stood and bowed her head to him.

"Miss Sawyer." He nodded back, then turned to her brother. "Hello, Calvin."

"Hey, preacher. I'd rather have beer, but Mrs. Wedington is going to get me some milk and cookies. Do you want some?"

"No, thank you."

"Have a seat, Reverend, and I'll be right back," Verbena said, and backed out of the room.

"Thank you, Mrs. Wedington."

Verbena hurried to the kitchen. She found a plate of cookies and the tea pot which Minerva had left on a tray. She grabbed a glass, filled it with milk, picked up the tray and hurried back to the parlor. All the time, she was thinking of what she was going to do to Tobias when he showed up again. If she thought she could find another couple to do her bidding at the rate she was paying the Johnsons, she'd fire the both of them today. She was going to make them think she was going to let them go, anyway. A good warning might make them realize she wasn't going to put up with their disobedience. She was certainly not going to pay them this month. That would teach him not to disappear when she needed him the most. It would make Minerva work a little harder, too, though the woman hadn't done anything wrong. She could have at least kept up with where her man was going and when he was coming back.

When she entered the parlor Cedric Calhoun was saying, "So you like to come to visit Mrs. Wedington, Calvin."

"Yes, sir. I get milk and cookies here. Hilda don't let me have beer with my cookies at our house, either."

Before the preacher could reply, Verbena set the tray down on the table. "And here are your milk and cookies, Calvin."

"Goody, goody." Calvin turned toward the tray and ignored everyone in the room as he grabbed a handful of cookies and his milk.

"He seems to be happy today." The Reverend took the cup of tea Verbena handed him. "Does he have any idea what's going on?"

"I'm going to be in a program." Calvin's mouth was full of cookies and crumbs cascaded down the front of his shirt as he spoke.

Verbena started to say something, but the preacher said, "Please, Mrs. Wedington. I need to talk to Calvin without interruption."

"But…" Hilda said.

"Both of you need to let me discuss this with Calvin and not interfere."

Though she looked doubtful, Verbena said, "We'll be quiet."

The Reverend turned to Calvin. "What kind of program are you going to be in, young man?"

"I get to say a line and the cripple girl will say a line, then I get to live here."

"Is that what you want to happen?"

"Sure. Hilda said Mrs. Wedington was going to get me a dog."

"Does the cripple girl want you to live here, Calvin?"

"I guess so. I told her I'd run with her dog since she couldn't walk." He turned to Verbena. "Are you going to get her a dog, too?"

"If she wants one."

"Somebody has to push her chair out there because I can't push it. I make her fall."

Cedric frowned. "What do you mean, Calvin? How do you make her fall?"

"I pushed her chair, but she fell out. We were going to see the place where me and the dog can play." He looked as if a sudden thought crossed his mind and he turned to Mrs. Wedington. "You said she'd show me the yard when I came back. When is she coming to show it to me?"

"Soon, Calvin. Soon."

"Well, Mrs. Wedington, it looks like Calvin is happy about getting married to your niece. If she feels the same way then I see no reason not to proceed with the ceremony."

Hilda looked relieved and Verbena almost sprang from her chair. "I'll bring her in here now, Reverend Calhoun, then you can marry them."

"Then can I go see where I can play with the dog?"

"Yes, Calvin," Hilda said. "Then you can go see the place where you'll play."

Verbena smiled at Hilda. "I'll be right back."

♥♥♥

Though she was still in a half daze, Hannah thought Minerva looked nervous when Verbena entered the informal parlor.

"She's still not good and awake, Miz Wedington. Maybe you should wait a little while."

Things seemed a little foggy to her, but Hannah said, "I'm awake."

Verbena ignored Minerva and asked Hannah, "Are you able to sit up?"

"Yes, ma'am." She didn't want to disappoint her aunt. The woman was being extra nice to her for a change, so maybe if she did what Verbena wanted, she wouldn't be punished.

Verbena moved beside Hannah's chair and Minerva moved to the other side. "She can't keep her head up long," Minerva muttered. "She's be awake one minute, then her head will fall and she goes back to sleep."

"Hannah." Verbena looked down at her. "Are you sleepy, now?"

She couldn't understand why everyone was so concerned about her sleeping. Wasn't sleep a natural thing? "I'm awake," she said again.

"Good. Do you know who I am?"

Hannah looked up at her aunt with a silly grin on her face and wondered why Verbena was asking such an inane question. "Of course, Aunt Verbena."

Verbena patted Hannah's shoulder. "I'm glad you do, dear. Now, would you like to go visit our guests?"

Hannah had no idea who the guests were, but she said, "Sure, if you want me to."

"I do." Verbena looked at Minerva. "Why don't you go get a cup for Hannah so she can have some tea? She likes my special tea, don't you child?"

"Oh, yes, ma'am." Hannah grinned. "I like it very much. Thank you for letting me have some of it."

"Would you like to do something else that will please me, Hannah?"

Hannah felt the sudden urge to close her eyes and go to sleep again, but she forced herself to say, "Yes, ma'am."

"Good. Do you remember Calvin and Hilda?"

"I think I do." Hannah wanted to add that she didn't like them, but even in her drugged state, she knew this would displease her aunt. She didn't want to do or say anything that would make Aunt Verbena mad. She was looking forward to the tea, and knew if she displeased her aunt she might be sent to her room without it.

"I'm glad you remember them. They're anxious to see you again. Reverend Calhoun is also here. He wants to talk to you."

"I like Reverend Calhoun."

"He likes you, too, dear." Verbena turned back to Minerva. "I thought I told you to go get a cup for Hannah's tea. What are you waiting for?"

"I thought Miss Hannah might need me."

"I think I'm capable of taking care of my niece, Minerva. Now, do as you were told."

"But..."

"Are you going to dare argue with me?"

Minerva bit her lip. "No, ma'am."

"Then obey me this instant. I don't know what's gotten into you and Tobias. I've never seen you two be so disobedient."

"Yes, ma'am." Biting her lip, Minerva backed out of the room.

Hannah wanted to tell her aunt not to be so hateful to Minerva, but she could only say, "I like tea."

"I'm taking you to the other parlor now, Hannah. Be on your best behavior and it won't be long until you get to go back to bed."

Hannah didn't want to answer her. She wanted to go back to sleep right now, not wait, but before she could doze off she felt a sharp jab in her back.

"Ouch."

"Wake up and stay awake. You're going to be sorry if you don't."

Hannah knew her aunt didn't make idle threats. She would have to force herself to stay awake. "Yes, ma'am."

As they entered the formal parlor, Cedric Calhoun said, "Miss Hannah, I'm delighted to see you."

She nodded at him and fought to keep her eyes open. "I'm glad to see you, too, Reverend, sir."

"Do you want Miz Wedington to get you a dog?" Calvin blurted.

"Be quiet, Calvin. The Reverend is talking with Miss Hannah and you shouldn't interrupt." Hilda grabbed his arm.

"I was just asking if she wanted a dog."

"Shh. Now's not the time to ask."

There were a few more things said between Hilda and her brother, but Hannah couldn't stay awake long enough to know what they were. All she wanted to do was get this visit over, drink a little tea and go to sleep. Why couldn't they see this was what she needed to do?

Reverend Calhoun was speaking. "Hannah, are you aware that there is supposed to be a wedding here today?"

"Weddings are nice."

"Yes, they are."

"Would you like to get married, Hannah?"

She smiled. Was he the one person in the world who could understand that her greatest wish was to have a husband to love and one that loved her? Maybe somebody like Jarrett MacMichael. She didn't voice this though. She only said, "Of course."

"What do you think of Calvin Sawyer?"

Hannah looked around the room and frowned. "He pushed me out of my chair and cut my arm."

Aunt Verbena blurted, "You know he didn't mean to do that, dear. He accidently ran into the door facing and you slipped out of the chair."

Even in her almost stupor, Hannah could tell she'd said the wrong thing. She wanted to make it right with her aunt. "You're right. I remember now."

The preacher went on. "Would you be good to Calvin, Hannah?"

"Yes." She started to say something else, but was interrupted by the preacher.

"Well, Mrs. Wedington, it looks as if Hannah is agreeable to this marriage. Why don't we set things up and get started with the ceremony?"

Hannah wondered who the preacher was talking about getting married, but she decided it didn't matter. They probably wanted her to be present with the bride, probably as a bridesmaid. At the moment all she wanted to do was get the wedding over with, go to her room and get back into bed. She didn't even think she'd wait to have the tea, and wondered how long this was going to take.

Chapter 18

"Mr. Jarrett, does you think we gonna make it back in time?"

"We're going to try, Tobias." Jarrett mounted the gray mare he'd rented as Tobias climbed on Verbena's horse.

"Oh, my Lord, I hope we makes it. I don't see why Miz Wedington would do such a thing as this to poor little Hannah anyway."

Jarrett was wondering the same thing. He knew he'd never forgive himself if he let this happen to such a special person as Hannah. "I'm sure she has her reasons, Tobias, and when I get a chance to go through this paper I just came into possession of, maybe I'll know why." Turning his horse's head, he added, "Now, let's ride. We have about fifteen minutes to get there."

They rode faster than they normally would through the streets of Savannah. Though Jarrett was calm and collected to all appearances, he was shaking with anger inside. How could anyone do this to a sweet young woman like Hannah? A woman who deserved a man who would appreciate her, not use her the way her aunt was doing. No better than he knew the young woman, he knew the beautiful girl deserved better treatment. Tobias and his wife certainly cared more about Hannah than her own flesh and blood. According to her father, she was nothing but a cripple who would never be in his life again. Her aunt certainly didn't think much of her, or she wouldn't make her spend most of her time in her bare room sewing dresses for every woman in town except herself.

Of course, her sisters cared, but Lydia's hands were tied. She did her best to support Hannah, but no court in the land was going to allow an innocent woman who couldn't fend for herself to live over a saloon. Though he'd never met her, he knew Drina cared, too. Why else would Aaron Wilcox hire him to come to Savannah to check on Hannah? He realized the problem Drina faced was that she lived all the way west in Arizona, where she couldn't take an active part in Hannah's life. Therefore, there was no way she could make sure things were right for her sister without outside help.

Thoughts began to run through his head. *That's why you're here, MacMichael. You have to make sure Verbena Wedington's evil plan doesn't work. You need to get Hannah out of that house any way you can. You know it won't be easy, but you have no choice. You can't let Verbena marry the beautiful young woman off to some idiot. If, for some reason, a wedding has to take place and there's no other answer, you'll marry Hannah yourself.*

Though he knew this thought was ridiculous, it made him push his steed harder. He had to get there as quickly as he could. Hannah's future depended on it.

When they rode the horses to the front of the mansion, Tobias shouted. "Maybe we should go in the back door. That way we can get in without Miz Wedington knowing."

Jarrett nodded and galloped his horse across the front yard without slowing down to avoid her flowers. He was at the point he didn't care what happened to the lady's pristine lawn.

Minerva must have heard them, because she opened the back door and waved them inside. "Hurry. They's done started the wedding."

Jarrett threw his reins around the post at the back steps and leaped off the horse. Tobias followed. He and Minerva were on Jarrett's heels as he hurried across the kitchen, through the dining room and into the entry toward the formal parlor.

The preacher was saying, "If there's anyone here who objects to this wedding let him speak now or forever hold…"

"What the hell's going on here?" Jarrett's booming voice filled the room as Verbena and Hilda both let out little screams. The preacher almost dropped his book. Calvin, with a scared look on his face, ran to Hilda, and Hannah turned to look at the interrupter with glazed eyes and a smile on her face.

Verbena seemed to gather herself first. "Mr. MacMichael. I'm afraid you arrived at a bad time. We're in the middle of a private ceremony here."

"I see what you're up to here." He strode to Hannah's chair and knelt beside her. "What's happening, Hannah?"

She closed her eyes then opened them. "I think there's a wedding."

"Who's wedding is it?"

"I'm not sure, but I think I'm a bridesmaid."

"I see." He stood and looked around. "Minerva, would you and Tobias take Hannah out of here for a little while?"

"Tobias, don't you dare take her anywhere." Verbena looked furious when she came up to Jarrett and grabbed his arm. "Mr. MacMichael, you're interfering in something that you know nothing about."

"Maybe not, but it looks to me as if somebody needs to interfere here. How could you do this to a sweet woman like Hannah?"

"I'm only doing what she wants and what's best for her. Now, I'm asking you to leave. You've created enough of a distraction."

The preacher spoke for the first time. "Sir, I don't know you, but let me assure you that I talked with Miss Hamilton before the ceremony began and she assured me she liked the idea of a wedding."

"And you believed she was in good enough shape to agree to getting married?"

Reverend Calhoun looked insulted. "I asked her if she liked Mr. Sawyer."

"Did you ask her if she liked him well enough to marry him?"

"Well, no. I assumed Mrs. Wedington had discussed the situation with her."

"Why don't you want me to say my part?" Calvin looked at Jarrett as if he didn't know what was happening.

"What part were you supposed to say?" Jarrett glared at Calvin.

"I just had to say the words 'I do' then when the crippled girl says her words Mrs. Wedington is going to get me a dog."

Jarrett shook his head. "Do you realize you'll be married to Miss Hannah after you say those words?"

Calvin frowned. "I don't believe you. Hilda told me it's just a part."

"I don't care what Hilda or anybody else told you, it's not just a part. You're getting married, even if you don't realize it."

He frowned again. "Is that right, Hilda?"

"Well…"

"Yes, it's right." Jarrett turned from him to Verbena. "I thought you were a better woman than this."

She lifted her nose in the air. "As I said, Mr. MacMichael, I'm only doing what my niece wants me to do."

"So, you're telling me that Hannah wants to marry a man-child?"

Cedric interrupted. "I think you have the wrong idea, Mr. MacMichael. Isn't that the name Mrs. Wedington called you?"

"Yes, that's my name and no, preacher, I don't have the wrong idea, you do." He glanced at Hannah, who was slumped in her wheelchair with her eyes closed. "Can't you see that Hannah is not herself? She's been drugged so she will go along with this fiasco. She has no idea what's going on. Didn't you hear her say she thought she was a bridesmaid?"

The preacher looked perturbed. "I did hear her say that."

"That should have given you a clue as to what was going on here! For some reason, Mrs. Wedington has decided to marry Hannah off to this man." He glanced at Hannah's aunt, who looked as if she was going to try again to throw him out of the house with her words. "I wonder if it has something to do with the paper she signed the summer before her sister died?"

Verbena not only looked stunned, but frightened as she began to tremble. Without answering, she dropped into the pull-up chair.

Jarrett looked at Hilda. "I think it's time you took your brother home. There isn't going to be any wedding today. If you're set on getting him married, you're going to have to find him a wife somewhere else. He's never going to marry Hannah Hamilton. I'm here to see to that."

Hannah stirred in her wheelchair and they all looked at her. "Is the wedding over?"

Minerva and Tobias had been standing faithfully by. She reached over and patted Hannah's shoulder. "It's over, honey."

"Oh, I must have dozed off. I'm so sorry I missed it."

Jarrett nodded to Tobias. "Take her to the other parlor, please. I don't want to upset her by what I'm about to say."

Hannah smiled up at him. "Hello, Mr. MacMichael. I didn't know you were here? When did you arrive?"

He bent toward her and felt relieved that he'd arrived in time to save her. "I've been here for a little while."

"Did you see the wedding?"

"The wedding has been called off, Hannah." His voice was soft.

"Oh, I'm so sorry. The bride must be devastated."

"I think she'll be happy about the situation. She was marrying the wrong man."

"Then, I'm glad." She smiled at him, then turned to look at her aunt. "Aunt Verbena, you look upset. Did you want the wedding to take place?"

She ignored her niece and glanced at her servants. "I think Mr. MacMichael asked you to take Hannah out of here. Take her to her room."

He glanced at Jarrett and he nodded. Tobias returned the nod and said to Verbena, "Yes, ma'am."

As Tobias rolled Hannah toward the door, she called, "Good-by, everyone."

"I'll see you in a few minutes, Hannah," Jarrett said. Nobody else said anything until she was out of the room. He went on. "Now, I want to know exactly what's going on here. Why were you rushing Hannah into a marriage she knew nothing about, and why were you pushing this man to do something he didn't understand?"

The preacher spoke first. "Mr. MacMichael, I take full responsibility for my part in this. Mrs. Wedington told me this was what her niece wanted, and after I asked her a few questions, I thought this was the correct thing to do. I never dreamed the girl was under the influence of medicine, and didn't realize what was going on."

Verbena seemed to gain back her composure. "I have talked to Hannah and she told me she wanted to get married. I knew no normal man would ever want her, so I suggested Mr. Sawyer."

"Are you still going to get me a dog since I didn't get to say my part?"

"Forget about the dog, Calvin." Hilda stood and took her brother's arm. "Maybe the man is right. I think we should leave now."

Verbena looked at the two of them. "Maybe we can work something out later."

"Don't count on it." Jarrett shook his head at both of them. "I think you two women are through playing God with other people's lives."

"How dare you say that to me!" Verbena shouted. "This is my house and you have no right to come in here telling me what I can and cannot do."

He scowled at her. "Mrs. Wedington, I have a document in my pocket which I think will clear up everything." He reached in his vest pocket and pulled out a yellowed paper. "I bought this from Burl Hamilton this afternoon."

She gasped and placed her hand on her heart. "Why?"

For some reason, he didn't think he should tell her in front of the preacher. "I think that is something you and I should discuss in private."

She looked as if she might argue, but changed her mind. "Maybe you're right."

Jarrett turned to the preacher. "Sir, I don't think you're needed here any longer."

The preacher seemed confused. "Are you asking me to leave?"

"Yes, sir. Mrs. Wedington and I have some things to discuss. If she wants to make you aware of them later, that is her prerogative."

The Reverend looked at Verbena.

"I think he's right, Reverend Calhoun. This is a family matter."

"Will you call me if you need me?"

"Yes, I will. Thank you for coming today, and I'm sorry for the misunderstanding."

Still looking unsure, the preacher took his leave.

♥♥♥

When they were alone, Verbena gave Jarrett a guarded glance. What was he up to? Why had he bought the damaging paper from Burl, and why did Burl agree to let him have it? That is, if Burl really sold it to him. If so, how did Jarrett know about it in the first place? Did Reginald Phillips tell him, unknowingly or outright? The two seemed to be getting close behind her back. Now, she wondered if she could trust the man she'd thought about marrying.

Jarrett hadn't spoken since the preacher left, so she decided to break the silence between them. "I think you owe me an explanation, Mr. MacMichael."

"Maybe I do, at that." He unfolded the yellowed paper and began to read.

"I'm not sure that document has anything to do with me, but if it does, I don't think that it is any of your business, sir. I demand that you hand it over to me."

"Not a chance, lady."

She pursed her lips, flipped her head around and called, "Tobias, come in here."

In an instant, the butler appeared in the room. "Yes, ma'am."

"Throw this man out of my house."

Tobias glanced at Jarrett then turned back to Verbena. "I'm sorry, Miz Wedington. I can't do that."

She saw a sneaky smile cross Jarrett's lips, though he kept reading and didn't say anything.

She grew furious. "How dare you refuse to obey my command, Tobias Johnson. I pay you to do what I say, and you're supposed to do it. After all, you're nothing but a servant."

Tobias ignored her. "Miss Hannah has gone back to sleep, Mr. Jarrett. Minerva is with her."

"Good. Have a seat over there in one of those chairs," Jarrett said.

Verbena gasped. "He can't sit down in my presence!" She couldn't believe that Jarrett MacMichael, even with all his strange ways, would suggest a Negro servant sit down in her parlor, but before she could complain further, Tobias sat and Jarrett began folding the paper.

"I think I've read enough to know what's going on here."

She bit her lip and eyed him. "What have you read?"

"As I said, enough. I now understand why you were so hell bent on getting Hannah married before her eighteenth birthday."

Though she was scared at what he was going to say, Verbena fought back in the only way she knew how. She used her words. "Even if you know, you have no right to interfere with anything I say or do. This is my house and my business."

"It's time you quit trying to finagle your way out of this, Verbena Wedington."

"Whatever, do you mean?" Oh Lord, what could she do to make this man see she had a right to do what she'd set out to do today?

♥♥♥

Jarrett decided it was time to confront her. She'd been lording it over everyone long enough. "First of all, I will tell you that I'm not who you think I am."

"Then who are you?"

162

"It's true that Jarrett MacMichael is my name, but I'm not a businessman who has come to Savannah to build a hotel."

"Then why are you here?"

"I'm a private investigator from Flagstaff, Arizona. I was sent here to investigate you and your treatment of Hannah."

She stared at him. "Who would send you to do such a thing?"

"I'm sure they won't mind me telling you. Aaron Wilcox hired me for his wife, Drina. She was worried about her sister and wanted to make sure she was well taken care of. If not, then I was supposed to make sure the bad treatment of her stopped."

Verbena's brow wrinkled. "I've always taken good care of Hannah."

This didn't set well with him and he began to spit questions at her. "Then tell me why Hannah lives in a room that isn't as good as one a person would supply their servants? Why does she go around dressed like a beggar's daughter? Why can't she have pretty dresses since she's an accomplished seamstress? Why isn't she allowed to have the special tea except at the times you have visitors? Why do you banish her to her room without her wheelchair as a punishment for some small infraction? Why did you not give her the letters her sister wrote her and why didn't you mail the ones she wrote to Drina?"

He stopped to take a breath, and she covered her face with her hands for an instant, then removed them. He thought she was going to sob, but she didn't. She only muttered, "Why are you being so cruel to me?"

"I'm not trying to be cruel, but I think it's time some of this information came out in the open so people will see the real Verbena Wedington. What did you plan to do? Wait until Burl Hamilton died so you could destroy your copy of this document and hope his never surfaced?"

"Of course not. I only wanted what was mine." Her eyes bored into his. "I'd have had it, too, if you hadn't poked your nose where it wasn't welcome."

Jarrett ignored her statement and turned to Tobias. "Please go to Hannah's room and have Minerva pack all the clothes the girl owns. Then, come back. I want you to go to the livery and turn in the horse I rented. Bring back a wagon of some kind. I'm getting Hannah out of here tonight. The livery stable man knows who I am, so I'm sure you won't have any trouble if you tell him you're renting the things for me." He took money out of his pocket and gave it to Tobias.

"You're not taking Hannah anywhere," Verbena shouted.

Jarrett gave her a sinister look. "Try to stop me and I'll send Tobias for the sheriff while he's out. I think you and I both know what that would mean."

Verbena sank back on the divan as if she'd slapped her back.

Tobias rose from his chair, took the money and headed for the stairs.

"If you go up those stairs, you're fired, Tobias. So is Minerva. If you disobey me, pack your own clothes, too and get out of my house." Verbena shrieked at his receding back.

Tobias paused.

Jarrett said, "Go on, Tobias. Do what she says. I'll take care of you and Minerva."

"He's lying," she screeched.

Ignoring her, Tobias nodded at Jarrett and continued up the steps.

Jarrett turned back to her. "Now, Verbena, go get the jewelry and bring it to me."

She looked startled as she turned from glaring at the butler going up the stairs. "What jewelry?"

"Come off your imaginary throne, lady. You're not going to be acting queen around here any longer. Get the jewelry, and be quick about it."

"I don't have any jewelry here."

"Where is it?"

"In the bank vault."

He shook his head at her. "I don't think so. The paper said you were to keep it in your home safe until it was time to give it to Hannah. And if I remember what I read just a few minutes ago, she's to get it if she isn't married by her eighteenth birthday."

"She won't be eighteen until next year."

"Don't try to pull that. She'll be eighteen in a couple of days. Do you want me to sit here and wait until the clock strikes midnight two days from now before you hand it over?"

Verbena looked at him as if she'd like to kill him.

"Don't you dare try to lie your way out of this. Your sister put it in her own handwriting that you were to abide by her wishes. Your sister and her husband signed it. So did you. Therefore, it's a legal document that will stand up in any court in the land."

"I've done my part. I've provided a home for Hannah when nobody else wanted her."

"That's not so. Lydia wanted her."

"No, she didn't."

"Oh, yes, she did. I know she tried to get Hannah to come and live with her, but you wouldn't let that happen. You knew if you did, you'd lose out on everything."

"Lydia is not a good influence on Hannah."

"And you are?" His eyes bored into hers.

"Listen to me, MacMichael. Hannah has a good home here. She's not mistreated, and she seems happy with her life."

"Do you really believe what you're saying? You keep her locked in this house like a prisoner and most of the time she's banished to her room. She isn't allowed to learn to walk or to have friends. Not to mention the fact that you beat her when she was a little girl for the least infraction. How would you like to live your life the way Hannah has?"

"What do you mean learn to walk? Hannah will never walk." She took on the stubborn look again.

"Have you never heard of crutches?"

Her shoulders slumped. "You have the answers to everything, don't you?"

Before Jarrett could reply, there was a sharp rap on the front door.

Chapter 19

"What's going on, Tobias?" Minerva stared at him when he asked her to start packing Hannah's clothes. She couldn't help being a little nervous.

"Mr. Jarrett says he's taking Miss Hannah out of this house today. We's got to pack our things, too. He wants everything ready to go when I get back."

"Where're you going?"

"I'm taking his horse back and renting a wagon for him."

"Will that there livery man let you rent a wagon?"

"I'm shore he will when I tell him it's for Mr. Jarrett."

"Miz Wedington is gonna be mad."

"She's already mad, Minerva."

"Does you think she'll fire us?"

He chuckled. "Honey child, she already has. That's why you gotta pack our clothes, too."

"What?" Minerva looked frightened.

"Don't worry, wife. Mr. Jarrett said he'd take care of us."

"And you believe him?"

"Yes, I do. You should've heard what he's telling her. I think Miss Hannah and maybe us, too, are goin' to be fine when we's get away from here."

"What makes you think that, Tobias?"

"I'll explain later. Best you get to packing Miss Hannah's things."

"Does you think Miz Wedington is gonna let her go?"

"She's got no choice. Mr. Jarrett is determined."

"What will we do with no jobs, Tobias?"

"As I told you, Mr. Jarrett said he'd take care of it. If'n he don't, we's gonna worry about that later." He reached over and patted his wife's shoulder. "We's will be fine. Jest you wait and see." He leaned down and kissed her forehead.

She nodded and got up from the chair she'd been sitting in beside the window. "I's trust you, Tobias. I'll get her stuff packed. Then I's go pack ours. What should I put it all in?"

"Don't she have something?"

"Don't worry about it. I'll find something. You go do what you have to and I'll take care of Miss Hannah's things and ours, too."

Tobias went out the door and Minerva walked to the bed. She looked at Hannah. Making sure the young woman was still sleeping, she decided she'd go downstairs and get one of the valises she'd seen in the linen closet. Since she'd been fired, she didn't figure Miz Wedington could do her any more harm. All kinds of thoughts were running through her head as she went out of the room. *I's might even get one of them bags to pack mine and Tobias's things in. 'Course if I does, she's so mean she'll probably have the both of us hung from that big oak tree in the town square.*

The sound of the knocking on the front door broke into Minerva's thoughts. Knowing Tobias was gone, she automatically went to the door.

"Hello, doctor," she said.

"I've come to check on Mrs. Wedington's niece. Would you please tell her I'm here?"

"She's right here in the parlor, sir. I'm sure she'll want to see you."

Without saying anything further, he followed Minerva to the parlor.

Verbena didn't seem to know what to do when he walked in. Finally, she said, "I assume you came to check on Hannah."

"Yes, I did." He eyed Jarrett. "Would it be better if I came back later?"

"Not at all." Jarrett stood, introduced himself and stuck his hand out to the doctor. "I'm glad you came by. It seems Mrs. Wedington has given Hannah her medicine wrong and you should check her over."

"I left clear instructions as to how the medicine was to be administered."

Verbena swallowed. "I just got mixed up."

"Then would you please escort me to Miss Hamilton's room?"

Verbena glanced at Jarrett.

He said, "I'm sure Minerva can show you the way. Mrs. Wedington and I are in a business discussion."

He gave them a strange look, but only said, "Very well."

Though Minerva was surprised, she didn't argue. She turned toward the stairs, "This way, doctor.

♥♥♥

Jarrett turned to Verbena. "Now that we're alone again, shall we continue?"

She looked defiant as she sat. "What is there to continue? You're determined to ruin my life."

"I don't think I'm doing that, Verbena. You did it to yourself when you decided to live your life the way you wanted to instead of the decent way your sister expected you to do."

"I'm a decent person, and I've done nothing wrong. I go to church and try to do right by my fellow Christians."

"Have you done the right thing by your niece? The one person you should have cared the most about?"

She bit her lip and he went on. "What decent aunt would have tried to trick her niece into marrying a man with the mind of a child? That was an evil thing to do, and you know it."

When she still said nothing, he said, "You might as well admit it was because you're greedy. You wanted her mother's jewelry for yourself and you were determined to get it, regardless of how it hurt Hannah."

She turned her head. "You're going to believe what you want to believe, Mr. MacMichael, no matter what I say."

He patted the pocket where he'd returned the paper he'd bought from Burl. "I believe in facts, Mrs. Wedington, and the facts on this document tell me all I need to know about you." He held out his hand to her. "I'll accompany you to wherever you have the jewelry. We have plenty of time to get it before the doctor returns, so we might as well get it now. There's no need to try to fight me about it. I don't intend to leave here tonight without it."

Verbena set her face in a stubborn scowl. "Hannah won't be eighteen until day after tomorrow. She has no right to it until then."

"Then, as I said before, you and I will wait right here until Hannah's birthday. As I said, I'm not leaving without it."

"Why not?"

"Because I don't trust you, Verbena Wedington. I know what you do to people who don't do the things the way you think they should. I don't intend for Hannah to be the subject of your wicked mind any longer."

Verbena didn't say anything, but stared at him with hatred in her eyes. He knew she'd decided there was no way out of the situation when she sighed, stood without taking his hand, and headed down the hall. He followed her to what had probably been her late husband's study. She moved back a portrait hanging over the desk. Jarrett figured it was of Hector Wedington when he was a young man. Behind the picture there was a safe fitted in the wall. Knowing there might be a gun inside it, he refused to turn his back as she began to dial the numbers.

When it opened, she reached in and took out a small ornate box. "This was all Ella left. If you'll check the document you'll see each piece that is described in the document is here."

"Rest assured, I'll check it carefully."

By the time they returned to the parlor, the doctor was coming down the steps.

"How was Hannah?" Jarrett asked.

He shook his head. "She's had too much medication. I know I gave you

168

clear instructions of had to administer it, Mrs. Wedington. You should have been more careful."

Verbena dropped her head without replying.

Jarrett said, "I plan to take Miss Hamilton to the hotel where she can be more comfortable, doctor. That is, if you have no objections."

"I think it'll be fine to move her. Just let her sleep off the effects of the laudanum and she should be all right."

"Then, would you please come by the hotel tomorrow and check her again?"

"I'd be happy to."

Jarrett gave him the name of the hotel and his room number, then thanked him.

Verbena walked him to the door and came back into the parlor. "Is there anything else you're going to demand of me today?"

"Not today. As soon as Tobias returns with the carriage, we'll be leaving."

"My friends are going to wonder where Hannah is and why she isn't here to do their sewing any longer. What am I supposed to tell them?"

"I've always thought the truth would suffice."

She cut her eyes at him. "Like you were truthful with me?"

"I was only doing the job I was hired to do, so I had my reasons for lying, Mrs. Wedington."

"So did I, Mr. MacMichael." When he only looked at her, she shrugged. "Well, then get Hannah, and be off with you. I'm ready for my supper and Minerva hasn't even started it."

"I'm afraid you'll have to get your own supper, ma'am."

She frowned. "What do you mean?"

"With my own ears I heard you fire both Tobias and his wife. I've decided I'm going to hire them to look after Hannah."

"You wouldn't dare."

He cocked an eyebrow at her. "Oh, wouldn't I?"

She said nothing more.

Hannah stretched and opened her eyes. She had had some strange dreams. She'd been to a wedding and then Jarrett MacMichael showed up. In her dream, she wanted to marry him, but Tobias took her away before it could happen. Then, Jarrett came back and lifted her up in his arms and they went for a ride in a carriage of some sort. It was so real she could feel the wind on her face, and she thought he was taking her away to marry her, but sleep overcame her and she couldn't keep her eyes open any longer…and it didn't happen. Now it was morning, and she was back in her real world. Or was she? Something was different. This bed was soft and comfortable, and she was lying on two fluffy feather pillows. Was she still dreaming?

She sat up and gasped as she looked around. The walls of this large room were painted a soft blue. There were white ruffled curtains at the double windows and there were a small sofa and two chairs covered in a silk flowered material positioned around a small table at the large double windows.

Hannah didn't know where she was or how she came to be in this lovely place, but she knew she wasn't in her room at Aunt Verbena's house. The only familiar thing here was her wheelchair sitting in the corner. She glanced down and saw she was wearing her regular cotton nightgown, though it was only pulled up over one arm. Her cut arm with its sling was outside. How did she get into her night clothes and who managed to get it over her sore and bandaged arm? She shook her head and continued to look around. She didn't see any of the clothes she thought she'd worn earlier, but she couldn't be sure of what she had on before coming here. She then spied a valise sitting near the mahogany wardrobe and wondered if her clothes were there. But how could they be? She didn't have a valise.

A knock on the door at the side of the room made her jump. She couldn't help being a little afraid, and wondered if she should answer.

The knock came again and a man's voice asked, "Are you awake, Hannah?"

He sounded familiar, but it wasn't Tobias. She said nothing and the door opened. She relaxed when Jarrett MacMichael stuck his head in the door.

Again he asked, "Are you awake, Hannah?"

"Yes," she said in an almost whisper. "I'm awake."

"Good because I'm coming in there." As soon as he was through the door, he said, "Good morning, Hannah."

Surprised and happy to see him, she quickly pulled the covers up to her shoulders, only leaving her injured one outside the sheet. Without returning his greeting, she took a deep breath and asked, "Where am I, Mr. MacMichael?"

"I think I asked you to call me Jarrett."

"Then, where am I, Jarrett?"

He stepped into the room and came to the side of her bed. "You're in a room in the hotel where I'm staying."

She frowned. "It's a beautiful place, but why am I here?"

"I'll explain later. How are you feeling?"

"Confused." She turned her head and looked at him. "But good morning to you, too. Now, please tell me why I'm here."

"It's simple. I brought you." He moved his head close to hers and looked into her eyes.

She leaned back a little. "Why are you looking at me so closely?"

"I want to make sure your eyes are clear." She frowned at him and he smiled. "You have beautiful eyes, by the way, and they're nice and clear."

"Thank you," she said, but she didn't quit frowning.

"You're welcome." He backed up.

"Now, please explain to me what's going on."

"Minerva should be here shortly to help you get dressed, then we'll go downstairs for breakfast."

"Won't Aunt Verbena be furious that I'm not in my room?"

"She's furious already. She didn't want me to bring you here, but she had no choice."

"Why?"

"You sure do ask a lot of questions beginning with the word 'why' don't you?" There was a knock on the door that led to the hallway and he opened it without saying anything else.

"Good morning, Mr. Jarrett."

"Good morning, Minerva. I'm sure glad you're here. She keeps asking questions even after I told her I'd explain everything later."

"I's help her get dressed then she can ask you her questions."

"Did Tobias go to bring Lydia?"

"Yes, sir, he did. He'll be along with her shortly."

"Good." He waved his hand toward Hannah. "See if you can get her dressed without her badgering you with her questions and I'll wait in my room."

"I'll do that, Mr. Jarrett."

Jarrett turned to Hannah, winked at her, and disappeared out the door he came through.

"Minerva, what in the world—"

"Don't start asking me you questions, Miss Hannah. Mr. Jarrett said he'd 'splain it all to you, and I'm sure he will. It ain't my place to do it. Now, let's get you dressed."

Hannah realized she had no control over the situation at the moment, so she decided to be quiet and put on her clothes. At least he promised to answer her questions later. She just hoped whatever was going on wasn't going to make Aunt Verbena punish her too harshly when it was all over.

♥♥♥

Jarrett ran his fingers through his hair as soon as he closed the door between his room and Hannah's. What in the world was the matter with him? Sure, he thought the woman was pretty. Well, maybe not just pretty, but beautiful. And yes, he enjoyed being with her, but why did his heart have to almost beat out of his chest when he looked into those deep blue eyes? Though he could admit, the eyes were special and could excite any man, but what about the mussed hair? The tangled mass of blonde tresses needed a brushing badly. It stuck up, not only on the top of her head, but it stuck out in the back as well. Why did he have the urge to reach out and smooth it down for her? It was a woman's job to fix hair, not a man's. Then why did the glimpse of her naked shoulder peeking out from the edge of her cotton gown where her damaged arm was on top of the covers give him a jolt? He's seen women in nightgowns before—silk ones that revealed a lot of a woman's body. Felicia often wore fancy gowns that were low cut and often split almost to her waist. She never wore the rough cotton kind that came up around a woman's neck as it appeared Hannah's did. Then why did the one Hannah have on affect him more than the fancy ones Felicia owned?

He had to stop this stuff. After all, Felicia Newell waited for him in Flagstaff. Or did she? What the hell did she matter anyway? He knew full well he had no intention of marrying Miss Newell, though he'd tossed around the idea of marriage eventually to somebody he had yet to meet. He shook his head and started to pour himself a whiskey from the decanter on the table.

"Man, what are you doing? It's eight o'clock in the morning and you haven't even had breakfast." He sat the decanter down and moved to the window.

Looking down on the bustling street, he let his thoughts take him where they would. *I've got to get out of this town and get back to Arizona where normal things happen. I can handle fist fights, gun battles, saloon women, wild horses, even marauding Indians, but what do I know about a woman who is devious enough to try to marry her niece off to a man who has the mentality of a child? And why did that beautiful woman who slept with only a wall separating us last night keep me awake most of the night? Why can't I simply finish up this job, send her to her sister in Arizona, or leave her with the sister here in Savannah, pocket my money and go home and forget I ever met Hannah Hamilton and her aunt?* He shook his head. *I know why, damn it. It's because I don't want to forget Hannah, that's why. I might as well admit it. That girl has done something to my heart that no other woman has ever done. Certainly not*

172

Felicia Newell.

♥♥♥

A knock sounded on the door to Hannah's room.

"Come in."

Minerva wheeled Hannah through the door. Her hair was combed and was tied back with a blue ribbon. It looked pretty, but Jarrett still liked the way it looked when he first saw her this morning, and the way he wished he could see her every morning. At this moment, she no longer wore the cotton gown, but was dressed in the blue flowered dress he'd seen her in several times. It's time to get her more clothes, he thought.

"Are you ready to tell me what's going on, now Mr...I mean Jarrett?"

"I was hoping to tell you and your sister at the same time. Tobias has gone for her."

She looked almost scared. "Then, I guess I'll have to wait."

He made a quick decision. "You're not going to have to wait much longer." Turning to Minerva, he said, "Take her back to her room and clean off the table at her window. I'm going downstairs to order breakfast for us. Would you like something?"

Minerva looked at him as if he'd said something she didn't understand. "You means you would get me something?"

"Sure, I would."

She bit her lip and smiled. "I done eat some breakfast, but a cup of coffee would be nice."

"Coming up. I'll get Tobias one in case he gets back while we're eating." He looked at Hannah. "What would you like this morning?"

"Whatever you're having will be fine."

He nodded. "I'll be back shortly."

♥♥♥

Verbena went into her kitchen and looked around. There was no coffee brewing on the stove. There was no breakfast cooking. The stove wasn't even hot. For some reason, she thought Tobias and Minerva would change their minds and be at their respective jobs this morning, but she'd been wrong. She decided to check their room, but found their few personal items and their clothes all gone. There was nothing else missing.

"Damn Jarrett MacMichael," she whispered. Though she wasn't a woman who cursed often, she felt justified this morning.

Moving back into the kitchen and going to the cabinet, she took a glass and intended to fill it with milk. She then realized there was no milk, because Minerva hadn't left the jug outside for the boy who brought it daily. She filled the glass with water and took a slice of the bread Minerva had made the day before. Maybe she'd been too hasty in firing her servants. She should have waited until she'd hired replacements for them. Finding someone else might not be easy.

Spreading some of the strawberry jam that Minerva had made last spring on her bread, she ate it quickly and drank her water. She decided she'd hurry to the market and pick up some things already prepared so she wouldn't be caught like this again. There were always good breads, pies and cakes as well as all kinds of fresh vegetables.

It then dawned on her that Tobias wasn't here to hitch up her buggy. There was no way she could walk to the market. That would be unseemly for a woman of her standing, anyway. Only the servants of the rich were shopping there this time of morning. No. She'd have to make do with what she found in the kitchen, and if need be, she'd build a fire in the cook stove. After all, she'd done it when she was younger. Surely, she hadn't forgotten how.

Once again, she said out loud, "Damn Jarrett MacMichael and Minerva and Tobias and Hannah and especially Burl Hamilton. I'll see to it that they all pay for what they've done to me."

♥♥♥

Standing beside the table in Hannah's room, Jarrett watched as she stared at the food the waiter put out for the two of them. There were eggs, ham, bacon, potatoes, biscuits, jellies, some type of sweet breads, an assortment of little cakes and a pot of tea, as well as a big urn of coffee.

Jarrett's heart seemed to do a little dance in his chest when she glanced at him with a twinkle in her eyes. She didn't say anything until he closed the door behind the waiter, then she laughed as she asked, "Do you really expect the two of us to eat this much?"

"Of course." He took the chair across the table from her. She looked so much like a child on Christmas morning that he had to smile. "I'm hungry, and I wanted to make sure you had something you liked to eat, but first, I'm going to pour Minerva a cup of coffee and let her go sit in my room and enjoy it while we talk. I'll also send one for Tobias."

"Thank you, Mr. Jarrett." Minerva took the coffee and turned to Hannah. "Now child, you relax and Mr. Jarrett is gonna 'splain everything to you."

"I'm not sure…"

"Now, Miss Hannah, has Minerva ever steered you wrong?"

"No, Minerva, you haven't."

"Good." She turned and went through the adjoining door to Jarrett's room and closed it behind her.

"Now, start filling your plate, and we'll talk." Jarrett passed her the eggs.

"There's so much to choose from here."

"As I said, I want you to have something you like."

"I'm not hard to please, Jarrett. I'm used to eating whatever Aunt Verbena sends up to my room."

"But you must have your favorite dishes."

"There are some I like better than others, but as long as it's filling, I don't think I should complain about what I eat."

"Then it's time you had some of your favorite things."

"Don't spoil me, Jarrett. Whenever I go back to Aunt Verbena's house, I'll probably have to pay for being here with you now."

He reached over and took her hand. "You're never going back to Verbena's house, Hannah."

She stared at him. "How can I not?"

"I'll tell you as soon as you fill your plate and start eating. Would you prefer coffee or tea?"

"I'll take coffee first, then I'll have tea, if it's alright." She put a few eggs on her plate and added a slice of ham, then picked up a biscuit.

"It's fine." He filled her cup and handed her the sugar. "I've seen you put sugar in your tea. Do you want it in your coffee?"

"Yes, please."

He knew as soon their plates were filled, he had to start telling her what had happened. He just wasn't sure where to begin. He didn't want to upset her. He decided not to tell her who he was yet. Instead, he started with the fact that Verbena had given her too much laudanum.

Hannah was shocked. "I know she doesn't like me much, but I can't believe she'd do that."

"Well, she did. When the doctor came to check you last night, he was firm with her about what she'd done. She tried to pass it off like she'd got confused about how to administer it to you."

"Maybe she did."

"No, Hannah, she didn't. She had her own sinister reason to keep you in a drugged state. I'll get to that in a minute." He took a bite of ham.

"What reason could she possibly have?"

"We'll get to that. You need to start eating before it gets cold."

She sampled her meal and glanced at him. "This is delicious."

He noticed how her eyes glowed with pleasure, and he wanted to reach out and touch her cheek, but he didn't dare. He looked down at his plate. "I'm glad you like it."

"I do, very much. Now, please go on with your story."

He was still having trouble deciding what to tell her and what to keep to himself for a while. Finally, he said, "I'm sure you remember Calvin Sawyer and his sister."

"They're friends of Aunt Verbena."

"Yes, and the sister and Verbena had cooked up a scheme to marry Calvin off. I have no earthly reason why."

"I only met them once, but it didn't seem to me Calvin Sawyer had the mental capacity to become a husband."

"That's true, but according to what I've been told, the sister's fellow wouldn't marry her unless Calvin was out of the house. She must have decided to have him marry some unsuspecting girl whose guardian would let him live in their house with the bride after the wedding. That way, the sister would be rid of him and could pursue her own goals for her life."

"That's a cruel thing to do."

"I agree. It would take an evil person to do that." He chose his next words as carefully as he could. "A person like your Aunt Verbena."

"Oh, Jarrett, Aunt Verbena wouldn't…"

"She did, Hannah. She drugged you and was setting you up to marry Calvin. If I hadn't gotten there when I did…"

She dropped her fork and it clattered on the table. "Oh, no." Tears began to slide down her cheeks. "Please tell me that's not so."

He stood and rushed to her. Kneeling beside her chair, he wrapped his arm around her and whispered, "Don't cry, sweetheart. You're safe here with me." As soon as he said the words, he knew she was safe, not only now, but for the rest of her life. He was always going to be there to take care of Hannah, no matter what.

Chapter 20

Lydia was confused when Tobias showed up and told her Jarrett MacMichael wanted her to come to the hotel to meet with him. It wasn't that she minded talking with the man, but she was sure Bradly had been a little jealous when he'd come home and found them together. Of course, this would have to be the one day her husband had to go up to Tybee Island on business. Would he get back before she finished her meeting with Jarrett?

Then, Tobias told her the meeting was concerning Hannah, and she knew it must be important. If he did return and find out she was there, Bradly would have to understand. It wasn't that Lydia was hiding things from her husband. It was just that he'd acted a little strange and stand-offish since his return. As for this meeting with Jarrett, she planned to tell him all about it later. She just wanted to be sure he was in a good mood when she did.

The desk clerk eyed them as they went up the stairs to Jarrett's room. When they reached the top, she said, "I thought they were going to stop us, Tobias."

Tobias shook his head. "Mr. Jarrett told them they better not stop me or Minerva whenever we went up the steps to his room. I guess they's afraid Mr. Jarrett will get mad if 'n they say anything to us, or to anybody with us."

"Jarrett does demand respect, doesn't he?"

"Yes, Miz Lydia. He shore does. He's a good man." Tobias knocked.

Minerva opened the door. "I's glad you back. Hello, Miz Lydia."

"Minerva, what in the world are you doing here?"

"I's work for Mr. Jarrett now, Miz Lydia."

Lydia was startled. "You what?"

"She's right, Miz Lydia," Tobias said. "We's both works for Mr. Jarrett now."

"Come on in. Mr. Jarrett is in Miss Hannah's room." Minerva stood aside.

"Hannah's room? What's going on here?"

Neither of them answered her, but Minerva showed her through the open door between the rooms.

She took one look at her sister and went running toward the small couch where she sat with Jarrett. "My goodness, Hannah. What happened to your arm?"

"I fell out of my chair." Hannah reached up with her good arm and hugged her sister. "I'm so glad you're here. Jarrett has told me part of what happened and he promised to tell me what got me to this point, but he said he wanted to tell the rest to you and me together."

Lydia took one of the chairs facing the two of them. "Well, I'm stunned to find you here. How did you talk Aunt Verbena into letting you out of the house?"

"You aunt had nothing to do with it. I took Hannah out of that house for her own protection." Jarrett motioned for Minerva to pour tea for Lydia, then for her and Tobias to take a seat.

"Thank you," Lydia said to Minerva. To Jarrett, she said, "What do you mean 'for her own good'?"

"Why don't you tell her how this all started, Tobias?"

Tobias nodded. "I overheard Miz Wedington making plans to marry Miss Hannah off to marry Calvin Sawyer. I told Minerva we had to do something to stop it."

Minerva said, "We knowed we couldn't let that happen to her, but we didn't know how to stop it. So I told Tobias to go find Mr. Jarrett. We both knowed he'd know what to do."

Jarrett smiled. "I got there in time to stop the wedding, and when I found out Hannah had been drugged, I wasn't about to leave her in that house a minute longer with her devious aunt. I didn't know what that woman would've tried next."

Lydia looked mad. "What a horrible thing for Aunt Verbena to do. I don't understand why she'd do such a thing in the first place."

"I don't know why either, Lydia, but I know Jarrett's telling the truth. Even Minerva said I was drugged."

Lydia looked at Jarrett. "I've never met the Sawyer man, but I'm sure Hannah is like every other woman, if she marries she'll want to pick out her own husband."

"Calvin Sawyer has the body of a man and the mind of a child," Jarrett said flatly. "And Hannah is right, Verbena had drugged her so she wouldn't know she was being forced to marry him."

"When did you fall out of your chair and break your arm?"

"A few days ago, I'm not sure how many. Calvin and his sister were visiting Aunt Verbena. She told him to roll me out to the veranda. He tried, but he couldn't control my wheelchair. It hit the door facing and I tumbled out."

"Why didn't you let me know about this? I could have come and got you."

"Actually, Tobias told me it happened the evening before Verbena arranged the wedding. A doctor had seen Hannah's arm and the Johnsons thought the important thing was to stop the wedding."

"I can understand that." She looked around. "Of course, Hannah can't stay here with you, Jarrett. I'll take her with me."

"I thought that same thing, Lydia, then it occurred to me that Verbena would find a way to make sure Hannah wasn't allowed to live with you. I don't want to see her sent back to live with her aunt."

"I don't think Aunt Verbena would try to take me away from Lydia now that you know what she's capable of."

"I think you're probably wrong, honey." Lydia patted her arm. "If Aunt Verbena would try to marry you to someone like you say this Sawyer man is, she'll do anything to make sure you and I are not together."

"That's why I wanted you to come here today, Lydia," Jarrett said. "I haven't talked this over with Hannah yet, but I think the best solution is to take her to Arizona."

Lydia frowned. "What in the world would she do in Arizona?"

"I'd be with Drina," Hannah whispered.

"Of course, that's the answer. Though I'll miss you something awful, you'd be where Aunt Verbena could never hurt you again."

"I'd miss you, too, Lydia, but I've wished many times I could have gone to Arizona with Drina. Thanks to Jarrett, it looks like this is one wish that can come true."

Lydia turned to Jarrett. "When would you be leaving?"

"Shortly, but not until after tomorrow. I know that's a special day for Hannah, and I think she should spend it with her sister."

"What's tomorrow?" Hannah frowned, then it was if a light went on in her memory. "Oh, it's my birthday."

"Your eighteenth birthday, if I'm not mistaken." Lydia smiled at her. "You will be a grown woman tomorrow, baby sister."

Oh, yes and what a beautiful woman, Jarrett thought, but he kept it to himself.

"I feel like I'm a woman already."

"You've had enough happen to you to prove that you are a woman in every sense of the word," Jarrett said.

"You're right about that, Jarrett. I don't know many people who have faced the problems that Hannah has had thrust upon her and handled them with such grace. I'm really proud of my sister."

"Thank you, Lydia."

"You're welcome." Lydia patted Hannah's shoulder then stood. "I hate to leave, but I need to get back to the saloon. Bradly is out of town for the day, but he'll be back soon. I need to see that things are going well at work."

"I understand, and I thank you for coming." Jarrett stood with her.

She looked at Hannah. "What time shall I pick you up tomorrow?"

"Pick me up?"

"Yes. I want to take you out to lunch then maybe to do some shopping and…"

"No, Lydia." Hannah shook her head. "I want you to come and spend the day with me here. I don't want to go out except maybe to the dining room downstairs. We can have lunch and then come back to this lovely room and spend the rest of the time together."

"Are you sure?"

"I'm sure."

"Then, I'll see you about noon tomorrow." She kissed Hannah's cheek and Jarrett walked her to the door.

"Maybe she'll change her mind," he whispered. "I think she's overwhelmed by being here in the first place."

"I think you're right." She held out her hand. "Thank you for everything you've done for her, Jarrett."

♥♥♥

In the middle of the night, Jarrett was jarred out of a restless sleep by a piercing scream. Knowing the scream came from Hannah's room, he grabbed his gun off the night table as his feet hit the floor and dashed to her room. His mind dragged up all sorts of scenarios as he ran. Did Verbena send someone to kidnap her niece? Had someone entered the room to rob or harm the woman? Did someone frighten her? He didn't bother to knock or call out, but hurried through the door and didn't stop until he was beside her bed.

From the moonlight coming through the window, he could see there was no one else in the room. Hannah was huddled in her bed, and she was crying.

Jarrett put his pistol on the table and sat down on the edge of her bed. He reached down and touched her arm. "Hannah, wake up. You're having a bad dream."

She continued to shake and he whispered, "Hannah, honey. It's all right. I'm here and I'm not going to let anything or anyone hurt you."

She surprised him when she opened her tear-filled eyes, seemed to recognize him, then threw her good arm around his mid-section and cried against his chest.

He didn't know what to do, so he just held her and let her cry.

In a little while, she muttered, "I thought Aunt Verbena was here and she had a big knife. She said she was going to kill me if I didn't marry Calvin."

He held her tightly. "Your aunt is nowhere near here, Hannah. Even if she were, there's no way I'd let her get close you. Unless you want to, you never have to see that woman's face again."

"Oh, Jarrett. I feel so safe with you."

"I'm glad you feel that way, because you'll always be safe with me."

"I don't know how I can ever thank you for all you've done for me."

"You don't have to thank me, Hannah. I just want you to feel safe and be happy."

She was quiet a moment, then without warning she whispered, "I love you, Jarrett."

Flabbergasted, he wasn't sure what to say or do. He cared for Hannah, he really did—but love? He wasn't sure about that. Still, no other woman had made him have the feelings she'd made him feel. This very night he'd not been able to sleep for an hour or two just thinking about her and how her presence was affecting him. He knew it was close to eleven when, after his third glass of whiskey and much tossing and turning, he'd finally drifted off. Now, there was the hint of light creeping through the window. It was the next day.

Knowing he had to acknowledge her statement in some way, he did the only thing he could think of to do. He took hold of her chin, lifted her face toward his, looked down in her trusting eyes and without saying a word, he slowly pressed his lips to hers.

If he wasn't the practical man that he was, he would've sworn he'd felt something magical happen in that moment. Never before, after kissing a woman, had he wanted to stand up and scream as loud as he could, 'this woman is mine,' though he did say it in his mind. He also knew, without a doubt, that he'd one day say it to the world in spite of all he could do to stop himself.

It soon dawned on him that he couldn't, in good conscience, continue to kiss her. He mustered all the strength he could and forced himself to pull away. Deep down, he had the feeling Hannah wouldn't have refused him if he'd made love to her right then, but he couldn't do it to this innocent young woman. Not now. Not yet. Of course, his body and his human instinct told him to take advantage of the situation, but he knew it wasn't the right thing to do. Not to someone so young and innocent. It then dawned on him she was eighteen today. She was a woman, not a child. But it still didn't make her anything but a naïve young woman who knew nothing about life or the way men reacted to the stimulus of being so close to a beautiful half-dressed woman.

Finally, he realized there was something he could say in response to her saying she loved him without declaring a commitment to her. He pulled away enough to look into her eyes. "It's your birthday morning and I want to be the first person to wish you a happy birthday, Hannah."

She smiled. "It is my birthday, isn't it?"

"Yes, it is, but it's still too early to get up. Why don't you try to sleep a little longer and we'll have a big breakfast together to celebrate when you wake up."

"I'll look forward to having breakfast with you, but please don't order so much this time."

"I'll see if I can control myself." He winked at her and stood. "I'll see you a little later."

"Do you have to go?"

He nodded. "I think it's best if I do, Hannah." He leaned down and kissed her forehead. "It won't be long until I'll be back. Now, lie down and get that extra sleep. Lydia will probably keep you busy today."

She cuddled down, but took hold of his arm. "Will you kiss me again?"

"I just did."

"I don't mean on the forehead."

His breathing became heavier, but he again leaned forward and pressed his lips to hers. Knowing this couldn't continue to go on, he pulled away and said, "Now, go to sleep and I'll see you later."

"Thank you, Jarrett."

"I told you not to thank me for protecting you, Hannah. I want to do that."

She gave him a half smile. "I appreciate that, but I was thanking you for the kiss. You're the first man who has ever kissed me, and I liked it very much. In fact, it was wonderful."

He was startled at her words. Swallowing, he muttered, "You're welcome. Now like I said, go back to sleep."

He hurried out of the room before she could say anything else.

It was ten o'clock in the morning when Verbena finished washing the one dish she'd used to eat some canned peaches and a slice of stale bread. As she'd completed the job, it crossed her mind that this was Hannah's birthday. The stupid girl had won. Not on her own, but thanks to that interfering Jarrett MacMichael, she'd won anyway. She now had the jewels that should have rightly belonged to Verbena. After all, they were family heirlooms and Verbena felt she should be the one to get them. Never mind the fact that their mother had left them to Ella, the eldest daughter. So what if Ella had thought the jewels would be the way for her poor crippled child to hire somebody to take care of her if Verbena threw her out of the house when she was eighteen. It wasn't right. Those jewels should be hers, and she didn't like what had happened at all.

Someday, Hannah was going to pay. So would everybody that had helped her win, including Mr. Jarrett MacMichael and Burl Hamilton.

Saying a few choice words about her family, Verbena crossed the dining room and started down the hall to her room. A rap on the front door from the brass knocker stopped her. She paused and wondered if she should answer it. It could be that MacMichael fool coming back to claim something else. When he read further in the paper he'd bought from Burl, he'd find there were other things Hannah could claim.

The rap sounded again. This time louder.

Taking a deep breath to prepare herself for anything, she moved to the door and opened it. Hilda and Calvin stood on the other side. "Please let us in, Mrs. Wedington. It's important that we speak to you."

"What do you have to say that hasn't already been said?" Verbena didn't want to deal with them this morning. Her business with them was over and they were only a nuisance to her now.

"I think you'll be glad we came by, but please let us in so we can tell you something."

Verbena stood aside and they entered. Without asking, they went directly to the formal parlor.

"Are you going to give me cookies and milk, today?" Calvin asked.

"Not today." Verbena knew her voice wasn't very pleasant, but she didn't care. They shouldn't have come calling without being invited. She turned to Hilda, who had taken a seat in one of the chairs in front of the settee, again, without being invited. "Well, out with it. What was so important that you had to come by so early this morning without an invitation?"

"You don't have to be rude, Mrs. Wedington. It's after ten o'clock. You must have slept late."

Verbena raised an eyebrow. She was surprised it was so late, because she never slept this long in the morning. But she had been exhausted from lack of sleep since Jarrett left with Hannah. "I'm sorry, Hilda. I'm not sleeping well, but you're right, I shouldn't take it out on you."

Hilda smiled. "That's all right. I just wanted to warn you about something."

"What's that?"

"Everybody at church is talking about us and I wanted to let you know what people are saying so you can be prepared."

"What are you talking about?"

"Undoubtedly, Reverend Calhoun told his wife that you and I were trying to force Calvin and your niece to marry without their knowing what was going on. She must have called on some of the women in church and told them. Now it seems everyone in town knows about the wedding. They're thinking of asking us to drop out of the Ladies' Bible study group because they're saying what we did was a sin against God's holy ordinance of marriage. They've already decided to ask us to resign from the decorating committee at church."

Verbena dropped to the settee. "This can't be happening."

"They say they believe we duped the Reverend and if some businessman from out west somewhere hadn't come in and demanded we stop the wedding, a travesty would've taken place here that day."

Verbena frowned. "After all I've done for that church, I can't believe Reverend Calhoun is trying to make people think he didn't have anything to do with the situation."

"It seems that he is doing that very thing, but when you get right down to it, he didn't have much to do with it. I think he actually thought he was doing what Calvin and your niece wanted." She shook her head. "We were fools to think we could pull something like that off without any repercussions, weren't we?"

"Maybe, but if Burl hadn't …" A thought crossed her mind. This was all Burl Hamilton's fault. If he hadn't sold that paper to MacMichael, Calvin and Hannah would be married and the jewels would be hers. She wasn't going to take it from any of them. Somebody was going to pay for what they'd done, and she might as well start with her brother-in-law. Abruptly, she stood, startling both Hilda and her brother. "Calvin, can you hitch up a buggy to a horse?"

"Yes, ma'am. I been doing it for Hilda for a long time, haven't I Hilda?"

"Yes, Calvin you have, but what's that got to do with..."

"Never mind, Hilda." She turned to Calvin. "I want you to go to the barn and hitch up my horse and buggy. I have somewhere I need to go this morning and I need to get started."

"Mrs. Wedington, don't you want to discuss this further?"

"What else is there to say? We can't stop those gossipy ladies, but I have a score to settle with someone. I can certainly make him pay for what he's done to me, and I'm going to do it."

"Are you talking about the man who came in and stopped the wedding?"

"I'll get to him later. Right now I have to go visit my brother-in-law. He's a horrible man, and he's the one who really messed up our plans."

Hilda looked confused. "How?"

"He's the one who let MacMichael find out what we were up to."

"How did your bother-in-law know?"

"Stop asking questions, Hilda. I need go get going." She turned to Calvin.

"Go do as I ask. Hitch up my horse."

"Will you give me a dog if I do?"

Verbena was disgusted with Calvin and his asking for a dog. She turned and yelled at him, "No, I won't. You don't need a dog. Now, stop stalling and go hitch up my buggy like I told you to do, and do it now."

"You look as if you're ready to murder someone, Mrs. Wedington. Maybe Calvin and I should go with you."

Verbena started to tell her they could go along, but she then thought better of it. She turned back toward Hilda and ignored Calvin. "No, Hilda. Not this time. Maybe when I go after MacMichael, you can come along."

"But he scares me."

"You have to remember, he's just a man. There isn't a man on earth who can outsmart a woman. Especially when he doesn't know you're coming for him. Hector learned that the hard way."

"I don't understand."

"It's best you don't." She frowned at Calvin. "Are you still here? I thought I told you to go hitch up my horse."

"I don't want to."

Verbena turned toward Hilda. "Make your brother mind me."

Though Hilda saw Calvin frown, then pick up Verbena's prized marble statue of David, she didn't get a chance to answer Verbena or stop him. Because in the next second he came down on Verbena's head with it. Without a sound, the woman crumpled to the floor.

"Oh, my Lord, Calvin, what have you done?" Hilda cried.

Calvin's voice was flat and without compassion when he said, "She should've got me a dog."

Chapter 21

"Oh, Lydia, it's been a wonderful birthday." Hannah clapped her hands and sat back on the small settee in her hotel room. "The pretty yellow dress you gave me is perfect. The lunch in the dining room was delicious, and I've enjoyed being here with you so much. It's the best birthday I've ever had."

"It has been wonderful spending it with you, little sister. I'm so glad Jarrett was thoughtful enough to give us this time to ourselves."

"Yes, it was thoughtful of him. He's a wonderful man."

"I'm so glad he had the doctor see you today and bring you the crutches, and I'm glad the doctor said you were well enough to travel." Lydia smiled at her sister. "It was sweet of Jarrett to give you that lovely cape, too."

"He said I'd need it in Arizona this fall."

Lydia reached over and took her hand. "Being eighteen is special, and you need to share it with those you love. I'm so glad we got to be together most of the day."

"It's certainly been different from the birthdays I spent at Aunt Verbena's house."

"I know. I remember how she'd only allow me to visit you for about an hour, at most." She squeezed the hand she was still holding. "You never have to worry about spending another birthday at her house."

"I'm happy about that." She smiled at Lydia with bright, shiny eyes. "Jarrett told me this morning that he'd always protect me, and I know he will."

"I'm sure that as long as he's around, he'll do just that, and when you get to Arizona, you'll have Drina and her husband to protect and love you."

"I'm sure I'll still have Jarrett, too."

"I know he'll be your friend, but you won't see him much after you move in with Drina and her husband."

Hannah gave her sister a coy look. "Oh, I think I will."

Lydia frowned. "What makes you say that?"

Hannah wasn't sure she should tell her sister, but she felt she had to share her happiness with somebody. Still smiling, she said, "He kissed me, Lydia."

Lydia raised an eyebrow. "Why did he do that?"

Hannah knew since she'd started, she had to tell her sister the details. She explained about the bad dream, her calling out, and Jarrett coming in her room to comfort her. "And when I told him I loved him, he kissed me." She sighed a contented sigh and leaned back against the flowered pillow of the settee.

Lydia frowned. "How dare he."

"What do you mean? It was wonderful."

"Did he do anything else?"

"No. He said he had to go back to his room and he wanted me to go back to sleep."

"And that was all?"

"Well, I did thank him for the kiss, and asked him to kiss me again."

"Did he?"

"Yes, but it was quicker the second time, and he hurried out of the room before I could tell him I wanted it to last longer."

Lydia sat upright and glared at her sister. "You must never do that again, Hannah."

Hannah was confused. "Do what?"

"Oh, Hannah, you're so naïve. A woman never tells a man she loves him before he tells her, and she certainly doesn't ask him to kiss her."

"Why not? He didn't seem to mind. When he kissed me the second time, I knew he loved me, too." Hannah went on. "I told you how we had a wonderful breakfast together, and how he left for a while, then came back with the doctor and those crutches. As soon as the doctor left, he gave me the cape. He said for the rest of my birthday present he was going to teach me to walk."

"I'm glad he's doing that. I suggested crutches to Aunt Verbena once, but she said you'd fall and hurt yourself. I knew it was useless to argue with her."

"Well, Jarrett has faith in me. He held me up and walked me around the room to strengthen my good leg. He said in a day or so, he would let me try the crutches, but only when he was here to make sure I didn't fall."

"I'm glad he's so attentive, Hannah, but you must remember, he's not doing these things because he loves you. Drina's husband hired him to come here to investigate Aunt Verbena and to make sure you were all right. Once he collects his money for doing the job, his responsibility for you will be over. I'm sure he plans that once you get to Arizona, he'll leave you with Drina and you may never see him again."

Hannah frowned. "What are you saying?"

"Surely, you knew he was only doing the job Aaron Wilcox paid him to do."

Hannah felt her heart plummet to her knees. So Jarrett didn't kiss her because he loved her. He was only doing it because she asked him to. How could she have been so stupid? To keep Lydia from seeing how crushed she felt, she smiled and said, "Well, at least he got me away from Aunt Verbena."

"That's true." Lydia stood and looked down at her. "Now, when he gets back today, don't you dare ask him to kiss you again. Just be thankful for the reason he came into our lives, and look forward to going to Arizona to live with Drina."

"I promise to do as you say, big sister." Hannah reached for her. "Let me hug you good-bye, and thank you again for spending my birthday with me."

Lydia hugged her. "We'll spend more time together before you leave."

As her sister went out the door, Hannah let the tears she'd been able to hold back slide down her cheeks. So Jarrett didn't care for her. He'd only kissed her because he was a man, and they did that sort of thing. How could she have been so unwise as to think he loved her? And how was she going to keep her broken heart from showing the world how she felt about the man? A man she knew she'd fallen in love with, not because he was being good to her, but because he was the type of man she'd always wished for.

It was a good thing she had all the experience of hiding her feelings from Aunt Verbena through the years. She just hoped she could continue the ruse with Tobias and Minerva. And especially, Jarrett. She only hoped he thought her confessing her love for him was just a slip of the tongue, or merely gratitude. Not the truth that it really was.

"Good morning, Miss Hannah." Minerva opened the drapes as Hannah began to stretch. "Did you have a good birthday yesterday?"

"It was wonderful. For the first time, Lydia and I weren't interrupted, and we got to spend a lot of time together."

"Good. Mr. Jarrett said you was tired last night and went to bed early."

"I did, and I slept wonderfully." She sat up and looked at Minerva. "I've been meaning to ask, where are you and Tobias staying?"

"We's has some friends we stay with."

"I wish you could stay here with me."

Minerva grinned. "Mr. Jarrett said he'd get us a room, but we's told him not to try. There ain't no way this here hotel would let us stay here. We been free for more'n twenty years, but white folks still don't want to associate with us."

"That's such a shame, Minerva, but I don't guess we can do anything about it."

"Mr. Jarrett says it won't be as bad in Ariezonie."

"I'm so glad you're going to Arizona with me."

"We's always said wherever you go away from here, we goes, too." She moved to the bed. "Now, let's get you dressed. Mr. Jarrett done asked Miz

Lydia and her husband to come and have breakfast with you and him this mornin'. Does you want to wear the new dress your sister give you?"

"I was going to save it, but since they're coming, yes, I will wear it. I want Lydia to see how nice it looks on me."

"I's glad you's gonna wear it. I think yeller will look purty on you."

"Thank you." She took the pan of water Minerva brought over and began to wash with the soft washcloth. "Did Jarrett say why he'd invited Lydia and Bradly to come for breakfast?"

"No, Miss Hannah. He didn't tell me nothing. He just sent Tobias to get them."

"Then I better hurry. I don't want then to have to wait on me."

Thirty minutes later, Minerva rolled Hannah into Jarrett's room. He stood and laid the paper he was reading aside as they entered. "My, don't you look pretty this morning. Yellow is a good color on you."

"Thank you. Lydia gave me this dress for my birthday."

"She did a good job picking it out for you." He moved to take the back of the wheelchair from Minerva. "I'm going to go ahead and roll you up to the table. Everyone should be here soon, and they'll serve breakfast. In the meantime, I have some tea for you."

"Thank you," she said again, and tried to avoid his eyes. She wished he wouldn't be so nice. It was making it hard for her to hide her feelings from him.

By the time she stirred the sugar in her tea, Lydia and Bradly arrived. Soon after the greetings, the waiter arrived with the breakfast trays. Again, Hannah was amazed at the amount of food, but everyone else seemed to take it for granted. She guessed it was because she was so used to what Aunt Verbena sent her. Unless Minerva slipped her extra food, she was often relegated to one or two things on her plate.

"It was nice of you to invite us this morning, MacMichael," Bradly said as they all sat at the table.

"I think what I have to tell you is of interest not only to Hannah and Lydia, but to you and the Johnsons as well." He looked around at them. "I know you said you'd already had breakfast, Tobias, but I want you and Minerva to join us, even if you only have coffee."

They were reluctant at first, but were finally persuaded to join the others at the table. After the plates were filled and everyone was settled, Jarrett said, "Tobias is aware that I visited Burl Hamilton a couple of days ago and was able to convince him to let me have the paper that was drawn up between Verbena, your mother, and your father." He looked at Lydia, then Hannah. "The only other person to know what the document said was the banker who drew it up and is now dead, like your mother. Until I got a copy, the only two people living who knew what the paper contained were Verbena and Burl."

He took a deep breath and went on. "In return for what I paid for the paper, Burl signed an agreement saying that when something happened to him or if he failed to keep up the taxes on the place, the farm was to go to you, Lydia."

"What about Hannah and Drina?" Bradly asked.

"Drina is in Arizona and I already knew I was going to take Hannah there so the farm would do neither of them any good. The place is so rundown it isn't worth much, but I thought maybe you and Lydia could sell it for a little profit."

"I see."

"Lydia, you told me about the meetings your mother had with Verbena and your father, though you were too young to know what they were about." She nodded and he continued. "Of course, Hannah was only a baby and knew nothing of what was going on. One thing the paper says is that there was some family heirloom jewelry that was handed down by your grandmother. This jewelry was to be given to Hannah on or around her eighteenth birthday to be used to pay someone to look after her. The only stipulation was that if she was married by then, the jewels would go to Verbena to pay her for raising Hannah to this age."

Hannah couldn't help blurting, "That's why she tried to marry me off. She wanted the jewels."

Jarrett reached over and took her hand. "That's right, honey. When I stopped the wedding, I foiled her plans. I had already read some of the document, and I knew what she was up to. I wouldn't leave there that night without making her give the jewelry to me. It's over there in the wardrobe, and as soon as we finish eating, I'll give the box to you."

"Why didn't she just destroy the paper and take the jewels?" Bradly looked puzzled.

"She probably would have, but she knew Burl had a copy of it. As long as he was alive, there was no way she could get away with anything. He agreed to go along with their plans because she was to keep the taxes paid on the farm, bail him out of jail when needed, and give him a little money along the way."

Hannah looked at him. "Why did she go along with it after mother died? She could have thrown me out at any time."

"She had no choice." Jarrett still had hold of her hand and he squeezed it. "She knew if she tried anything until you were eighteen, her world would crumble."

"Why?" Lydia stared at him.

"I don't know any easy way to tell you this, but your mother and Burl knew something that could have sent Verbena to prison for the rest of her life."

"I don't understand." Hannah saw Tobias nodding. "Do you know, Tobias?"

"No. I didn't know, but Minerva and me had our suspicions. We jest couldn't prove nothing."

"What had Aunt Verbena done?"

"It is all documented in the paper. But the gist of it is, your mother had come to see her sister to ask her to raise Hannah because she knew she wouldn't live to do it. Of course, being the selfish person she is, Verbena refused to do so. Your mother was upset, but had to accept the fact that you would probably be put in a home since your father didn't want you. It was too late for her to go home, so Ella decided to stay one more night at the Wedington's house. Verbena and Hector had a big fight before they went to bed that night and the lady was livid. The paper didn't say what the fight was about, but the next morning, Verbena got up first, put a string across the top of the stairs so when Hector started down he'd stumble. Which he did. The fall didn't kill him, but he was unconscious, He never regained consciousness, and died a few days later. Verbena probably would have gotten away with it, but your mother had you with her, Hannah. And as little ones often do, you were fussy and your mother started downstairs to get you some milk. She witnessed the entire thing."

Both Hannah and Lydia gasped. Bradly looked stunned and Minerva nodded her head.

Finally, Lydia asked, "If she murdered her husband, what kept her from doing the same to Hannah, and then claiming the jewels?"

"There is a line in there that says if something happens to Hannah before she is eighteen, the jewels are to go to you and Drina."

"So, she had no choice but to keep me in her house, though she never wanted me." Tears came to Hannah's eyes. "I guess I've never had anyone but my mother and my sisters who really cared for me."

"Now, Miss Hannah, you knows Tobias and me cares about you."

"I'm sorry, Minerva. I know you do, and I appreciate it."

Jarrett touched her arm. "I care about you, too, Hannah."

She wanted to say, "As long as you're being paid to do so," but she didn't. She only muttered, "Thank you."

Lydia asked, "Is there anything else in there we should know about?"

"The only other thing is that if something happens to your aunt, the three of you get the house she lives in. The rest of the Wedington fortune goes to some nephew of Hector's. He lives in Atlanta."

"I don't particularly want her house. Do you, Hannah?"

"No, and I don't think Drina will, either."

"Well, the fact that the woman is alive makes the point moot," Bradly said.

"You're right." Jarrett nodded. "The other things in the document simply detail how Verbena is to raise Hannah until she marries or is eighteen and gets the jewels. I'll be glad to let you read it, but the main thing I want to do is ask you what you want done about the crime Verbena has committed."

"Maybe we should ask Drina, too. She also has a stake in all this." Lydia took her husband's arm. "I say we check with her. What about you, Hannah?"

"I agree. She should be told."

"I'll wire Wilcox today." Jarrett pushed back his chair. "Then, let me get the jewelry so you can see what your mother left."

♥♥♥

Five weeks later, Everett MacMichael walked into his Flagstaff, Arizona office and found Jarrett slumped over his desk, writing.

"Well, speak of the devil. When did you get back?"

"I wasn't speaking of the devil, but I got back this morning."

"How did things work out?"

"Fine. I have the money ready to be deposited in the bank." He tossed it to his twin.

Everett looked at the amount written on the slip of paper wrapped around the bundle of money and his eyebrow shot up. "Wow. Wilcox must have been pleased with your work."

"He was, and his wife was ecstatic."

"That's all well and good, but I'm surprised you came into the office so quickly. I figured you'd be down on Chester Street as soon as you got home."

Jarrett shrugged. "I'm in no hurry to go there."

Again, Everett's eyebrow went up. "Uh-oh, something must have happened to you in Georgia."

Jarrett ignored him and handed him the paper he'd been writing.

"What's this?"

"My report on the job I did in Savannah."

"If I read this, will it give me a clue as to your attitude?"

"What do you mean?"

"You know what I mean, Jarrett. You usually get back from a job, rush to see Miss Newell and live it up with her for a few days before you get back to work. Now, here you sit on your first day back, working away."

"I figured you and Miss Newell had cut me out while I was gone."

"I haven't seen much of the lady. There's a new banker in town who seems to have attracted her attention. Besides, I'm tired of fighting you for her affections."

"I thought we were having a friendly little competition."

"The truth of the matter is, I've kind of lost interest."

Jarrett eyed him. "That doesn't sound like you."

"Well, there's a new minister in town…"

"Don't tell me you've had some kind of strange religious experience."

"No, Jarrett, I've not had anything of the sort. The religion we were brought up in is good enough for me. It just so happens that Reverend Dench has a daughter I've kind of taken a liking to. Been going to church every Sunday just to get to take a walk with the pretty redheaded lady after the service ends."

Jarrett stared at him. "Are you telling me you've fallen in love with some preacher's daughter?"

Everett shrugged. "Could be heading that way."

Jarrett stood, put on his Stetson and held out his hand. "I've got to digest this. Give me the money back. I'm taking it to the bank."

"Gonna stop on Chester Street?"

"I don't know."

"Maybe you should. Might put you in a better mood."

Jarrett shook his head and went out the door without further conversation.

On the way to the bank, Jarrett let his mind wander over what had just happened. It wasn't that he thought Everett would never meet the right woman and want to get married; it was just that he thought that right woman would be somebody more like Felicia Newell, not some preacher's daughter. A preacher's daughter wasn't off limits. In fact, mom and dad would be thrilled to see Everett settle down with any woman, and a preacher's kid would be a bonus. Though the MacMichaels had always gone to church and tried to live right, Everett was the one who rebelled the most. Said he didn't need church to make him a good man and he didn't have much to do with it. Now, he was saying he was going to services every Sunday so he could walk around with the Reverend's offspring. It didn't make a lot of sense.

Wonder what he'd say if he knew I can't get sweet Hannah Hamilton off my mind? I miss that young woman more than I thought I'd ever miss anyone. Maybe Everett is right. Maybe I should make a trip down to Chester Street and see if it makes me forget what might have been.

But he didn't go to Chester Street. He went back to the office. As he came through the door, Everett said, "Now, I know."

"Know what?"

"Why you're in such a rotten mood, and why you're not interested in going to Chester Street."

"How do you know I didn't go?"

"Look, Jarrett, for one reason, you haven't been gone long enough to go down there and back, much less spend any time with Miss Felicia. For another, you're in love with Hannah Hamilton."

"Who says so?"

Everett held up the report. "You do. You say it on every page you write. That woman has your heart clutched in her little hands, and you might as well admit it."

"I admit I like Hannah a lot, but she's as naïve as they come. Besides, she's only eighteen years old. That's too young for me."

"Who says age has anything to do with it? Miss Dench is only nineteen, and I lied to you when I said I was only interested in getting to know her."

Jarrett's brow shot up. "Then tell me what you're trying to say."

"Have a seat. This may come as a shock."

Jarrett sat, but he didn't say anything.

"I met Callie the day she and her father arrived in town. I've never believed in such a thing, but I swear, Jarrett, it was love at first sight. She seems to feel the same way, because I asked her to marry me two days ago...and she said yes."

Jarrett stared at him. "How do you know it's love and not just lust?"

"Brother, I know, just like you know how you feel about Miss Hamilton."

"I said I liked the girl. That's all there is to it. I'm not ready to tie myself to any one woman–even the beautiful Miss Hamilton."

"Deny it all you want to, brother, but it won't change the facts. You're in love with this woman, whether you want to admit it or not."

Jarrett shook his head and changed the subject. "So, when do you plan to marry this Callie Dench?"

"We want to get married soon, but there's only one problem."

"What problem?"

"She's hesitant because of my job."

Jarrett frowned. "I don't understand."

"I hate to tell you this, but she says she'd worry about me traipsing all over the country trying to find criminals and poking into other people's business where I might get shot or some such thing. To ease her mind, I told her when we were married, I'd give up the detective business and find something to do that is more stable and can be done around here so I wouldn't have to travel. Hell, I might even go back into ranching. The older I get, the more interesting it becomes."

Jarrett was surprised. "So, you're just going to walk out on our business?"

"I wouldn't do you like that. I'd stay until you found a new partner."

Jarrett frowned. "That's nice of you."

"Well, it's the truth, and as a matter of fact, I may have already found a partner for you."

"Oh?"

"Remember I mentioned a new banker in town? Well, he's not only interested in Miss Newell, but he's interested in buying into our firm. You'll like him. He has the assets, and he's had some training with Pinkerton."

"I don't know about this. I'm not sure I'd like working with a stranger."

"Then we could sell him the entire business and you could start your own firm." Everett grinned at him. "You might even want to set it up in this town called Hatchet Sprigs instead of Flagstaff. That way, you could be close to your lady love."

Still somewhat stunned, Jarrett muttered, "I'll think about it. In the meantime, tell me about Miss Dench and why you're willing to give up everything we've built here for her."

Chapter 22

It was three in the afternoon when Drina pushed the door open to Hannah's huge room. "It's time you took a break. I brought you some tea."

"Good. I'm ready for it." Hannah laid the pink dress she was sewing for Geneva Ragsdale aside. "I've had to sew this tucked front three times and I'm still not sure I have it right."

Drina smiled. "That's not like you, honey. You never seem to have any trouble with your sewing back in Savannah. What's the matter?"

"I'm not sure. Maybe it's the change in scenery." She took the cup Drina handed her.

"I think it might be more than that. I know you were glad to get away from Aunt Verbena, but for some reason, you've seemed a little blue since you arrived. Do you miss Lydia?"

"Of course I miss her, but she was glad that I was getting out of town. Especially after Aunt Verbena's house burned down."

"As much as I detested our aunt, that was a terrible way to die. I don't understand why she chose to burn herself to death."

"Neither do I, but we decided it might be because we'd found out she killed her husband and was afraid she'd have to go to prison."

"That is one way to look at it."

"Of course, nobody knew that fact except us. The paper speculated she killed herself because she must have gone soft in the head."

"You and I both know Aunt Verbena would have never gone soft in the head." Drina looked at Hannah and sighed. "You don't suppose somebody killed her and set her house on fire, do you?"

"I have no idea. Jarrett said he'd stay in town and investigate if we wanted him to, but Lydia said since the police had ruled it a suicide, let's just let it go. I agreed with her."

"I guess there is nothing that can be done about it now." Drina sipped her tea. "Speaking of Jarrett MacMichael, Aaron and I were thrilled at the job he did in Savannah. Not only bringing you here, but also in finding out why you'd had to live with our aunt for so long."

Hannah dropped her eyes. "Yes, he's a good man. It's too bad…" Her voice dropped off and a tear slid down her cheek.

Drina set her tea aside and reached for Hannah. "What's the matter, little sister?"

"Oh, Drina if I tell you something, will you not laugh at me?"

"Of course I won't laugh. Tell me anything you want to."

"I thought when I got here it would stop, but it hasn't. It seems to get stronger and stronger."

"You're frightening me, Hannah. What is it?"

"Don't be frightened, Drina. It's just that I thought when I got here and saw you and started my sewing business, I'd forget it, but I can't."

"Forget what?"

"That I love Jarrett MacMichael. And before you say anything, let me assure you, I know how I feel. I've tried to look at other men and think I could love somebody else, but I can't. It always comes back to the fact that Jarrett is the man I wished for and the man I fell in love with." She snuffed and added, "I wish that he would love me back."

"Oh, Hannah, I don't know what to say."

"You don't have to say anything, Drina. There's nothing to be said, anyway."

"I will tell you this. When I first got here, it didn't take me long to fall in love with Aaron, but he wanted nothing to do with me."

Hannah pulled back and looked at her. "But when I see the two of you together, you act as if you're very much in love with each other."

"Oh, honey, we are, now. It took him a while to feel that way about me, but I didn't give up. He eventually realized that we could be happy together, and then he fell as much in love with me as I am with him."

"Do you think if I just be patient—"

"I don't know, Hannah. Jarrett lives a long way away from here, and Aaron and I were actually in the same house. But I don't want you to give up wishing. You never know what will happen. It wouldn't hurt to say a prayer here and there, too."

"Oh, Drina, I do that. In fact, my wishes often come out as prayers."

The next week turned into a busy one for the MacMichaels. Late on Sunday, their mother and father arrived for Everett's upcoming wedding. They took rooms at the hotel and insisted on meeting their sons for supper at the hotel dining room. Of course, Callie Dench and her father were invited to meet Everett's parents. It turned out the Reverend Dench was a pleasant man, and they all enjoyed getting to know him and his delightful red-haired daughter. Unfortunately, Mrs. Dench had died when Callie was twelve, and there were no siblings. Abigail MacMichael assured her that as soon as their daughter and her husband and their twins arrived, there would be enough family around to celebrate...not only the wedding, but every event that came up in the future.

Jarrett looked forward to seeing his sister and her family. It had been a long time. The only problem was, he kept wanting to tell his family about Hannah, but he refused to do so. He didn't want to take away any of the attention from his twin brother at this special time in his life.

Instead of selling the entire business, the MacMichaels decided to sell only the cases that had never been solved, which didn't amount to very many. They decided to let their father take the closed files back to his ranch and store them for a while.

"What do you plan to do with the rest of them?" Cyrus MacMichael asked Jarrett when they began cleaning out the office on Monday.

"We've already weeded out the pending files and sent wires or got in touch with the people involved to ask if they want their cases handled by the new man."

"Have you got any answers?"

"Most of them have come back and said they did want to stay active. Everett has gone to the telegraph office to see if we have any more replies."

"Looks like you have it all taken care of."

"Most of it, anyway."

"I know Everett is set, but what do you plan to do without this company, Jarrett?"

"I'm not sure."

"You can always come back and work on the ranch."

"I know, but I've been thinking about something else, Dad."

"What's that?"

"I'm not sure yet."

Cyrus didn't say anything else, and the two men continued to work. In a few minutes, Jarrett paused. "I want to ask you something, Dad."

"Sure, son. What?"

"How did you know you were in love with Mom?"

Cyrus laid down the file he had in his hand and looked at his son. "It may sound trite, but you'll know it when it happens. Oh, you may fight it for all you're worth, but it won't do you any good, because you're in love."

"Is that the way it was with you?"

"It sure was. You know I was pretty wild when I was a young man. Made my living rambling from here to there, picking up any odd job I could land. Then I met your mama in Phoenix, and my rambling days were over."

"So you just quit rambling and settled down."

Cyrus chuckled. "Not by a long shot. I left there as fast as I could and made my way through New Mexico and Texas, but nothing I did would help me forget that auburn-haired young woman who made my heart turn flips, not only every time I saw her, but every time I thought about her, too. I finally gave up and went back to Phoenix. Two months later, I bought a little spread nearby and married Abigail Millsap in spite of her father's protest. Been a happy man ever since. As you know, that spread has grown considerably and believe it or not, so has my love for Miss Abigail."

Jarrett smiled. "That sure answers my question."

"I'm assuming you've met someone who makes you have these feelings, but you're running from it, just like I did."

"That I am. I've even thought about resuming an old affair I was having before I went to Savannah and met Hannah."

"Tell me about this Hannah, son."

Before he could stop himself, Jarrett was telling his father all about Hannah and the way they met. He even recounted how he'd saved her from the horrible marriage and took her to his hotel. "One night, out of the blue, she told me she loved me, Dad. It threw me for a loop. I didn't know what to say or do."

"So what did you do?"

"I kissed her."

"And?"

"That's it. I just kissed her. Well, not 'just kissed her'. I don't think I'd ever been moved by a woman's lips like I was by Hannah's."

"I've only got one thing to say, Jarrett. You know it will be hard to be married to a woman who will never be able to walk, but on the other hand, if you love her, it'll be harder to live without her."

Jarrett nodded. "You're right, Dad. I'm not going to say anything to anyone else until after Everett and Callie are married, but as soon as all the festivities are over, I know exactly what I'm going to do."

"What's that?"

"I'm going to Hatchet Springs and convince Hannah Hamilton to marry me."

♥♥♥

Geneva Ragsdale twirled around in her new pink dress. "Well, Hannah, I just love my new frock. I didn't know a seamstress like you would ever come to Hatchet Springs, but I'm so glad you did. You're such an asset."

"I'm pleased you like your dress so much."

"I just wish you were in town instead of way out here on the Wilcox ranch. You'd have a lot more business if you were there, I'm sure."

"I probably would, but I'm staying fairly busy now."

"Well, there are several ladies who plan to come out here and have you design a dress for them. I hear them talking when they come into my emporium. Your fame with the needle is spreading rapidly."

"I do the best I can, Mrs. Ragsdale."

"Now, dear, I want you to call me, Geneva. I'm proud to have you as a new friend and as a business woman in Hatchet Springs."

"Thank you." Hannah stood on her crutches. "Do you plan to wear your dress, or should I wrap it up for you?"

"I'm going to wear it, dear. I have to stop by Preacher Elliott Jamison's house and I want his wife to see your remarkable work. I'm sure she'll want a dress, too. That is, if she can get it made before they move."

"Oh, I didn't know they were moving."

"Yes, and it's such a shame. We'll be without a preacher in Hatchet Springs until we can find one who wants to come here."

"I'm sure you'll be able to do that. And if Mrs. Jamison wants a dress before she goes, I'd be happy to make one for her."

"I'll tell her, dear."

Hannah didn't say anything. She simply smiled at Geneva and wrapped the brown dress the woman had worn into the shop and handed it to her.

Geneva paid her the three dollars for the dress and bid her good-by.

Hannah followed her to the door and waved as she climbed into her buggy.

"Boy, that woman shore can talk," Minerva said when Hannah came back into the room.

"You're right about that." She took a seat in the stuffed chair beside the fireplace. "Minerva, is Beulah getting more comfortable letting you come into her kitchen to make things for me?"

"She's being plumb nice, but I can tell she's not used to anybody being in what she considers her part of the house."

"Then, if it isn't too much trouble will you please get me a cup of tea? Drina told me Beulah keeps hot water on the stove all the time for her."

"I'll be more than happy to. You need to take a break afore you cut out another dress." She headed for the door, then paused and looked at Hannah. "Sometimes I worries about you 'cause you works too hard."

"I enjoy being busy, Minerva. I don't like just sitting around doing nothing." She didn't tell the dear woman that the busier she kept herself, the less she thought about Jarrett. Though, at unexpected times, he'd cross her mind. When Geneva had told her she'd have more business in town, she wished that someday she and Jarrett would have a house in town and she could work from there. Then, she'd wondered if he was working hard. Then, her mind asked her if he was with another woman and kissing her the way he had her? Most of all, she wondered if he ever thought of her. She couldn't help hoping he did, at least occasionally, but logically she knew he probably didn't. Most likely, he was on another job with another woman he had to help or rescue. A woman who would, more than likely, fall in love with him the way she had.

Shaking thoughts of Jarrett out of her mind, she looked around her room. Aaron and Drina had provided well for her. It was a huge room. One side was her bedroom, curtained off from the rest of the area. There was the sitting area around the fireplace and on the other end, roped off by heavy curtains, was where she'd set up her dressmaking business. She liked the room very much because it afforded her not only privacy, but access from the side door to a veranda which was surrounded by a flower garden. It was also the door the public used when they came for fittings and to pick up their finished dresses.

At the end corner of the room was a closed off stairway that led to the room Aaron and Drina had provided for Minerva and Tobias. So far, it had worked well. Minerva's job was to take care of all of Hannah's needs and since Hannah had become proficient with her crutches, Tobias wasn't needed as often to lift her to her chair. He could now be found almost daily working in the barn area tending the horses. He had become fast friends with Aaron's right hand man, Salty Andrews, and the two of them spent time repairing saddles, reins, and other gear the ranch and the cowboys needed.

It was a good living and a good place to live. Hannah knew she should be thankful every day, and she really was. The only thing that would make it perfect was if she could get Jarrett MacMichael off her mind.

Hannah jumped when her door flew open and an excited Minerva ran into the room. "Miss Hannah, Miss Hannah, come quick."

A little frightened, Hannah grabbed her crutches. "What is it, Minerva? Has something happened?"

"You's never gonna believe it. I's hardly believe it myself. Hurry."

Hannah knew she wasn't going to find out what was going on unless she came to the front porch. Drina came around the house with a basket of vegetables in her hand. Beulah came outside and took them. Minerva was practically jumping up and down.

Shaking her head, Hannah looked in the direction of the approaching horse and her heart came into her throat. Was it? Could it possibly be? Were her eyes deceiving her? No, they weren't.

Jarrett! She almost called out, but she dared not. He could be here for some reason other than to see her. He probably had business with Aaron. Even so, it was wonderful seeing him.

With Minerva's help, Hannah managed to get down the steps to the yard. Maybe she should go back on the porch. She didn't want to seem anxious.

Then he reined his horse to a stop, jumped down and let the reins fall to the ground. He didn't pause as he ran toward Hannah. Without saying a word, he folded his arms around her and kissed her full on the lips.

Stunned, she let her crutches fall to the side, threw her arms around his neck and kissed him back. "Oh, Jarrett, I love you so."

He smiled at her. "I wanted to say that first, but it's wonderful to hear you say it. I was afraid you'd forgotten me."

"I could never forget you."

He kissed her again. "I love you, Hannah Hamilton. I love you with all my heart. Will you marry me soon and put me out of my misery?"

"Oh, yes, Jarrett. I'll marry you. I want to marry you, and I want to marry you *soon*."

Oblivious to all that was going on around them, Jarrett swooped her up in his arms and headed into the house as Beulah held the door open. Minerva ran down the steps and picked up the crutches. Tobias and Salty came around the house and watched the couple disappear through the door. Tobias took the reins of Jarrett's horse. "Guess I might as well put him in the corral. Looks like Mr. Jarrett's gonna be here for a while."

"Who's he?" Salty asked.

"The man who rescued Miss Hannah from her mean old aunt."

Salty nodded as if that explained everything and followed Tobias to the barn.

Aaron came up, put his arm around his wife's shoulder and looked down at her. "What's going on?"

"Jarrett MacMichael is back."

"And that means?"

Drina smiled, kissed his cheek, then put her arm around his waist. Looking up at Beulah, who still stood on the porch, Drina said, "It looks as if Hannah's biggest wish is coming true. I figure that means we're going to have another wedding around here very soon, doesn't it, Beulah?"

"Yes, Miz Drina. It shore does."

"Then I think you should get my wedding dress out and press it. I'm sure there's not going to be enough time for Hannah to make another one."

Chapter 23

Three weeks later, the buggy stopped in front of the large Victorian house in Hatchet Springs, Arizona. Hannah looked over at her husband. "This place is beautiful. It can't be ours, can it, Jarrett?"

"I told you we wouldn't have to live with Aaron and Drina for more than a month until I moved us into our own home and, yes this is ours, sweetheart." He grinned at her. "How did I do finding the perfect house for us?"

"Like I said, it's beautiful, but..."

"No buts." He winked at her. "My wife deserves the best."

"But..."

He wrapped the reins around the brake stick and shook his head. "I told you, no buts. Do you think we can live happily here?"

"Yes, Jarrett, I can live happily anywhere with you. A house, a barn, a cave. It doesn't matter."

"I agree, but we might as well be as comfortable as we can." He slid his arm around her. "Now, let's go see our house."

"Yes, my love."

He jumped down and reached for her. He held her in his arms until she grabbed her crutches, then let her drop her good foot to the ground. They walked side by side up the flower flanked walkway to the front porch.

It surprised her when Minerva opened the door for them. "Come in Mr. and Miz MacMichael."

"Thank you." Hannah smiled at her. "How did you get here?"

"Mr. Jarrett brung us this mornin' and we's been doing some work around here."

"I hope you've picked out your rooms."

"No, Miz Hannah. We's got a 'partment all our own. Can you believe that? It's connected to the back and we has a bedroom, a little tiny kitchen and a nice setting room. Me and Tobias is gonna be happy here in our own little place."

"That's good, Minerva. You deserve your own apartment."

Tobias came out and greeted them. "I's git your stuff into the house, then put up your horse and buggy. You has a nice stable in back, Mr. Jarrett. I's gonna like working around here with you as much as I did on Mr. Aaron's ranch."

"I'm glad you feel that way, Tobias, because I plan to keep you busy. You may end up being a detective yourself."

"My Tobias is too old for that sort of thing, Mr. Jarrett, but he be a good person. He'll shore help you out."

"Now, Minerva, I might not be as old as you thinks I is." He shook his head.

As Jarrett and Hannah started inside the house, Hannah said, "I heard Tobias say that was your buggy. When did you buy it?"

"I got it so my wife could have it to get around town in... and it's *our* buggy, not just *mine*. Everything I have is as much yours as it is mine, now."

"I only have a necklace and a few other odd pieces of jewelry to share with you."

"You keep your jewels, my love. I know you shared with Lydia and Drina, but what you have left should someday go to our future daughter."

She looked at him and her eyes grew big. "Do you mean you want me to have children?"

"Yes, but if you don't want any..."

"Oh, Jarrett, I'd love to have children, but Aunt Verbena told me that crippled women couldn't have them. I didn't think I could."

"Hannah, I want you to promise me you'll stop thinking about what your aunt told you. That woman filled your head with a lot of untruths and half lies. From now on, what you and I decide together is what will be happening with us."

"I like that." She smiled at him. "Now, let's look around."

"All right, we'll do that. If you notice there's a door on each side of this entry. On the left is the perfect size room for my office. I want to set my business up there."

She nodded. "It will be nice to have you working at home."

"I think so, too." He waved an arm to the right. "On this side of the hall is an even bigger room. I thought if you want to continue your sewing, it would be the perfect place for your dressmaking room. Each of these rooms have an outside entrance and that's the way the public will come in to do business with us. We'll keep the front door shut except for our own use and for guests."

"And the doors into the hall?"

"That's where we'll stand to kiss good-bye in the mornings, and where we'll meet for lunch, and for anytime we feel the need or want to see each other about during the day."

"Jarrett, you're a rascal."

"I know. That's why you love me." He leaned down and kissed her forehead. Straightening, he said, "Now, this leads to the parlor. I guess here is where we'll entertain our special guests."

"I think all guests are special."

"Of course they are. Off to the side are doors that lead to the dining room. And behind it is the kitchen. The room to the left is a nice, comfortable family sitting area. It's probably where we'll spend a lot of time holding each other and maybe kissing and such."

"I like that." She giggled as they went through the dining room and into the kitchen. She pointed at a door near the pantry. "Where does that go?"

"That leads to the Johnsons' apartment."

Back in the entry, she looked up the long, winding stairway. "Is our bedroom up there?"

"It is."

"I'm not sure I can maneuver my crutches to get up those steps."

"And you're not going to have to. I look forward after our long day's work to carrying you up the stairs to our bedroom every night."

"But what if you're not here?"

"I'll be here most of the time, but in case there's an emergency, there's a bedroom downstairs. When I get too old to carry you, we'll sleep there."

"You have it all figured out, don't you?"

"I do." He swept her up in his arms. "I want to practice taking you to our bedroom."

She laughed as he went up the stairs and didn't even breathe hard. When they entered their suite, she gasped. "Oh, Jarrett, what a beautiful bedroom suite."

"Do you really like it?"

"Oh, I do. It's the prettiest one I've ever seen."

He smiled. "It pleases me to know you like it. When my family came for our wedding, they brought this suite for us. It belonged to my grandparents."

"Your brother and sister were married before you, how did we luck out and get it?"

"The story goes that when I was a little boy, my grandpa bought this suite for grandma. When he brought it home, I thought it was pretty. They say I looked up at grandma and said, 'When you die, can I have this bedroom stuff?' It was left in their will that it come to me whenever I got married."

"Oh, what a wonderful story, Jarrett. I'll always cherish this suite because of that. It's something else we can pass to our child."

"You're wonderful, Hannah." His eyes were misty as he sat her on the bed then sat beside her. "I promise you that there'll be a lot of love and maybe more than one child made in this bed, just as it was for my grandparents. They'd be proud to know how much you like it."

"Maybe they do know, Jarrett. Maybe they also know how much I love their grandson. You may think I'm naïve and inexperienced, but I know there's no other man anywhere in this world for me. I think I've told you before that you're just what I always wished for in a husband."

"All I know is, the moment I walked into your Aunt Verbena's parlor and saw you sitting there looking like a princess in your faded dress, I knew you did something to my heart that no other woman has ever been able to do."

She looked at him and smiled. "It's still a while before supper time and I know Minerva will probably be making something special for our first night here. I think that might give us time to try out your grandparents' bed. What do you think?"

"I think I might be the man you wished for, but you're the woman I've wanted and needed all my life and didn't know it until our wedding day." He removed her hat and reached for the buttons on her dress. "I love you, now and forever, Hannah MacMichael."

Hannah surrendered to his kisses and knew that no matter what happened in the future, all her most important wishes had already come true.

About the Author

In 2012, Agnes Alexander's first western historical romance was published. Agnes has lived all her life in her home state of NC, but loves to travel. Though she has visited 48 of the 50 states, she says she has an affinity with the west and loves writing and researching this genre. Other than traveling, her most favorite thing to do is spend time with her two grandchildren.

LINKS:

www.Agnesalexander.com

https://www.facebook.com/agnesalexander.549?sk

www.Pinterest.com/agnesalexander8

DRINA'S CHOICE by Agnes Alexander

To escape her terrible father, Drina Hamilton feels she has no choice but to make the long trek to Arizona to become the wife of a rancher she only knows from the one letter his uncle has written her. Unknown to Drina, to have the mortgage taken off his Rocking Chair Ranch, Aaron Wilcox is being forced to marry the woman his uncle has chosen from the answers he received from the mail-order-bride ad he put in the Savannah, Georgia paper. As Drina and Aaron struggle with the situation they've been forced into, they are unaware there is a plan in the works to murder Aaron and force the sale of the huge ranch.

WISH FOR THE MOON by Celia Yeary

At the dawn of the Twentieth Century, sixteen-year-old Annie McGinnis wishes for a chance to see more of the world, since all she's ever known is the family farm in North Texas. A mysterious visitor arrives who will change not only her life, but her family's as well. To save Max Landry from a bogus charge, she follows him and the Texas Rangers back to the coal-mining town one county over where a murder occurred. The short journey sets Annie on a path of discovery—new horizons, an inner strength, and quite possibly…love.

www.prairierosepublications.com

Made in the USA
Charleston, SC
27 February 2015